BOUNDLESS

Nothing is as it seems

MIRACLE AUSTIN

BOUNDLESS

ISBN-13: 978-0-9986182-0-3   ISBN-10: 0-9986182-0-9

Authored by: Miracle Austin
Cover Design by: Mia Hoddell
Edited & Proofread by: Kitten Jackson
Edited & Formatted by: E & F Indie Services

Wings & Fangs
PUBLISHING

Published in (United States of America)
10 9 8 7 6 5 4 3 2 1

Dedication

I'd like to express my deep gratitude to Stephanie Morris and J.D. Mason. I met both of these outstanding authors a few years ago at a book conference. They never had to take time to visit with me about the twists and turns of the writing and publishing world, but they did.

They shared some amazing information with me, which planted seeds of confidence and perseverance within me. I thank you two both so very much for spending those few minutes with me because that little time ignited me to continue on my writing journey. Stories for **Boundless** were just taking shape back then, as well, with no intentions to ever publish, as a future collection.

I would also like to take time to thank two very dear friends of mine, Erica B. Barfield and Jacqueline (Jackie) E. Smith, amazing author of *Boy Band* and *Cemetery Tours* series, for always showing their *unconditional support* towards my works. I so appreciate their inspirational and enduring messages to me.

Erica, thank you for your solid friendship over the years. Jackie, thank you for creating fantastic promos on social media outlets of my works with your special, artistic magic—I'm deeply grateful.

My appreciation runs deeper than y'all will ever know. May peace and countless blessings always follow each of you.

-Miracle Austin

Introduction

Boundless, my first eclectic collection of free-verse poems (*minimum punctuation at times*) with mini stories intertwined and short stories—ranging from over two thousand words to under twenty words—received approximately **315** rejections in almost a year with four hopeful bites, which all fizzled out.

I fell into a deep, hopeless hole and began to convince myself that no one would ever publish or want to read it. **Boundless** almost had its final date with the delete button.

Luckily, my hubbie convinced me in the knick of time before I pushed the button. He encouraged me to re-read a few individual reviews from others who read my works.

Some have been published in anthologies and/or ezines, which I'm extremely grateful for; while many have never been published. I finally decided that it was time to share **Boundless**.

As you read this collection, I hope that you allow your mind to be opened up wide because my colorful imagination is sometimes not only outside, all around, over, and under the box, but sometimes beyond the box.

Some of my works are light, while others are much darker. My diverse works will provide morsels of fear, romance, heartache, betrayal, fantasy, suspense, faith, comedy, mash-ups, and will illustrate various social issues within some of my storytelling on multiple levels.

I hope that you enjoy one or more works from **Boundless**, and it inspires you in some way. You'll find a little questionnaire at the end about the collection, along with a few other surprises. Thank you for taking time to read and support **Boundless**. It means so very much to me.

Reviews

Infinity

"You have one active imagination, and I'm continually surprised at the range of your writing. This creature seemed to encompass many different types of the abilities that we credit to those dark night beings that prey on us. Good work."

~Cal G.

Dishonorable Path

"Your poem reminded me of Baudelaire. A grim picture painted by the words. '*Of sores, molds, and mud have erupted beauty and new things.*' --Charles Baudelaire, loosely translated (*The Flowers of Evil*)."

~Gianinas

Meat Lover's Special

"Well, I couldn't stop reading this one. Now, what kind of mind comes up with that and where do you go shopping? Fantastic dialogue, perfect timing, and scene cuts work well. Your characters and setting are believable and visual…Dash was the only 'normal' one there. I was pulling for her all the way. Damn, this was a good read!"

~E.L. Ekey

Study Break

"A dramatic, attention-grabbing introduction. Good use of flashback and natural sounding dialogue. A gruesome story, paced well, and filled with horror."

~Brooke B.

Reviews

Dark Place

"Miracle, this is a very insightful and extremely powerful. You've gotten inside the head of a person who struggles with mental illness. Excellent writing."

~Writingdimension

Table of *Contents*

INFINITY   **1**

HORROR/PARANORMAL TALES

Study Break	3
Ex-Change	26
Slippers	27
Crooked Shadows	30
Meat Lover's Special	32
Dishonorable Path	41
Lock	43
Krisper	47
Unleashed	49
Toxic	68
The No-No	71
Almost Extinct	73
Creep	89
Sweet Secrets	91
Stalker	100
2nd Annual Z-Run	101
Lights Out	103
Infinity	108
Snow's Secrets	109
Double Trouble	110
Birthday Surprise	121
Last Pass	122
Monster	131
927 Ghost Trails	132
Zeke: The Unfreak	145
Damaged II	151
One-Way	156
App	157

Table of *Contents*

HIDDEN   **181**

FANTASY TALES

The Gift	182
Stormie's Birthday Wish	189
Rebirth	193
Hidden	197

WINGLESS   **201**

AWARENESS TALES

Pens	202
Side Effects	204
What If	205
Faded Dreams	206
Waiting Games	207
Haunting	208
Atlanta	209
Trial	210
On & Off	211
Believe	212
Prisoner	213
Heartless	214
Damaged	215
Tricks	216
A Glimpse	217
One Knock	218
UnBelievable	220
Gone	221
Buried	222
Rushed	223
Penelope	224
Birthday Candles	226

Table of Contents

Hero	228
Sixty Minutes	229
Invisible Ones	230
Wagon	231
Hate	232
Trip	233
Poisonous Voices	234
Rescue	235
Venom	236
UnFallen	237
My Closet	239
Dark Place	240
Choose	241
Cherish	243
Broken	245
If	247
Wingless	249
Transformed Restrictions	251

HEAVY EYES — 254
WOUNDED TALES

Alone	255
Crave	257
Willow's Dress	258
Rumors	262
Solo	263
Heavy Eyes	264
Dear Ms. Margaret	265
Lost Beauty	266
Dream Thief	267
Hope's Wishes	268

Table of
Contents

Crushed	270
Porcelain Girl	272
Un-Goodbye	273
Silencer	276
Beast	277
Flood	279
Excluded	280
Heart-Stopper	281
Death of One Musketeer	283
Unjustified Heartbreak	289
Temporary Wish	291
Infinite Stranger	292
Fired	293
Evaporated Love	294
Locked Out	295
Flypaper	296
Shattered	297
Bloodsuckers	298
Trust	299
Miss Blue	300
Finish Line	301
Love Punisher	302
Chances	304
Fatality	305
Mr. Heartbreaker	306
Without My Consent	307
Unjoy	309
Stranded	310
Daydreamer	311
Confessions	312
Trapped	318

Table of
Contents

Un-Kissed	319
Doubt	320
Enemy	321

1958   **322**

LOVE TALES
Love Stew	324
Southern Lover's Tale	325
Awoken	326
You	327
One	328
Second Chance	329
Dancing Flames	330
Stampede	331
Dream Destination	332
Union	333
Exposed	334
Thousand	335
1958	336

EXTRAS
Short *Boundless* Questionnaire	337
Doll Reviews	339
Sneak Peak #1	342
Sneak Peak #2	347
Acknowledgements	353
Author Bio	355
Works Previously Published	356
Helpful Resources	358
Reader's Notes	361

BOUNDLESS

Nothing is as it seems ——————————————

Infinity

————————————————— Horror/Paranormal Tales

Dedicated to
Nelson W. Pyles

Study
Break

Catalina stroked Ivory's hair while kneeling over her on the bloody carpet and whispered under her breath, "It's my fault. We never should've come here."

"No one will believe us. Let's go!" Ryder screamed, perching himself on the balcony rail with his hand extended towards her.

Within minutes, cop cars and fire trucks lined up on the side of the high-rise with swirling red and blue emergency lights.

Catalina grabbed Ivory's purse and Ryder's hand.

"You trust me?" Ryder asked.

"Yes."

Ryder pulled her close to his chest and leaped off the balcony.

Butterflies cartwheeled over and over again in her stomach—they were flying into the darkness below.

Catalina wrapped her scarf around her face and squeezed him tighter around his slender waist for extra warmth.

Explosive, country pine and vanilla aromas from Ryder's long hair whipping in her face ignited automatic sedation and allowed her mind to drift back to eight hours earlier.

InFinity

"Ivory, please turn the music down. I can't concentrate," Catalina pleaded. "Finals start on Monday."

"Why are you making such a big deal out of it?" Ivory blurted out, twirling a long strand of hair with her perfectly manicured finger and popping bubble gum loudly. "You know this stuff, Ms. Dean List Queen."

Catalina giggled, covering her mouth with her hand to hide the railroad braces cemented onto her teeth.

"Let's do something tonight. It's Friday. Please," Ivory begged.

"I…you need to study."

"You don't play enough, Catalina. That's what's wrong with you. You're such a bore, like everyone says." Ivory parked herself on the bed and crossed her legs, pretending to read from her Latin book.

"You really think I'm a bore?"

"Yes. You never go out."

"I'm on scholarship, and I have to maintain my grades. You don't have to worry about things like I do," Catalina said, her voice clipped with annoyance.

"What's that supposed to mean?"

"Come on, Ivory, you know you got it made."

"So what?"

She rolled her eyes.

"Sorry. It's just…I really have to work hard, you know."

"Yeah, I get it, but Catalina, you work *too* hard. A girl needs her fun, too."

"Maybe you're right. Okay, let's do something fun." Catalina closed her books and shoved them off the twin-sized bed.

"Are you really game?"

"Yeah."

"Okay, my friend told me about this amazing club called Twin Twisters—it's in the city." Ivory jumped on Catalina's bed to show her the neon yellow flyer she pulled from her hot pink Hermes Birkin

Study Break

handbag.

"The city?" Catalina questioned, shrugging her shoulders and pushing her oversized glasses farther back on her sweaty narrow nose.

"Yeah, so what?"

"It's just…"

"What? Spit it out, Catalina!" Ivory shouted.

"You know what happened to those girls there three months ago?"

"No."

Ivory shook her head.

"They never found them," Catalina said, pausing after each word.

"Who told you that?"

Ivory scoffed and flipped her hair back with both her hands.

"Benjamin Payne."

"Benjamin. He's so weird. He believes in UFOs and fairies, too," Ivory whispered, laughing.

"Really?"

"Oh, yeah. He just tries to freak people out with his crazy made-up stories. He's such a freak."

"Let's do it, then," Catalina said, biting the side of her lip.

"Come on, girl. We're going to have the most amazing time!" Ivory insisted with a huge grin planted on her face.

"Wait, Ivory, I don't have anything to wear. Look at me."

She stood up in her baggy flannel pajamas, oversized t-shirt, and fuzzy slippers.

"Yep, you need an Ivory makeover. I'll pull out that hidden beauty of yours. Jump in the shower, so I can begin my magic."

Ivory walked into her closet and hunted for the perfect outfit for her friend, while shoving countless items back and forth. As Catalina showered, Ivory laid out black lace panties with a matching push-up bra and red fishnet stockings on the bed.

Catalina walked out with a beach towel wrapped around her thin, petite frame.

Infinity

"Are you sure about this?" Catalina cocked her head to the side and held up the peek-a-boo goodies. "I've never worn anything like this."

"Yeah, I know. I picked up a few things at Priscilla's Closet last weekend. We're about the same size. They'll fit you perfectly."

"Okay, if you're sure."

"I am. I'll do your hair and makeup, too."

Ivory walked towards the bathroom and leaned back through the doorway to look at Catalina. "You're going to look so sexy when I'm done with you."

"Can I ask you something, Ivory?"

"Sure."

"Why are you being so nice to me now? You usually ignore me when walking with your friends or in the dining hall," Catalina pointed out, fastening the bra around her back and pulling straps around her shoulders.

"I know. I've been a real bitch to you this year. I want to be a better roomie to you, which is why I invited you out tonight. Hell, we'll be graduating before you know it."

"Time is flying by so fast."

"Catalina, we need this, and we deserve it!"

"Yeah, I guess you're right."

"Of course. I always am."

Ivory curled Catalina's thick golden-auburn hair into cascading twirls and added some sparkling mini bows on the sides to fasten some of her hair out of her face.

She looked like an 80s rock star in a tight blue jean mini skirt, fishnets, a raspberry silk blouse draping off her shoulders with a loose silver chain-link belt, and sparkly flats to finalize the look.

"Catalina, you almost look better than me. Almost."

Ivory winked and turned around to open the door of their room.

Catalina grabbed her backpack from the floor and carried it behind her. She followed Ivory out and walked towards her convertible

Study Break

Corvette.

"Ivory, can you pop your trunk?"

"Why?"

"Need to put something back there."

"Hope it's not books." The lid opened up. "You won't need those tonight."

Ivory cranked the car to life, as Catalina tossed her backpack in the trunk, which shut automatically after a few seconds.

Catalina walked around to the passenger side and jumped in, and then they were off to the city.

Ivory popped in a mix CD.

"Turn it up. I love this one," Catalina said, as she began to sway back and forth in the leather bucket seat.

"You're finally letting loose! We're going to have some fun-fun tonight."

They sang *West End Girls* out loud to each other, laughing, as the cool wind danced in their hair.

The neon sign for Twin Twisters led them into the packed parking lot.

Ivory parked and touched up her lips with Cherry Bomb lip gloss.

Catalina could feel the loud bass penetrating her chest, and they weren't even inside yet.

"It's really loud!" she shouted.

"Yeah, I know. Clubs are loud. Come on."

Ivory grabbed Catalina's hand and pranced to the door.

"Hello, ladies. I hate to ask, but I need to see some ID. You know this club is 21 and up?" the bouncer asked, as he smiled at both of them while licking his lips.

"Oh, yes. Here you go, sugar," Ivory said, while she placed their IDs in his hand with a slight massage, as she slipped him a hundred-dollar bill. "Everything okay?"

The bouncer glanced at the IDs quickly and said, "Yeah, it's all good here. Step on in, ladies. Enjoy."

He pulled back the purple velvet curtain, with his eyes fixed on every bounce their bodies displayed through their skimpy clothes.

Colorful lights twirled in every direction. People were dancing on multiple dance floor levels, on poles, and in cages with water raining down on them. The scent of strong alcohol and smoke filled the air, as loud techno music thumped.

"I've never been in a place like this, Ivory."

"I know. You've been stuck in your little country town way too long, sheltered one. You'll be unsheltered tonight!"

As a line dance song came on, Ivory pulled Catalina onto a glass dance floor.

"You remember when I told you that I have two left feet?" Catalina asked with a nervous laugh.

"Oh, come on. Just watch me and follow along."

The floor was packed already, but it multiplied, as everyone joined in. Catalina tried to follow Ivory's steps, but she ended up trampling on her feet and bumping into other dancers. Ivory noticed some of them frowning and laughing at her.

"Honey, you better sit this one out." Ivory pointed towards the bar. "Hey, go save us a seat. I'll be over in a bit."

"Okay."

Catalina walked slowly off like a puppy with its tail between its legs. She flopped down at the bar near the end and watched her roomie glide on the dance floor like a pro.

All the guys flocked to Ivory. She was perfect in every way—her hair, lips, complexion, body, and especially her moves.

Catalina began to bite her nails and decided to walk out to the car to retrieve her backpack from the trunk. That was the perfect time for her to reunite with what she felt most comfortable with: her books. They were always there for her. She never had to face embarrassment or rejection from them. They were her best friends.

Study Break

After getting the keys from Ivory, she went out to the car. The bouncer started to give her a hard time when she returned to the door, but after Catalina reminded him of Ivory earlier, he waved her inside for the second time.

She found the same seats still open at the bar and glanced at the dance floor. Ivory was still the queen out there.

Catalina sighed and placed her backpack on the empty barstool next to her, unzipped it, and pulled out her organic chemistry book to read for several minutes.

"Hey, you," a bartender yelled out, as he fixed a drink.

Lifting her head up out of her book, she asked, "Who, me?"

"Yeah, you, the cute bookworm."

"What?" she asked, straining to hear him over the deafening music.

"I've met a lot of people before, but never a cute bookworm, especially in a club, of all places."

He walked towards her and then placed his arms in front of her, leaning in.

"I probably look really stupid."

Smiling, he said, "No. Just…you should be out there dancing and having a good time."

"Yeah, but I can't even two-step. I love music and people-watching on the sideline."

"Oh, one of those."

With a frown, she asked, "One of what?"

"A pretty wallflower."

She smiled, and they both laughed.

"Can I get you a drink?"

"Oh, no," she said, shaking her head.

"My treat."

"I mean I don't drink alcohol."

"Oh, okay. What about a Shirley Temple?"

"You're sweet, but I just told you that I don't drink."

Infinity

"It's virgin."

Eyes opened wide, she said, "What?"

"That means it's a non-alcoholic drink. You really don't get out much, do you?"

"No, I don't. This is my first time. I think I would like a Shirley Temple."

She breathed in deep and exhaled with a soft sigh.

"Well, I'm going to make you the best one I've ever made."

He mixed the drink up and added lots of cherries for an extra splash of color for her.

She took a sip while pushing her glasses further up her nose.

"Yummy. Thank you."

"So, what's your name?"

"You first."

"I like that. It's Ryder."

"Nice."

"Your turn."

"Catalina Harper."

"Beautiful name to match a beautiful young lady. Nice to meet you, Catalina Harper."

Ryder held out his hand, and after a pause, she shook it. It felt extremely warm.

"So, what are you doing here by yourself?" Ryder asked while staring into her eyes without blinking.

Catalina's face transformed from rose to a dark raspberry tint.

"I'm not alone. I'm with my roomie. See her over there? She's the one in the electric blue cage, surrounded by all the guys."

"Oh, that one. Yeah, I noticed her earlier."

"I see."

She frowned, slammed her drink down on the bar, and stared at the floor.

"No, I don't mean it like that."

Study Break

"Sure. All guys look at Ivory like that. I'm okay with it," Catalina said, shrugging her shoulders.

"You're not going to let that one go, are you?"

She smiled and shook her head, and then she picked up her drink and continued to sip it.

"Next topic, quick. What's your major, Catalina?"

"Premed and business."

"Interesting combo."

"I know it sounds boring, but I have a photographic memory. I just soak information up like a sponge," she said, as she snapped her fingers.

"That's amazing."

Ryder grinned.

"You think so?"

"Oh, yeah. I've been taking a few classes at the community college. Not as impressive as what you're doing, though," he said with a wink.

Catalina smiled and mumbled, "I'm not impressive at all."

She stared down into her drink, as she picked out the cherries with a stiff straw and popped them into her mouth.

"Catalina, you're very impressive. How many people do you think, right here in this bar, have photographic memories?"

"I don't know."

"None, no one but you. See?" She smiled and stared into his forest-green eyes. "Where do you go to school?"

"Rhodan College."

"Double impressive. That's not an easy place to get into."

"I guess so."

"You know I'm right."

She squirmed in her chair, as she pulled up the fishnet stockings on her legs and tugged at the scratchy bra.

"Hey, I've been meaning to ask you, is that outfit really you?" he asked, leaning into her more, almost touching her hand.

Pulling back slightly, she said, "Why?"

"You're beautiful. You just look a little uncomfortable to me."

"Oh. No, it's not me. Another brilliant idea from my roomie. She thought it would make me look sexy for our night out."

"Gotcha. You're definitely—"

Before Ryder could finish his sentence, Ivory popped up next to her.

"Hey, girl, who's this?"

"Ivory, this is Ryder."

"Hey," Ivory whispered, leaning toward him in her low-cut Victorian blouse, exposing most of her merchandise.

"Nice to meet you," he said, avoiding the free show by focusing his eyes on Catalina instead.

"Listen, I met a hot guy, and he has a hot roomie. They invited us to their place to listen to some music and stuff. They're friends with my favorite band. They showed me pics of them hanging out together. Plus, they're senior frat boys. You know how I love my frats. Let's go."

"Ryder, please excuse me."

"Sure, I'll be over there."

"Thanks."

He walked away.

"Ivory, you don't really know them. I just don't know," Catalina said, as she began to twist her fingers repeatedly.

"Please? I promised him that you would go, so his friend would have someone to talk to."

"Why did you do that?"

Catalina pulled her hair behind her ears, both her hands trembling.

"He's so cute, and his roomie is, too. I've been dancing with them since we got here. They're so fun. Pretty please?" Ivory begged.

"Where are they?"

"Over there," Ivory said, waving her hands in the air to get them to come over.

Study Break

They worked their way through the crowded club until they stood beside the girls.

"This is Romeo and Dexter," Ivory said. "Romeo is all mine."

She pulled him close to her, resting her hands on his rear.

"Hi," Catalina said.

They both kissed her hand in greeting. They looked like fashion models, tall and perfect. Romeo had glistening, curly shoulder-length charcoal hair and dark blue eyes, while Dexter had short spiky dirty blonde hair, deep dimples, and sparkling hazel eyes.

"See? They're gentlemen—harmless and so yummy," Ivory purred.

"I don't know, Ivory," Catalina said, squirming in her seat.

"Guys, please give us a minute."

Ivory slapped them both on their rear ends, and they walked away from the bar, to an empty table, in their fitted jeans and t-shirts. They grinned back at her.

Ivory and Catalina turned around to face each other.

"Okay, what's the big deal here?"

Ivory propped one arm on the bar and tapped her foot to the beat of the music.

"Do I have to spell it out to you?"

"Yes, please do."

"We don't know them. You just met them tonight, and, well, they're strangers. Remember stranger danger…from when you were a little girl?" Catalina asked, as she rotated her body back and forth in the swivel barstool.

"I knew it. Don't know what the hell I was thinking, inviting you, of all people, to come out with me tonight."

Ivory began to walk away, with a wave of her hand over her shoulder. Catalina jumped off the stool and fell to her knees on the slippery floor.

"Wait!" she yelled, as she picked herself up and brushed herself off.

"What?" Ivory shouted, flinging herself around.

"You really think it'll be okay to go?"

"Yeah. They're cool. Plus, they're so delicious," she said, batting her thick eyelashes.

"Okay, give me a minute to grab my stuff."

Catalina turned around and placed her book in her backpack, feeling as though she was moving in slow motion.

She walked back towards Ivory and said, "Okay, ready."

"Thank you. I love you for going with!"

She hugged Catalina and ran outside to retrieve the car to swing around to the front of the club to pick her up.

As Catalina adjusted her backpack on her left shoulder, Ryder walked towards her.

"Look, I get off in 30 minutes. Please join me for a cup of coffee at the Gator House Diner about a block down. Great little place," he said with a grin.

"I'm sorry, Ryder. I'm leaving with my roommate. It's been nice talking to you. Thank you for the company and the drink. Sure I don't owe you anything?"

"No, it was on me. You sure you want to go with those guys? You don't even know them. Let your friend go."

"No, I can't do that. She's my friend. I can't let her go by herself."

"You always do what she says?"

"No, and you're being a jerk."

Before she walked out the door, Ryder grabbed her right wrist and spun her around.

"Catalina, wait. Sorry. Tell your friend to join us."

"Thanks, but no, thanks, Ryder."

"Please don't go," he said, squeezing her wrist tighter.

"She's waiting for me outside. Please let go. You're hurting me."

She stared down at his hand wrapped firmly around her wrist. Her eyes began to water.

"Sorry."

Study Break

Ryder released her hand and took a few steps backwards. She walked out and jumped into the car with Ivory, and he followed.

"Hey, let me give you my number, at least."

He fumbled through his pockets, searching for something to write his number down on.

"Just tell me, Ryder," Catalina said with a sigh.

"Forgot. It's 224-8011."

"Bye, Ryder."

She waved at him and turned to face Ivory.

"Ready, roomie?"

Ivory gripped the steering wheel with one hot pink lace-gloved hand and shifted the car into drive, so they could follow Romeo's platinum Ferrari.

Catalina looked back in the rearview mirror, as they drove off from the club, and noticed Ryder standing where she left him. He was waving at her. She also noticed a red mark on her wrist. Ivory noticed, too.

"How did you get that?"

"I must have hit it on something at the bar."

"Put some ice on it when we get to Romeo's and Dexter's place."

Catalina nodded.

When they pulled up to the high-rise complex the guys led them to, Ivory pulled out her cosmetic bag from her purse to powder her nose and glide more gloss onto her lips. She sprayed a few puffs of *Exotic Breeze* down her neckline and between her thighs.

"Want some?" she asked, holding the bottle out to Catalina.

"No, I'm fine." She pushed it away. "Why spray downstairs?"

"A girl must always be ready. You just never know when adventure will find you," she said with a wink and a giggle.

Catalina shook her head.

Ivory opened her car door and stepped out. She clicked her six-inch golden stilettos on the ground as she walked.

"You sure about this, Ivory?"

Infinity

"Of course. We're going to have a really good time. You'll be thanking me for taking you away from those boring books tonight."

Romeo slid in front of them and offered both of his arms to escort them inside. Dexter followed.

"Shall we, ladies?" Romeo asked.

"Most definitely," Ivory replied.

The four of them stepped into the elevator in the lobby and stopped on the penthouse floor.

"Wow, you didn't tell me you had all of this," Ivory whispered.

She tossed her hair back and forth and licked her glossed lips.

"There's more to see. Just wait," Romeo purred.

The door opened with one swipe of his finger. Everything was white and stainless steel, and nothing was out of place.

Romeo walked over to the bar. Soft music filled the room, as soon as he touched a button on a remote. He made some drinks and carried them over on a crystal tray.

"Thank you, but I don't drink," Catalina said.

"Oh, no, she doesn't. You have any soda, Romeo?"

"I have a little of everything. What kind?"

"Anything."

He walked back over to the bar and carried out five different soda bottles for her to choose from.

"You pick."

"Thanks."

Romeo bent down to whisper in Ivory's ear. He kissed her on the mouth, while his hand traveled to places Catalina thought should be forbidden, at least on the first date.

"Hey, roomie. Romeo and I are going to go back there. If you need me, holler."

"Ivory, can I ask you something in private really quick?" Catalina asked while squinting her eyes.

"Sure. Hey, guys, we're going to step out on the balcony for a bit.

Study Break

Be right back."

"All right. I'll be here waiting for you," Romeo whispered while staring at every part of her body.

The girls walked out onto the balcony. Catalina closed the glass door behind her, making sure it was shut tight.

"Ivory, are you sure you want to be alone with him?"

Catalina began to chew her nails.

"This is not my first, second, or third rodeo with a Romeo, especially a really hot one. I'm a big girl. I know what I'm doing. You'll be fine with Dexter. He's a kitten. Romeo, on the other hand, is a naughty tiger."

She smiled, as she massaged Catalina's shoulders with both of her hands. Ivory opened the glass door and walked back into the living room. Catalina paused and then followed.

Romeo grabbed Ivory's hand and led her back to his bedroom, as she slipped off her golden stilettos and carried both on one finger.

Catalina plopped herself at the far end of the massive leather couch, and Dexter scooted closer to her.

He asked, "So, where do you two go to school?"

"Rhodan College, about 45 minutes from here," she said while trying to scoot away from him.

"Oh, I know where that is."

He moved even closer to her.

"Really."

She slid so far away from him that she almost fell off the couch. He caught her with one hand in the split second before she hit the floor.

"You okay?"

"Yeah." She picked up the soda bottle from the coffee table and took a few sips with her trembling lips.

Dexter set his drink down on the coffee table. He ran his hand through her hair.

"You're so gorgeous."

Infinity

"No, I'm not," she said, as her glasses slipped down her nose.

"Yes, you are." He removed them. "Just what I thought."

"What?"

She blinked a few times.

"Beautiful eyes, hiding behind these. Can I kiss you?"

"I don't know. I guess."

She squirmed around and scooted herself down deep into the couch while holding the soda bottle in one hand.

He leaned in towards her and pressed his mouth to hers.

When she didn't kiss him back, he whispered, "Relax and open."

"Open what?" she asked, pulling back and spilling her soda onto herself.

"Your mouth, silly," he said. "You taste wonderful."

"My mouth, huh?" Catalina stood up.

"You're a virgin, aren't you?"

Dexter grinned, staring up into her widened eyes.

"No…maybe. It's none of your business. Where's your bathroom? I need to clean this. It's Ivory's blouse."

"Go down the hall and make a right," he said, watching her walk. "Hey, don't be embarrassed. It's okay. We'll take it slow. I won't do anything you don't want me to do."

She turned around and tripped on the thick rug, before entering the hallway.

"I'll be back."

"I'm not going anywhere."

He stared through her as if he could see what was underneath her clothing.

She rushed into the bathroom, shut the door, and locked it. She then grabbed a towel hanging near the sink, turned on the faucet, soaked it with water, and pressed down on the stained blouse.

Come on, don't be nervous. Don't be nervous. Go with the flow, she said to herself, as she stared in the mirror.

Study Break

She pulled down her stockings and sat on the toilet. Nothing.

She heard a faint buzzing. It was coming from the linen closet. She stood, pulled her stockings back up, and walked over to it.

The sound increased and stopped. She opened the door, and a pile of purses dropped onto the floor. A cell fell out of one of the purses. The battery symbol flashed a few times and disappeared.

She noticed a small piece of paper sticking out of one of the purses. She squatted and pulled it out. It was a stained receipt with faint scribble, but she finally made it out: *Get out! They'll kill you!*

Catalina stood up quickly, knocking into a table near her, and a glass fell to the floor, shattering into pieces.

She heard a knock within seconds.

"Hey, everything okay in there?" Dexter asked, leaning against the door.

"Yeah, I'm so clumsy. I dropped a glass. Sorry. I'm cleaning it up now."

"Okay, I'm going to surf Movie Carnival to find us something to watch."

"Great."

Her hands trembled, and she began to pant.

"Any preferences?"

She took some deep breaths and counted backwards from ten, before she said, "No, anything."

"Okay, just what I was thinking. Hurry up, now."

"I will."

She scrambled and scooped up all the purses from the floor. She stuffed them back into the closet, shut the door, gathered up the broken pieces of glass, and tossed them in the trash.

Leaning on the bathroom counter with her arms bracing her weight, she began to breathe heavy, sweat trickling down her back and the sides of her face.

I've got to get Ivory out of there, but how?

InFinity

She unlocked the bathroom door, opened it, and walked towards the room she watched Ivory enter with Romeo earlier.

"Ivory, I need a… *Pam* came early," she whispered, tapping on the door.

No response. Her tapping turned into harder knocking.

Nothing.

Catalina jiggled the knob a few times, but it was locked.

Something wet and warm began to saturate her cloth shoes.

She looked down and saw blood flowing from the room. She backed up and ran through the hall.

"Dexter, something's wrong! Look, there's blood in the hallway and on my shoes!"

She pulled at his shirtsleeve.

"What? Show me."

They ran towards the scene.

He saw the blood and cried, "What the hell?"

He pounded on the door. She stood behind him, as he yelled out Romeo's and Ivory's names. When there was no response, he slammed his hands hard against the barrier, knocking it off its hinges. It then collapsed into the bedroom.

Catalina screamed as soon as she saw Ivory lying on the ground, covered in blood. She was still, her throat slit wide open. Catalina flung herself to the floor beside her friend, the blood soaking through her stockings to stain her skin.

"You, bastard! What did you do?" Catalina screamed.

Romeo was standing on the balcony in black silk pajama bottoms and no shirt, his back turned away from her.

"Answer her, man! What did you do?" Dexter demanded.

Romeo turned around. Blood covered his mouth, neck, and hands.

"I tried to tell her to relax, but she resisted me. They usually give in so easily. Not this one. I enjoyed it, though—feisty!"

"You're sick, man," Dexter said.

Study Break

Romeo clapped his hands.

"And the Oscar for best actor goes to my man, Dex. Enough!" he roared.

"What are you talking about?" Catalina asked as she stood up.

"Look, Romeo, she's a virgin, and a little slow with common sense stuff."

"Okay. So, you have no idea what we are?"

Romeo grinned. His eyes appeared to transform into a darker shade with a slight glimmer.

"Romeo, I know what you are…a murderer. Not sure about you, Dexter."

She began to back up, as tears ran down her face.

"Let's show her, Dex."

"Cool. I just thought we could have a little fun with them before going straight to the kill. You definitely didn't waste any time with her friend."

"Nope," Romeo said.

Dexter's voice lowered and his words came out in a lustful growl. "How did she taste, Romeo?"

"So-so. I've tasted better."

"This one here is really sweet, and she'll be a very special treat. I'll share a little with you, Romeo, if you reel in an extra one for me next time. Virgins are a rare delicacy for us nowadays. Practically extinct." Dexter turned and licked his lips as he stared at her. "You'll be extinct in a few minutes, as well. Sorry, Cat."

"Let's get her."

They growled louder, jumped in the air, and high-fived each other.

"I don't understand." Her legs began to wobble as her lips trembled. "Why did you kill her? What are you both?"

"You'll understand soon enough, but it will then be too late, Cat," Dexter whispered, walking towards her, as Romeo followed.

Catalina dashed down the hallway towards the bathroom. She

slammed the door and locked it. She pulled out the purses and dumped them all out, searching for the one cell phone she found earlier. She knew it had a little battery life left. She dialed Ryder's number from memory.

Her breathing grew heavier after each unanswered ring. Then finally, he answered.

"Ryder, it's me, Catalina!"

The call dropped. She glanced at the phone's screen; it was blank, and the battery symbol disappeared.

Catalina knew death was waiting for her outside the door. Her crying intensified, as trembles took over her body.

"Come out, come out, Kitty Cat," Romeo and Dexter chanted outside the bathroom, as they beat against the door.

Their beats grew louder and louder.

"I just called the cops," she shouted, rummaging through the drawers for a weapon.

She found a pair of scissors. She pointed them up towards the door with her shaky hands and stepped back into the bathtub. She slipped and hit her head against the tile. In an instant, she was out like a light.

When she woke, Ryder was standing over her. She jumped up, almost stabbing him in the chest.

"Whoa. I'm not going to hurt you." He grabbed the scissors from her and placed them on the counter behind him. "You fell and bumped your head. You were out for a bit."

"Ouch. I can feel the bump on the back of my head," she said, as she rubbed the throbbing guest now residing on her head.

"Ryder, where are they?"

"Who? Romeo and Dexter?"

"Yes, they're going to kill us! We've got to get out of here! How did you get here so fast? I didn't give you an address before the call dropped."

"Lot of questions. Will answer each one in time. I tracked you."

Study Break

"What?"

"Your scent. I smelled you as soon as you walked into the club."

She narrowed her eyes and whispered, "I don't follow."

She continued to rub the back of her head.

"I know you don't." He nodded and smiled. "Here, let me show you."

He pulled her up from the bathtub and guided her towards the bedroom, where Ivory's body remained.

"No, no…they're in there!" she yelled, pulling back.

"Catalina, it's okay. I took care of them. You're safe."

She saw two gruesome monsters on the bed, with heavy silver chains draped over the entirety of their hairy bodies—large fangs protruding from their mouths. Their eyes were black and flickered every few seconds. Long spikes of different sizes outlined their backs, curvy wooden horns adorned their heads, and razor-sharp twelve-inch claws throbbed in and out from the tips of their fingers.

"Where are Dexter and Romeo?"

"That's them."

"What? What are they?" Catalina asked.

"*Werevamcabras.*"

"What?"

"They're a lethal and predatory trio-hybrid—part werewolf, vampire, and chupacabra."

"Are you kidding me?"

"No. They've been preying on girls for a while now, especially at Twin Twisters. They can shift from monster to human form in seconds."

"I can't believe this."

"Believe it, Catalina. Romeo killed Ivory, and they were coming for you next."

"So, that story about the young girls from my college never being found is true?"

"Probably so. If not these two, then another hybrid type."

Infinity

"You telling me there're more?"

"Oh, yeah. Many. I cannot stand these hybrids. My late granddad couldn't either. We've been hunting them in my family for a long time."

"So you're like a hunter on one of those silly television shows, like *Amadeus, the Vampire Slayer*?"

Ryder laughed and said, "Something like that."

"What's that awful stench?"

She pulled a scarf from her pocket and held it against her nose.

"It comes from their anal scent glands. They use it to deter predators and their captors. It's very nauseating for some, to the point where they can become unconscious and easier prey for these vile creatures."

"Like a skunk's anal glands?"

"Sort of."

"It reminds me of hot spoiled milk and rotten meat, Ryder."

He pulled out a small tin square from his pocket. "Place this cream under your nose. It helps neutralize their stench some."

"Thanks."

She slid the top off the tin and pressed her finger into the thick cream. She rubbed a thin line under her nose, standing with her back turned to the creatures, so she could talk to Ryder.

Romeo and Dexter growled at Catalina and extended their sharp claws towards her. She could feel a slight pull, as Romeo's claw tore through the lower portion of her blouse, without touching her.

"Watch out, Catalina! Don't stand too close!"

Ryder pulled her towards him, where she fell to the floor next to Ivory, and he leaped high over her in the air, pulling out two weapons from the back of his jeans.

He stabbed both of them simultaneously with ultraviolet silver-tipped stakes.

Their bodies jerked violently for a moment and melted like lava onto the carpet.

Ryder walked outside the bedroom, into the hall, where he fetched

Study Break

a large kerosene can, which he brought along with him. He doused the apartment and their melted, smelly remains with the flammable liquid.

"We really need to go. The cops and whoever else will be here soon because of all the noise."

"We can't leave Ivory here, Ryder!"

"We have to. All the evidence has to be destroyed. It has to be done this way."

Catalina kneeled down to touch Ivory for the last time and grabbed her purse from the bloody floor. She stood up and looked at Ryder while wiping tears off her face with the back of her hand.

"Who and what are you, really?"

He perched on the rail of the balcony with a lit match in one hand and extended his other hand to her.

"Let me formally introduce myself. I'm Ryder Lycanhouse. Who and what I am is a long story. I'd love to explain it all to you. Now, what about that coffee?"

The End

Ex-Change

Dana Juniper only had five minutes left until shift change—she'd just worked a double. As she walked towards the break room to clock out, she heard an announcement over the intercom: *"Code green!"*

She froze for a moment and then rushed towards the hospital corridor. Rows of bloody gurneys with mangled bodies lying on them rolled in.

Dana saw her ex. He yelled out her name. She walked towards him, staring down at the tan and royal blue-speckled floor until she reached him. His face and clothes were saturated with ebony slimy gunk.

"I'm sorry, Dana."

She frowned and looked into his red watery eyes.

"Why?"

"For what I did tonight…and this!"

He rose up and clawed her bare arm.

Ex-Change

Slippers

The shining star of *El Circo Increible* belonged to Julia, the ballerina. She twirled up and down the flaming tightrope night after night, without a single pause.

The ringmaster, Galileo, begged her to allow him to add a net for her safety.

"You, silly little man! You've asked me this question too many times. The crowd loves it, and they love me. I'm Julia Diaz, the most famous ballerina of all, and I won't ever need a net because I'll never fall."

She swatted him away.

She was right about the crowd adoring her. They always tossed out silver coins and fluffy crimson canary roses.

In her dressing room, some of her wealthy fans frequently left her lavish outfits or expensive tickets to travel exotic lands when the circus was on break.

One night, after her performance, an 11-year-old girl on rickety crutches made her way through the crowd to reach Julia. She had attended almost a dozen of her performances over the years, and posters of the dancer painted her walls from floor to ceiling.

That night, she was going to finally meet her.

After multiple camera shots and interviews by the news media flock, the child finally had a rare moment alone with her idol.

InFinity

"Oh, Miss Julia, could you please, please sign my autograph book and take a photo with me? You're so beautiful, and I want to be just like you one day."

Her smile was intoxicating and full of life, although her front teeth were missing.

Julia looked at her and gently pressed her ultraviolet tutu down with both of her hands. She then brushed her hair up with her hands to make sure not one hair was out of place in her tight bun. She hugged her sixteen-inch waist, as she bent down to the girl's height. She signed her book and took the photo, but then she did the most horrible thing.

Before the child shuffled away, one hop at a time, Julia whispered into her ear, "Sorry sweetie, but there will never be anyone like me. I'm your one and only. You would never cut it as a ballerina. Plus, you'll never be pretty enough."

The little girl's eyes filled with tears, and she was eventually swallowed up by the crowd.

Halloween night arrived, which was one of the most special nights of the year, with costumes and fireworks.

Julia always represented the portrait of beauty, but that night, she looked absolutely breathtaking, with golden glitter shimmering in her hair. Her iridescent orange and black tutu lit up, with matching ballet slippers and sparkly purple ribbons, which laced up all the way to her knees.

She curtsied towards the crowd and pranced slowly to begin her climb up the 713 steps.

Before she climbed the first one, an older lady appeared out of nowhere. A scarlet cloak with an oversized hood covered her body. She held the most unusual bouquet of swaying black roses with silver tips.

Julia couldn't take her eyes off them. She reached out to touch one, but it pricked her index finger.

"Ouch!" she screamed, as she placed her finger in her mouth to suck the blood.

Slippers

"Get this crazy hag out of here!"

The lady smiled, as two security officers escorted her out of the big top.

Julia stood at the top of the platform to prepare what she had done over one hundred thousand times without a wobble.

As she started to twirl over the flaming tightrope, she felt something sharp inside of her slippers.

She continued to spin, until she went out of control and fell, her body shattered inside.

The crowd cried out and stood to their feet.

Galileo yelled out to workers to close the curtains immediately. He ran to her and stooped down.

Julia could barely speak, but she managed to point towards her shoes.

Tears streamed down Galileo's cheeks.

Julia's arms flopped down to her sides before she took her final breath.

When the stretcher arrived, Galileo helped to lift her body from off the ground, and that's when he noticed thin twirling glass thorns protruding from the top and bottom of her ballerina slippers.

He gasped.

Three months later, no one showed up at *El Circo Increible*.

Galileo packed up the last box in his office and found a note stuck behind a picture frame with Julia's photo on his desk.

He unfolded it, and it read:

"Sometimes beauty can be a curse—not just for one, but everyone..."

The End

Infinity

Crooked
Shadows

No one believed me, but they do…
They really do exist!
They live down there.
Deep down
Under the floor
Way below
Behind that rotten, chained-up wooden cellar door…
At night, I hear their barking moans and scratching against the cement
walls.
I hear their cold whispers climb up the vents and feel them tiptoe
down my spine.
I saw them once, I tell you.
Bobby Brewster, next door, triple-dog-dared me to walk down and
peep through the cracked wooden cellar door.
So I did…
What I saw was most terrifying.
Hunched and curved over transparent grey, twisted shadows…
I tell you, don't go down there
Way below
Deep down
Behind that rotten, chained-up wooden cellar door…
It's been 13 weeks now, and Bobby has not returned home.

Crooked Shadows

His pictures remain posted in all the grocery stores and nailed on lampposts.
They lured Bobby in 'cause he didn't believe me and went back alone.
I know they're still down there.
They live there.
They wait…
They pace up and down the dirt floors, waiting for the next one to recruit into their family.
One more.
Just one more…

Meat-Lover's
Special

For 60 seconds, Dash contemplated driving away from her life and never looking back.

Instead, she threw her sweater onto the leather driver's seat and slid down on top of it.

The steering wheel burnt her fingers upon touch. She jerked them back.

She popped in the car key, turned over the ignition, and pressed the air conditioner button to set it to full blast. The torturous Texas heat barely allowed for cool air to tickle her face.

She scooted forward in her seat, peeling her dress from the back of her sweaty thighs, which felt like sticky flypaper.

Her phone chirped.

Dash reached to her backseat to hunt for it in her stuffed purse. It tumbled onto the floor, spilling all its contents—cosmetics and a .38 Special.

She found it after the third ring and placed it on speaker.

"Hey, babe, I'm on my way to your place. I'll start the steaks once I get there," Jeremy, her fiancé, said.

"What?"

"Don't tell me you forgot that Vince and Stacie were coming over tonight?"

"Yeah, I guess I did," Dash said, as she reached back with her right hand to throw all the contents back into her purse. "Be home as soon as I can."

The call ended.

Dash shifted the car into reverse, sped out of the driveway, and drove toward the market to retrieve two T-bone steaks, a bag of salad, baking potatoes, sparkling cocktail juice, cheese cubes, crackers, pound cake, fresh strawberries, and strawberry glaze.

When she arrived at home, she saw Vince and Stacie walking towards the front door.

Dash pushed the yellow button of her garage door opener clipped to the visor above her and drove inside.

She hopped out of the car, throwing her purse over her shoulder, while scooping the paper grocery bags into her arms, and leaped towards the door leading into the house from the garage.

When she wasn't paying any attention to the bag with the juice, it gave way. The bottle dropped and shattered on the kitchen floor as soon as she opened the door.

Jeremy heard the noise from the living room, where he was entertaining Vince and Stacie.

"Hey, you guys, I'll be back. I think Dash needs some help."

"Sure, we'll surf through the channels," Vince replied, grabbing the television remote from the coffee table.

Dash was kneeling on the floor, picking up the large broken glass pieces and wiping up the juice as fast as she could with towels she pulled from the shelf next to her.

"Jeremy, I'm so sorry. I'll run back to the market to pick up another bottle."

"Never mind. Stacie brought over some." Then he whispered, "Why do you always mess things up?" as he pinched Dash hard under her right arm.

"Ouch, Jeremy, you're hurting me. Let go."

She jerked her arm back from him while staring down at her purse on the floor.

He shrugged his shoulders and said, "If you would just do what I ask, then things would be perfect. I told you to pick up the groceries earlier this week."

"Jeremy, I'm sorry. What else do you want me to say?"

"Toss me those damn steaks, so I can put them on the grill for Vince and me," he said with a sharp glare. "Wait until later. Don't think I'll forget about this little stunt."

Dash rushed to the bedroom and peeled out of her sweaty work clothes. She jumped into the shower for a quick wash-off, dried herself, and threw on a backless white summer dress. She then slipped on white tennis shoes. She squeezed two drops of Visine in both eyes, popped an Ativan into her mouth, and took a few deep breaths.

She walked back into the kitchen to prepare the salad, cheese and crackers, and dessert.

"Hey, you two," she said.

Stacie and Vince walked up to the island and hugged her.

"So good to see you guys. It's been a while. You look great," Stacie said.

"Thanks. I've been so busy with graduate school work and wedding planning," Dash said.

"Hey, Vince, grab us some cold ones from the fridge," Jeremy yelled out, as he poked his narrow head through the sliding door to scan the room like a military laser before exterminating its target.

"Dash, I thought you were going to wear the brown outfit," Jeremy said.

"Oh, it makes me look fat. I thought this one looked better. See?" she said, doing a half twirl.

"Vince and Stacie, come on out and enjoy some music. The juice is in the cooler," he said.

"Sure. Come on, Stacie," Vince said, grabbing a few cold ones from the fridge.

Meat-Lover's Special

He placed them under his arms and then shoved Stacie along with his body. They walked outside and sat down in the cushioned chairs.

Jeremy stormed back in and shut the door behind him without a sound.

Dash's hands began to quiver as if they were being submerged into freezing water.

Jeremy turned six shades of red within seconds.

"Why are you always challenging me?"

"I wasn't, Jeremy. I just thought this would be a better choice for the occasion."

His hands rested on his hips. The back of his right hand swung towards her mouth quicker than any pitcher's fastball.

Blood droplets exploded from her mouth and flung onto the front of the fridge, as well as her previously pristine white sundress. She fell down to the floor, pulling the salad on top of her.

He stooped down next to her.

"Now you have to change! Put on what I told you. Hurry. Our friends are waiting for dinner. Clean this mess up and you, too!"

He scooped up the potatoes.

She grabbed a dishtowel, held it to her mouth, pressed down gently, and shuffled to the bathroom to change into the baggy khaki pantsuit.

Dash stared up in the mirror, unzipping her stained dress. Thick tracks were painted under her eyes from her running black eyeliner. She wiped her nose with the hand towel resting on top of the wood counter.

She turned on the water and rinsed and dried her face. She then sat down in her vanity chair and opened up a drawer, where over a dozen plastic hospital emergency room ID bracelets covered her makeup.

She shoved them to one side and picked up the tube of liquid concealer. She squeezed a glob about the size of a quarter onto her fingertips, then blended it around her mouth. The powder came next, with a few dabs of neutral gloss on her lips.

Infinity

Dash reentered the kitchen, swept the mess up off the kitchen floor, and wiped the blood off the fridge's door with paper towels dipped in warm soapy water.

She opened up the fridge and rummaged through it. Luckily, she found a half head of lettuce, two plump tomatoes, and a few carrot sticks in the back of a drawer. She prepared a second salad.

She walked out onto the patio with a tray, where the salad bowl, dressings, and cheese and crackers rested.

"Okay, you guys, let's begin," she said.

"Hey, why did you change, Dash? Your dress was so lovely," Stacie said.

"I spilled something on it."

She stared down at the grass.

"You okay, Dash?" Stacie asked.

"Yeah, just a tough week. Here, have some salad."

They all sat down to eat, while Dash served them.

"Jeremy, my man, you know just how I love my steak. Enough grilling to knock that chill off. I like it warm and bloody. I don't get how our girls are vegans," Vince said with a stuffed mouth.

"Yeah, me too, man. There's nothing like a juicy steak and a cold one."

A few drops of blood ran down the side of Jeremy's mouth and landed on his hairy arms.

Stacie looked at Dash from across the table, as she nibbled on her salad and baked potato, mostly scooting the food around her plate with her fork.

After dinner, they all went back into the house to watch a movie and to have dessert and cold drinks.

Dash cleaned up, as she listened to her favorite jazz station. Stacie walked into the kitchen to help her.

"Stacie, I got this. Please enjoy the movie."

"It's too loud, and the movie switched to football. You know how it

Meat-Lover's Special

goes. Is there something wrong, Dash?"

"Nothing. Why do you ask?"

She scrubbed the plate with the dishtowel repeatedly, without looking up at her friend.

"It's written all over your face."

"I'm just tired."

"Okay, if you say so. I'm just going to keep bugging you until you tell me."

Suddenly, a breaking news report interrupted the ballgame.

"ATTENTION, LISTENERS... IF YOU HAVE PURCHASED ANY BEEF PRODUCTS FROM J'S GROCERY, EMMA'S MARKET, OR K&M WHOLE FOODS, THEN PLEASE THROW OUT IMMEDIATELY. ALL MEATS CONTAMINATED! REPEAT—THROW OUT. PLEASE CALL 1-800-000-0000 FOR MORE INFORMATION."

"Oh, my gosh, Dash. Where did those steaks come from?" Stacie asked, as her knees began to shake.

She slid down into the barstool.

Dash walked over to the trashcan. She lifted up some plastic bags with tossed salad on top and found the white paper the steaks had been wrapped in. She turned it over. It read: Emma's Market. She dropped it to the floor.

Stacie ran over to her.

"Give me the phone, Stacie," Dash commanded without blinking.

Dash dialed the number. A rep answered.

"Hello, I just heard the news report on the radio about the contaminated beef. My fiancé and his friend just consumed steaks super-rare from Emma's Market."

"Listen, you need to get out of the house now!" the rep yelled.

"What? Why? What is it contaminated with?" Dash asked frantically.

"That's not important. Get out now! You may have less than 15 minutes after consumption, before..." the rep replied, breathing hard and stuttering into the receiver.

"Please, tell me. What is it contaminated with? Before what?"

"Ma'am, ticks were genetically engineered with a lethal flesh-eating virus in a lab a few months ago, about 60 miles from your location. Somehow, they escaped and fed on a pasture of cattle. Those same animals were unknowingly slaughtered and packaged for sale in the stores listed on the announcement."

"So, you're telling me that my fiancé and our friend are going to eat me, like in those silly zombie movies?"

"Yes, that's exactly what I'm trying to tell you. Listen, whoever consumed the contaminated meat will transform into a mad feeding zombie with no memory of anything or anyone. I got your location, and a special termination squad will be headed to your home address soon."

"I can't believe this."

"Believe it, sister! This is for real. You need to leave. Get out of there, while you still can!" the rep demanded.

The phone call dropped with an irritating, dreadful buzz.

Dash repeated everything to Stacie.

"We need to go now!"

"I'm not leaving Vince. Someone's playing an awful joke, that's all, Dash. None of it is true. It's just a big, fat hoax to scare us. Remember that radio segment years ago by that famous guy that caused panic to so many listeners? This is the same kind of thing," she whined.

"Come with me, Stacie. I really think the rep is telling the truth. Anyhow, I almost didn't come home today. I was going to leave Jeremy for good. I know this is my out."

"What, your out? What are you talking about?"

"Stacie, I didn't want to tell you, but he's been abusing me physically and emotionally for months."

"Dash, are you sure?"

"Yes, I think I would know."

"He doesn't mean to hurt you. Vince has hit me, too, but not lately,

Meat-Lover's Special

because I know what irritates him now. Guys get angry, and this is how they react. You just have to figure out the things you do to make Jeremy so upset and stop doing them. He's always telling Vince how the two of you are meant to be together. He told Vince how he fell in love with you that night at the homecoming bonfire our senior year in high school."

"Are you kidding me? You think what Vince has done to you is forgivable? That I should listen?"

"Of course. Vince is a good guy. He works hard, and so does Jeremy. Give him another chance. They don't mean it. It hurts them just as much, Dash."

"No, I can't believe this. Tonight was it for me! Please come with me, Stacie, before something really bad happens."

"I can't."

Dash grabbed her purse off the counter and pulled out the .38 Special.

"Here, take this, at least."

Dash attempted to hand it over to her. Stacie pushed it away, hugged Dash, and walked back into the living room.

"Hey, you guys? What are you two doing?" Stacie asked, as her lips trembled and teeth chattered.

She noticed their shadows against the wall. Vince and Jeremy were hunched over on all fours behind the couch, as their bodies flinched again and again.

Stacie walked towards them with her arms pressed against her sides, touching her ruffled denim miniskirt. Her legs shook like Jell-O.

Within seconds, their heads cocked backwards like a gun trigger. Thick yellow drool ran from their mouths. Their eyes widened and transformed into bright iridescent lenses. Their cuspids protruded out, and within seconds, they were gouged in her voluptuous thighs.

Dash was already in the car. She had backed out of the garage and was driving toward a black van, parked in front of the house.

She heard Stacie scream twice and saw quick shadows move across the living room bay window.

The large bold white initials *Z.T.* were printed on the side of the van, with *Zombie Terminators* spelled out underneath. The driver scanned Dash's eyes with a lime-green light and waved her on.

She drove away from her house for the last time.

The End

Meat-Lover's Special

Dishonorable
Path

Each night…
They came
Never the same way
I tried to pretend not to see them or hear their crackled whispers.
They knew I saw and heard them.
Dragging their spiny fingers across my quivering, blistered lips
They made me watch.
Over
Over
And over again…
I tried to turn those memories off, but failed each time.
They never gave me rest.
Each night…
They came
All of them
The years grew clearer and clearer:
1969
1976
1989
1996
2002
2008

Infinity

2017
I could smell all of them.
Jasmine perfume, vanilla ice cream, sweet cranberries, burning hair, decaying flesh…
I knew each by name:
Veronica
Raynay
Shazia
Frances
Olivia
Constance
Zena
These were the ones who came to me each night.
They showed me what I wanted to dismiss permanently.
Their bodies were once young, beautiful, and full of warmth, now so cold and distorted.
My dirty, evil deeds transformed into night terrors.
Each night…
They came
They were my visible sins.
They would never allow me to forget, only to remember every detail of the gifts I gave them—personal tortures and eternal cries.
Each night…

Dishonorable Path

Lock

Gerrie Knots heard many tales about the Garmountsville Hotel throughout high school.

It sat up on Wasp Hill. Many swore the grounds were haunted, and they whispered stories about what they'd witnessed.

She never believed the tales. So she decided to stay at that hotel one night, just to prove her best friend, Hazel, wrong.

Hazel begged her not to stay there.

Gerrie refused to listen.

Hazel texted Gerrie the night before her trip.

H: **Gerrie, please, please, don't go!**
G: **Whatever! I'm going to prove to you that your crazy tale is just that…crazy!**
H: **If you stay there, then always lock your door and never forget to fasten the silver-chained lock after midnight.**
G: **Sure. I'll pack a dozen garlic cloves, a few wooden stakes, and special ultraviolet high beam flashlight while I'm at it.**

Gerrie drove to the hotel and checked into room 797. After she rested for a bit, she decided to tour the small city for a few hours. She ate dinner at Serena's Secrets, a family-owned Italian restaurant. Two refills of garlic fettuccine and several breadsticks later ushered her into her sleep zone earlier than planned.

By the time she made it back to her room, she just wanted to curl up in bed and drift off to sleep. It was almost 11:30 p.m.

Gerrie's cell phone beeped—a text from Hazel lit up the screen.

H: Please, please, don't forget to lock your door with the silver-chained lock before midnight.

G: Hazel, please...please, go to sleep. I am. See you soon.

Gerrie threw her cell on the bedside table and jumped into bed. After about twenty minutes, she heard something bumping at her door, and the door squealed unbearably loud as it opened. She turned over and grabbed her cell phone from the bedside table.

She turned the flashlight on and shined it all over the room. Her door was wide open.

Gerrie rose out of bed and walked over to the door. She saw nothing in the hallway. She shut the door and locked it. She noticed the silver chain swinging back and forth.

She heard something bump into the wall in the closet. She turned the lights on and opened the closet door. Only empty hangers swung back and forth, making a soft clanking sound; an ironing board rested on a hook inside and an extra blanket sat on a shelf, but there was nothing else to explain the noise.

She laughed to herself and mumbled, "Hazel's crazy text just got me wound up." She turned off the lights, peeled back the comforter and sheets, and lay back down in bed.

Gerrie drifted off to sleep after thirty minutes or so, then something fell onto the floor with a loud crash. She jumped up, her heart racing and cell phone in hand. She shined the flashlight in the area, only to discover it was the antique ceramic lamp from her bedside table that fell and woke her.

She was too tired to clean up the mess, and figured that she would

Lock

take care of it tomorrow morning before checking out.

She pulled the covers over her head and closed her eyes again… Then, she felt something cold licking each of her toes.

She opened her eyes and grabbed her cell phone once more. Gerrie slowly pulled the covers up off her feet. The licking ceased. She rose up and crawled down to the foot of the bed.

She saw nothing, so she pulled the comforter up on the side of the bed to look underneath. It was vacant, except for a few dust bunnies and scraps of paper.

Before she rose up, hot, stinging breath showered her neck as a deep, garbled voice whispered, "You forgot to use the silver chain to lock your door."

She turned around to see what it was, but before she could identify whatever it was, she felt its long claws piercing her neck. A line of blood dribbled down her chest and splattered onto the white sheet.

Before it could finish her off, her phone beeped. Gerrie tried to grab it, but whatever it was jerked it from her hand. Within seconds, it loosened its other claw from around her neck, leaped from the bed, and jumped out the window.

She was barely able to dial 9-1-1, and she didn't recall being transported by an ambulance to the ER for immediate surgery. Her vocal cords were severely damaged and swollen from the attack and surgery.

Gerrie was lucky the doctors and nurses were even able to save them. She overheard someone say that she may never speak again; when she tried, it hurt to even whisper.

The hospital contacted Hazel since Gerrie had no immediate family. She walked into Gerrie's room, grabbed her hand, and bent down to whisper in Gerrie's ear, "I told you to lock your door with the silver chain."

Gerrie pointed at a notepad and pen on her bedside table. Hazel grabbed them and handed them to her. Gerrie wrote as best as she could on the pad, her hands trembling with each letter she attempted to write: "What attacked me?"

"It's called a *Ta-Wan-De-Ran*," Hazel said.

Gerrie wrote out a few squiggly question marks as Hazel continued to explain. "Soul-stealers…they prey on those who don't believe. You see, that hotel's grounds have been infested with them for a long time, and only the silver-chained lock keeps them out. They hate silver, and the chain would've protected you, if you would've just listened to me. Your cell phone must possess silver accents, because the *Ta-Wan-De-Ran* retreated from your room before it could rip out your vocal cords to gobble up your unleashed screams and suck your soul out. Where's your cell phone?"

Gerrie pointed at the dresser next to the hospital bed. Hazel pulled the drawer open and picked the cell phone up. "Hold out your hand, Gerrie," Hazel said. Gerrie grimaced and held her hand out.

Hazel dropped the cell in her hand.

At first, it felt fine to Gerrie…and then it started to feel like someone was holding her hand over an open flame. She dropped it on the floor and noticed a bed of blisters inside her throbbing palm.

"Just what I thought, Gerrie…I'm so sorry." Tears ran down Hazel's cheeks. She pulled latex gloves out of her coat pocket, slipped them over her hands, and reached over to place her hands over Gerrie's nose and mouth.

The End

Lock

Krisper

Someone told me this campfire story last weekend.
There's a hidden and forgotten wooded area in Texarkana called
Whispering Bend.
Many believed a turbulent spirit haunted that place, a spirit with the
name of the Krisper.
They said, "Don't say its name out loud… even a whisper would be
too loud, and your life would be nevermore if you were ever near
Whispering Bend."
A group of high school seniors decided to test it out last October, after
Homecoming.
Some were too scared to go down the steep hill to Whispering Bend
and drove off, leaving a tornado dust cloud behind, while the rest
pulled out their fearless vests and nonbeliever sunglasses.
Once they climbed down and found Whispering Bend, they began to
chant out its name.
"Krisper… Krisper…"
They waited for a while, almost an hour.
Nothing…
They repeated the chant two more times.
More disappointment painted their faces.
They started back up the hill, one by one.
A high wind from the East slapped each of them down really hard,

temporarily numbing their limbs.

Before anyone could scream out, a deformed ten-and-a-half-foot creature with curvy, glistening blades for hands stood over them. Freshly burnt human body parts decorated her curvaceous body, like strips of tainted clothing...

The creature opened her mouth, which resembled moving rows of razor fangs.

It roared out a choppy, dreadful laugh that caused the weak branches and leaves from the trees to rain down onto its new victims.

One girl closed her eyes tight and hoped that she was having a bad dream. She whispered under her breath, "Please, please make it go away..."

The odor of rotten corpses and sewage settled over her like a heavy fog.

The Krisper kneeled down to her and whispered one word at a time, "You should've stayed with your wise friends up there. Now, you'll believe, and others will never forget me after tonight..."

Krisper

Unleashed

I thought Aunt Flow waking me up at 3:30 a.m. last summer, on my fifteenth birthday, was the worst thing that could ever happen to me. Nope…

My older brother's death and transformation into a monster… Those events were much more traumatic for a teen girl.

My grandma had always told me stories about our kind, ones that were passed down from her clan. I always ignored her and thought she was a little wacko, being almost 102 years old and all.

I now know her stories are true. I woke up in a pool of blood a few nights ago, but it's not what you're thinking. A mangled, unidentifiable animal swayed back and forth in a tree above me, as I lay in a bed of dirt and crispy leaves.

My mouth was wet. I wiped it with the back of my hand and pulled it away, only to find blood. I don't even recall leaving my bedroom last night.

✳ ✳ ✳

My name is KoKo Hawk, and I believe that I committed the unspeakable, because I just turned sixteen years old, which means shifting age and something far worse than being with Aunt Flow every

Infinity

month—Shifter Duels.

These duels occur every odd year. The Shaman Tribal Council, S.T.C., votes on which two tribes will compete. The shamans from various tribes make a selection based on a journal of names and crimes committed within each household.

A sixteen-year-old is chosen to fight someone from a different tribe until only one is left standing. I've heard so many awful stories about these bloody, barbaric duels over the years.

My name was chosen because of how my older brother died. He committed suicide, an unforgivable crime.

I'm part of Kiwaddo tribe. We originated from Southern Texas and our people were amazing bead-making masters. Most of my ancestors have traveled outside of Texas because many of them have been targets of the Shifter Duels over the last few years. The S.T.C. sent out hunters to bring the chosen ones back for the duel or terminated them with their immediate families if they resisted.

There are stories that my tribe was cursed many years ago. I do find it quite ironic, how a Kiwaddo teen is chosen the most out of all the others.

When I asked my grandma about the curse, she looked away for a moment, before scolding me with her eyes. I never asked again after that day.

I dreaded the end of the week because that was going to be the day of the Shifter Duel.

I never embraced my shift and knew my fate. In other words, I didn't practice the shifter arts. My grandma and mom begged me to years ago, so I would be prepared for that day.

After picking my backpack up off the floor, I carried it in my right hand. I went out the door and took note of the grey clouds hovering over me. The rain started as soon as I took a few steps away from my house. I unzipped my backpack, moved my hand to the side, and pulled out my mini umbrella. I opened it up and headed towards my school,

Unleashed

which was about 15 minutes from my house.

I approached a church after deciding to make a small detour in an attempt to change things up by taking a different path than usual. I walked up to the church door and pushed it open. I shook my umbrella off and folded it in, as I stepped inside. I looked around and noticed tall stained-glass windows on each side. Someone tapped me on my shoulder, and I jumped. My umbrella dropped to the ground.

A petite man dressed in a white robe with a golden roped belt around his waist bent down to pick it up. He handed it to me, and I grabbed it from him.

"I'm sorry to bother you," I said.

"You're not bothering me at all. May I help you?"

"Oh, no. I was just making a quick stop inside from the rain. My school is nearby."

I started moving towards the door.

"Something on your mind, Miss?"

"Koko... Koko Hawk."

"Nice to meet you, Miss KoKo Hawk." He extended his hand. "I'm Pastor Sage."

"Nice to meet you. Well, I better get going."

He turned around and started walking away from me.

"If you need to talk, then I have really good listening ears."

Pausing for a few seconds, I pulled my cell out of my backpack to check the time. It was about five minutes until my first class. I dropped my phone back inside my backpack, looked around, and saw that Pastor Sage was sitting in a pew near the front row.

I went inside and sat down behind him. I took several deep breaths before I could usher a word out.

"Have you ever wished that you could be someone different?"

"Yes."

My eyes opened wider.

"Miss Hawk, who do you wish you could be?"

InFinity

He turned his body halfway around, placed his elbow on the top of the wooden pew, and rested his head on his hand while gazing straight up into my eyes.

"I don't know… just…"

"Just what?"

"Oh, nothing. I should go."

"Are you sure?"

"Yeah."

"Miss Hawk, know that my door is always open."

Nodding slowly, I stood up and walked down the aisle. When I reached the door, I pushed on it, and it swung open wide. The rain had stopped. I stepped outside and hurried off to school.

After classes let out, I decided to take the same path I had taken earlier that morning.

As I approached the church, I stopped and saw Pastor Sage sweeping the sidewalk out front. He waved, and I waved back. I continued on towards my home.

After I opened the door, I threw my backpack onto the couch. Mom was still at work.

I walked into the kitchen, opened the refrigerator, and grabbed some leftovers in blue plastic containers. I dumped the food onto a plate and warmed it up in the microwave. I thought about Pastor Sage and how much I wanted to talk to him before the eve of the duel.

The front door opened; it was Mom. Her eyes were bloodshot, and her hair was wet. She slammed the door behind her and looked over her shoulder while turning the top and bottom locks.

I held a spoon of steaming macaroni next to my lips.

She swung around and whispered, "Koko, we're getting out of here tonight."

"Mom, what are you talking about?"

I watched her, as she scrambled all over the kitchen, opening cabinet doors one after the other. She then scurried over to the freezer

Unleashed

door and swung it wide open. Bags of frozen vegetables and meats fell to the floor.

I dropped my spoon and walked over to where she was. I started picking up the packages.

"What are you searching for?"

"It's gotta be here. I know it's here."

She continued to rummage through the freezer, and I had to move out of the way a few times to avoid something landing on my head. Then she slammed the door with one hand, holding a coffee can in the other.

"Here it is!" she yelled out.

I frowned and said, "Glad you finally found what you were searching for."

"Yeah, me, too. It's all we have in savings, and it's going to get us far away from here."

"Seriously, Mom? You actually believe that the council is just going to let us leave freely?"

I stood up with several packages in my hands, placed them on the counter, and opened the freezer door to find each one a new home, while Mom sat down at the table, tossed out the money from the can, and started counting.

"I'm not getting the council's permission. My only priority is to save you. I failed with John."

She wiped her watery eyes with a napkin from the table.

"Mom, what happened to John is not your fault."

"Enough, Koko! Now, go and pack a small bag. We're leaving tonight."

I tossed a few necessities in my overnight bag, as I thought about Pastor Sage again. I told Mom that I needed to run down to the store to pick up a few snacks.

"Hurry up. We don't have a lot of time."

"Okay, okay. I'll be back as soon as I can."

InFinity

"Koko, you know that I never wanted this for you, right?"

I turned around and shook my head.

"Yeah, Mom, I know. It's just my fate."

"Well, I'm changing that tonight. You'll not end up as another casualty in their stupid war."

I left and headed towards the church. The doors were still open. I thought it had closed already.

As I entered the building, I saw Pastor Sage preparing the altar.

Though he had his back turned, he said, "Miss Hawk, I knew you would come back to visit me."

Before I spoke a word, I took some deep breaths.

"Yes, Pastor Sage, I need to talk to you."

"Come in."

As I approached him, he turned around to walk towards me. His face was smooth, with a thin beard at his jawline. His eyes reminded me of a sparkling stream.

My heartbeat finally slowed down after my walk there.

"So, what's going on, Miss Hawk?"

As my hands quivered, I looked up at him. I didn't want to waste too much time because I knew that Mom would begin to wonder about me if I was gone for too long.

"I'm leaving town tonight with my mom."

"Oh, I see. Is there something wrong?"

"No."

He stared at me and shook his head.

"I understand. There are always solutions to any problem. You just have to have faith and be confident."

"Pastor Sage, I don't think I've ever had faith in anything. You see, after my brother died, my home was different, and now I'm changing."

"My condolences about your brother. What do you mean when you say you're changing?"

"Thank you. It happened several months ago. I'd rather not talk

Unleashed

about what's going on with me."

"I can respect your stance."

"You said something about faith."

"Yes, go on."

"If someone believes hard enough about something, is it possible that their life can really change?"

"Yes, I do believe that."

"Wish I could believe like that."

"You can."

"You make it sound so simple."

"It truly is. I want to share something with you."

He dug a little booklet out of his pocket and handed it to me. I flipped through it.

"Thank you."

"You're welcome. When you're unsure what to do next, I hope that you refer to it. You'll be amazed at what you may find in there."

When we stood up, I placed it in the back pocket of my jeans.

"Thank you again for your time, Pastor."

"My pleasure. I wish that you could've attended one of my services, but I do understand that your travels must begin. May I say a prayer for you?"

With a shrug of my shoulders, I said, "Sure. No one has ever prayed for me."

"Remember that there's a time for everything in life. There will be a time you'll take a stand and not be afraid."

He placed his hand on top of my head gently and said, "Dear Lord, please keep your child safe and strong. Help her find her own confidence and faith in time. Amen."

I walked out of his church doors and towards the mini-store to pick up some snacks, and then I hurried home.

As I approached, with a brown paper sack in my hand, Mom was packing the car.

Infinity

"Finally, you made it back. I just have to grab a few more things, and we're out of here."

She dashed back inside, and I looked around at our house. It wasn't a mansion or anything, but it was our home—one that my late dad built with his bare hands. He wanted us to have a nice place because he didn't have one when he was my age.

He told me plenty of stories about when he was young and how his family was homeless for many years.

"Mom, you really think we're going to get out of here?"

"Yes."

"You really think that they're going to let us go just like that?" I asked with a snap of my fingers.

Mom stared at me. She backed up next to the car and slid down, until she was sitting, with her eyes still pinned on me. Tears zipped down her face like small shooting stars.

Squatting next to her, I wiped away some of her tears.

"They'll find us, and they'll take me from you. There's nothing we can do. The Shifter Duel is my fate, as what John did was his. I gotta do this. You and I both know the consequences if we try to run." I took my finger and slid it across my neck, before pointing at my mom's. "They'll kill us off, just like they've done to the others who tried to run."

Her head dropped onto her knees. I patted her back for a few seconds, and then we stood up and took the items out of the car and put them back in the house.

"Mom, just rest and take an early bath."

Later, I jumped in the shower and replayed my visit with Pastor Sage. I fell asleep early that night.

The next day, I skipped school because the big day was fast approaching. I wanted to visit Pastor Sage again, but I backed out.

A red letter arrived Friday morning; it was from the council. Mom saw it and snatched it from the mailman's hand.

Unleashed

Thanking him, I grabbed the rest of the mail.

Mom ran into the house and sat at the kitchen table.

"Koko, come quick!"

I placed the other envelopes on the coffee table in the living room, then walked into the kitchen and sat in front of her.

Her hands were shaking, as she asked, "You know what this is?"

I nodded my head.

The letter made it official—that I was a participant in the Shifter Duels. It also disclosed the name of my opponent. I was finally going to be privileged to know.

Mom ripped the top of the envelope open with the sharp nail on her left index finger. She read it quickly and dropped it to the table.

"Mom, what? What's wrong?"

I grabbed the letter and read it.

~Greetings, Ms. Koko Hawk~
The S.T.C. has made our final decision to match you with
Megedagik Horn.
Please meet at Hummingbird Forest no later than 7:00 p.m.
tomorrow night.
We appreciate your participation in the Shifter Duels.

"His first name means *to kill many*, and he belongs to a very evil tribe, the Monaapho. They're always known to be extremely cruel and aggressive. Do you know why he was chosen?"

I shook my head and said, "No."

"Megedagik's dad killed his second wife and has never really been held accountable for his evil deeds because of special favors his dad committed for a powerful skin walker, who in turn helped him become untouchable in law enforcement's eyes, but not in the eyes of the S.T.C."

"So, this Horn kid, is he pretty good?"

Infinity

"He's beyond that. I knew of his family in high school. His only goal will be to destroy you."

Tears raced down her cheeks faster than before.

"Would Grandma know anything about his shifting abilities to help me?"

"Maybe. Let's go visit her tomorrow morning."

We jumped in the car and drove about 30 minutes to the country, not too far from Hummingbird Forest. The wind picked up and rocked the car a little on the road. We pulled up to a small wooden house, where almost a dozen dreamcatchers hung on the tall poles positioned all around the house.

Mom and I stepped out of the car at the same time and shut the doors. We walked along the curvy mocha-bricked pathway. I knocked on the panel of the screen door.

"Come on in. I've been expecting you two."

I pulled the screen door open. Grandma was sitting up in her floral-print recliner. Mom followed behind me.

"Sit down, you," Grandma said.

I saw two glasses of watermelon juice and a plate of bannock—flat quick bread. I grabbed two, stuffed them in my mouth, and then immediately drank half the glass of juice.

Mom stared at me, so I stopped chewing so fast and swallowed.

"Sorry."

"Luyu, hush, now. Let her eat. She's going to need all the strength she can absorb before tonight."

Mom shook her head, and tears filled her eyes.

"Grandma, do you know who my opponent is?"

"No."

Mom reached for the letter in her purse. She pulled it out and handed it to Grandma, who grabbed it and read it to herself. She was quiet for a few minutes, and then she stood up and walked into her bedroom.

I looked around the space. It must have been a while since I'd

Unleashed

visited her because I'd almost forgotten about all the dreamcatchers that decorated her walls.

Grandma was a big believer in bad spirits always searching for somewhere to hide, so she kept them out of her home by having dreamcatchers inside and out.

I remembered when she gave me my first one. I was about eight-years-old.

Grandma finally reentered the living room with something in her hand. She shuffled over to me.

"Bend your head down, Koko."

I did, and she tied a leather-like necklace around my neck, and it felt like it took her an hour to complete the knot. She instructed me to lift my head.

I picked the round necklace up to look at it closely; it was encased in leather.

"Grandma, is this a dreamcatcher?"

She nodded.

"This one is truly special. It'll provide you with protection tonight. You're going to need it because you've never prepared!" she snapped.

"Yeah, I know. I just hoped I would never get chosen."

"I've told you about our history. It was only a matter of time, KoKo, before the council chose you."

I stared down at the floor.

"Too late now to feel sorry for yourself. You gotta be strong and do your best tonight."

"Grandma, you never said anything about my opponent."

"He's strong, sneaky, and really mean. He'll try to take you out pretty quick. I knew his granddad and other relatives. You're going to have to watch him and be as fast as you can."

"Do you know what he may shift into?" I asked.

"Not exactly. He could turn into anything."

"Any other advice that you can give me?"

Infinity

"Wear the necklace and try to keep it on. I made it with that material, so it can stretch during your shifting."

"Thanks, Grandma.

"I don't even know what I'm going to change into in a few hours. I think I shifted a few nights ago, but I don't even know... I can't tell you what I turned into."

"Premature shifting a few nights before the full moon isn't uncommon, especially since you've never practiced. I so wish you had."

I bowed my head down and said, "Yeah, me too."

Mom placed her arm around my shoulders, pulled me in closer, and whispered, "We can still go. It's not too late."

I blew my puffy rainbow-highlighted bangs up with a long breath.

"It's okay, Mom. I know what I have to do."

I gave Grandma a hug because I knew she wouldn't be able to be there. I wouldn't have wanted her there, anyway, just to watch her last grandchild die.

Mom and I walked back to the car, opened the doors, and slid in. She looked at me before starting the car up and sighed, tears in her eyes. We drove away from Grandma's house towards my final destination.

"Mom, do you know what I could shift into?"

"Not really, KoKo. You didn't allow it to emerge. I could've helped you, but you refused. You didn't read or study any of the old clan books about it. I begged you so many times when you were younger, and again last year."

"I'm so sorry that I didn't listen to you."

"I wish that your brother was still here."

I sighed and whispered to myself, "I wish he was still here, too."

We finally made it to Hummingbird Forest. We opened the doors, stepped out, and shut the doors behind us.

The sun was still bright, with a golden-reddish tint, spanning onto the forest floor. The tall trees formed an extremely spacious archway

Unleashed

leading to the clearing where the duel would occur. A set of three-tiered bleachers lined the left and right sides.

"KoKo, this place will be dark soon and packed with the council and spectators. I want you to start focusing. Close your eyes."

My mom's arms rested on top of my slender shoulders. I looked up at her before I closed my eyes. Hers were full of unspoken emotion and tears. I placed my hand on top of hers.

"Okay, think about something mighty. I want you to also think about something that terrifies you."

I kept my eyes closed.

"Now, I want you to see it in front of you."

I closed my eyes tighter and tighter. I pulled away from Mom, stumbled backwards, and landed hard on my bottom.

"What did you see?"

"Absolutely nothing."

"Really?"

I nodded, and then Mom started to pace back and forth in a small space.

"This isn't good," she said, looking at her watch.

I heard noises, so I looked up and saw a row of cars driving along the winding path. I knew the time was getting close.

Mom walked over to me and extended her hand. I grabbed it, and she pulled me to standing.

"Again, and quickly! Close your eyes and really focus this time, KoKo. I mean it!"

Her eyes were different, with an iridescent glow that wasn't present in them until that moment.

"Mom, are you a shifter?"

She nodded.

"Have you ever been in a duel?"

"No."

"You've been holding back. You never told me."

Infinity

"Koko, why? You were never interested, so why waste your time?"

"Wow. Mom, if you had just told me, then maybe I would have gained a little bit of curiosity about it."

"Too late for that now. Focus!"

"One more question."

"Hurry up, the duel will begin soon, Koko. What?"

"What are you when you shift?"

"I'm a *Rodtugamuan*."

"A *Rodtu*… What is that?"

"I'm a trio—part rat, tiger, and chameleon."

My jaw dropped. I couldn't say a word.

"Let's try this for the last time. Think of the mightiest animal and something that terrifies you."

I closed my eyes slowly and a vision started to formulate slowly, but it was fuzzy.

"Can you see it, KoKo?"

"Sort of."

"What do you see?"

"Long, sharp claws and a glowing tail."

"Anything else?"

"No."

I opened my eyes back up.

"Remember what you saw, okay? You'll need to unleash the vision you saw in the ring when it's time."

"Then, what?"

"Allow it to emerge into your shifting."

"What if I can't get it to emerge?"

"Don't worry. It will, once you are pushed hard enough. Keep Grandma's necklace on."

I shook my head, as I felt a cold chill run down my entire body.

More cars drove into the area, as the others started unloading. They flocked to the bleachers, which filled up fast.

Unleashed

"This is when I leave you, Koko." She hugged me and whispered in my ear, "Remember to focus and allow your vision to unleash."

Nodding, I said, "I love you, Mom."

"I love you, too. Come back home to me."

She walked away and looked back a few times. She opened the door to the car, which was parked to face the ring of death, and flopped in.

A tall tribal councilman walked over to me. His face was chubby, with a thick salt and pepper mustache over his lips.

"Ms. Hawk, we're pleased that you're here tonight to pay tribute to an honor of our tribal world."

"You call this an honor? It's just unnecessary bloodshed!" I shouted, rolling my eyes.

"You have a right to your opinion. Regardless, you're one of the chosen who'll enter the ring."

For a moment, I stared at him, and then I walked away from him and headed towards the center of the ring. It felt as if everyone was staring at me.

The tribal councilman waved his hand to signal a few men. They held a long rope in their hands and walked over to the large open dueling area. They placed the rope around that space until both ends touched.

I looked around, but I didn't see Horn yet. I wondered if he had the same idea that Mom had earlier and went through with it, unlike us.

There were no clouds in the sky. The sun had begun to dip down behind the tall trees. The golden-reddish hues vanished.

Before I could blink, I noticed a rusty green Suburban driving down the path. I already knew who it must be. It came all the way up to the edge of the ring. The passenger door flew open, and a stocky six-foot-two guy jumped to the ground, which seemed to rumble briefly. He had a blonde crew cut, with red highlights on the tips of his hair. He wore ripped blue jeans and a black leather jacket with swinging chains on the pockets. His eyes were huge with bushy brown eyebrows above them.

InFinity

I wished that I had a set of clippers.

He walked towards me. Horn reached out both his hands to grab me, but the tribal councilman stepped in the middle before he could touch me.

"Okay, I think our two participants are ready to begin!"

A few spectators laughed and pointed at me.

The tribal councilman kneeled down and held his hands up. He rubbed them together several times. He closed his beady eyes and placed them on the rope, which lit up on fire, with sparks shooting up into the starry sky, towards the full moon. He then turned around and nodded his head.

Horn returned the nod and ripped off his jacket. He wore a sleeveless t-shirt. Tattoos, mostly wild animals and reptiles, decorated his arms and lower neck. I looked closer, and they appeared to move. A few peeled off his arms and floated into the air. He stomped the ground, and the loose dirt rippled up, and some of it flew into my eyes.

My vision became blurry for a few seconds. I wiped the dust particles from my eyes with the back of my t-shirt. I noticed how Horn slurped up the floating tattoos into his huge mouth.

He fell to his knees, and his arms and legs began to stretch out. His arms grew and formed three tentacles on each side. His head mutated into an unidentifiable elongated shape with miniature spikes on his jaws.

When Horn opened his mouth, I noticed protruding fangs on the top and bottom. His eyes glistened like large onyx glass marbles. Long twisted horns grew on both sides of his forehead and around his head. His legs expanded, and his feet transformed into large hooves. His back became a large hairy muscular hump.

He roared out, and the force of his voice made the trees wave back and forth for several seconds. I stumbled straight to the ground. His height seemed to have increased. He stood there, pacing back and forth on his end, like a rattlesnake about to strike.

Unleashed

I searched for Mom, but I couldn't find her through the crowd. I tried to get out of the ring, but I was unsuccessful. I felt as if I kept running into a brick wall.

Mom saw what was going on and ran from her car, so I could finally see her. She tried to enter the ring, but the same happened to her. I couldn't touch her, and she couldn't touch me.

She fell down to the ground and began to cry. She looked up at me and pointed at the necklace around my neck.

She mouthed, "Keep it on you."

I nodded, and then I recalled the booklet that Pastor Sage shared with me. It was still in the back of my jeans pocket. As Horn started to race towards me, I managed to pull it out and flip to the last page. There was a short handwritten message.

Believe in yourself, and you can conquer anything.

Before I could look up, Horn lifted me by my waist with his tentacles and flipped me several feet into the air.

Feeling as if I was falling back to the ground at a fast rate, I touched the necklace and focused hard. My descent slowed, and I levitated in midair.

Horn was looking at me, and I heard his heavy panting. He attempted to jump several times and reach up with his tentacles to pull me down, but he failed because I was higher than he thought.

Concentrating even more strongly, I thought about the words in the booklet from Pastor Sage, and I felt my fingertips and toes tingling.

My arms extended a few feet out and transformed into immense blue wings, while my hands turned into sharp raptor claws. My torso became slimmer. My feet sprouted talons, and I grew a long glowing fuchsia tail.

I turned around 360 degrees and flew towards Horn. His eyes were staring into mine.

With my talons aimed at his chest, I flew down and knocked him to the ground. I used my wings to hold his flopping body in place. My claws caught his flying tentacles; I clasped tight and sliced them in half.

In seconds, another tattoo lifted off Horn's body, and his tentacles regrew—more that time, though, and they looked longer. He flipped me over and wrapped them around my waist and neck. I reached up with my claws to pull the tightening appendages from around my throat. I felt really dizzy. Horn continued to grip tighter, but finally, I broke free. I attempted to fly away, but another tentacle attached to my left wing and broke it with an excruciating snap. When I fell down, they wrapped around my neck. As my eyelids began to grow heavier, I could see my mom running around the ring.

I heard Pastor Sage's voice, sharing the messages from earlier and opened my eyes. My tail rose up and slammed Horn in his face, which stunned him in what looked like a painful way. He landed on his back, as his tentacles flopped all over the ground.

My claws landed on his chest, and I knew what I wanted to do, but I stopped.

The crowd stood up and yelled out for me to complete the duel. I looked back down at Horn, as his tears spilled over.

Loud chants echoed from the crowd, "Finish him! Finish him!"

I stood up and looked at the crowd. The fire ceased from around the ring. Mom ran towards me and hugged me.

A sharp pain shot through my chest. Horn had crawled to his feet and driven his horn into my mom's chest and partially into mine, as well.

Mom fell to the ground, as he roared out a piercing laughter.

"Stupid, stupid girl! You should've killed me when you had the chance! I win!"

I kneeled by my mom, but her eyes were closed, as blood dripped down her chin from the corners of her mouth. Horn lifted me up in the air and wrapped a tentacle around my neck, before slamming my entire body to the ground a few times.

He then stooped down over me.

Unleashed

"Your brother was just as pathetic as you and your mom. My dad was right about your entire family." He spat thick brown mucous in my face and screamed, "I'm about to erase another weak bitch!"

As I looked at him, my tail flew up, remaining stationary for a few seconds. My hand brushed over Grandma's necklace. I could feel something sharp emerge out of my tail, pain piercing the tip, as it first broke through.

At what felt like lightspeed, my massive tail landed on Horn's head, slicing his entire body in half.

The End

Infinity

Toxic

Careless I became, night after night, due to my fading eyesight, a disability I obtained after a baseball injury in junior high. I think she sensed it, too.

Revisiting those dark alleys that I promised myself to avoid, but she begged me at her almost last breath to do it just one more time, as she'd done a thousand times before, and I did it without a hiccup.

Vicious thoughts tumbled over and over in my mind every time I closed my eyes to recall all my hideous crimes, which I'd committed for her in order to kiss, caress, and hold her again. Those memories of holding her... erased my evil deeds for only a moment.

I guess that's why I didn't mind cutting hearts out of the ones who'd been long forgotten on the streets. Slicing and sautéing hearts with garlic, onions, and peppers to satiate her cries and moans...

I'm not sure if I can continue much longer, but I must, in order to keep her alive—yet my nightmares trigger my mind to rewind.

I despise closing my eyes because I know what waits for me in the darkness. When I sleep, I hear their screams and smell the metallic splatters of blood flying onto my face, landing on my thick lenses, as I finish another innocent victim.

Some were so very young with innocence written all over them.

It was all worth it because her life and beauty were fully restored once again, and I could hold her in my arms at least for another night,

Toxic

before she figured out that my travels would soon cease.

I knew what would happen when that hour arrived.

I met her by accident seven years ago, when she spotted me peering in that fogged up window that Halloween night at the *Annual Ghouls & Freaks Masquerade Fest* in New Orleans. I was only 17 at the time.

I'll never forget how she shape-shifted from such a beautiful Egyptian Princess in costume and exotic makeup, who mesmerized me within seconds. She then transformed into a jaw-dropping beast that I'd never seen before in my life. I wanted to run, but my feet were stuck to the ground, as though someone had hammered ten-inch nails through the tips of my toes. I desired to see more.

Ripped mammoth-sized dragonfly wings that were pointy and opaque graced her back. She possessed a scorpion-like tail, long fangs, razor-sharp claws, with multiple spikes standing on top of her knuckles, and piercing pink eyes.

Her head jerked around, and she stared at me with a sinister grin that pierced my inner soul, as she shot her hand right into that guy's chest. She ripped out his heart, with veins dangling down to the ground, and stuffed it in her dark widened mouth. Blood gushed out like a rapid waterfall from its corners.

She wasn't prepared for the allergic reaction. Her wings flopped up and down rapidly, banging against the ceiling.

Thank goodness, my dad studied medicine. I knew just enough to save her that night.

I've loved her ever since I saw her that first time before I knew she was a murderer, who would transform me into the same. Her beauty nearly made me forget her beast.

She made me a promise that night: That she would be my mate as long as I hunted for her. Sightings of her kind were getting too frequent—it was too risky.

She told me that once I became too feeble to continue, she would take my life, as she had taken her ex-boyfriend's that night back in New

Infinity

Orleans.

I've been preparing myself for a while now so that when that day came, I would be ready.

She shape-shifted into that horrid beast I first saw years ago because she knew—and she needed to pass the hunter baton on to someone else before she grew weaker.

Her tail dangled back and forth, as she towered over me. Acidic droplets oozed out onto my chest, and each felt like flaming fireballs, as they singed my skin.

As I looked into her eyes for the last time, she wrapped my entire body in her tail, held me up almost ten feet in the air, and placed her puffy, blistered purple lips onto mine to suck my insides out slowly.

Before she could finish, she dropped me to the floor and started gagging.

My drooping eyes struggled to look up.

"What did you do?" she asked in a heavy snarl, as she bent over.

She brushed her mouth with the back of her claw and noticed an indigo crystallized powder.

"I'm finally setting us both free…"

Zara looked at me with those eyes and stumbled down to the floor, transforming back into the beautiful Egyptian princess I met a few years ago and fell in love with for the last time…

The End

Toxic

The
No-No

Once upon a time, there lived a reclusive vampire, Twiggie Bean, inside an underground oak treehouse on a high hill, covered with blooming bluebonnets and golden daffodils.
Two upper crooked fangs and one middle lower fang decorated Twiggie's mouth.
He only left a few times a week, not to do the expected of most vampires.
What Twiggie did was so forbidden that if his vampire clan ever found out, then his name would be written in the *Vampire Book of Shame*, for sure.
No hesitation!
I saw the crime that he committed, more than once.
I would turn him in myself, but I must make a confession:
I've also participated in the forbidden act.
Ssshhh… Don't tell anyone, because if it ever got out, then Twiggie and I would be burnt at the stake, like those witches in 1692 Salem.
So, do you really wanna know?
Can I trust you?
Promise me you'll never repeat this, even to a dead soul… Pinky and fang swear it!
Okay… we both attend B.A.G., for vamps who wish to make a change…

Infinity

"B.A.G. what?" you may ask.
Sorry, forgot to share that. Blood Anonymous Group. We're taking the pledge to no longer live the bloodsucker lifestyle—instead, we are Juicers!

Yep, red fruits and veggies, all the way, baby!

The No-No

Almost
Extinct

I'll *never* begin high school, attend prom, graduate, or make out with a boy… I'm the last zombie on Earth.

I survived, and no other human knows, except my mom, the spastic Dr. Ginger Hunter.

She's been keeping me hidden downstairs in a creepy cobwebbed secret lab basement, where she's been experimenting on me to cure my zombie cooties.

Oh, yeah, I forgot to tell you my name… Zoey Hunter.

Let's just say that she's been at this for a while now, since almost a year before the wars ended. The HZW—the Human-Zombie Wars— swept throughout the world from 2015 to 2018.

Humans killed all the zombies—at least, that's what they thought.

I never imagined that I would be living a life of solitude, like I was in a prison. My room was big enough to fit a twin bed, low bedside table, two small lamps, and a dresser.

The bathroom was worse. I had to walk sideways to get in, and the slender shower and low toilet were basically kissing each other. The lights were always dim, with a constant flickering.

There was one window in the bedroom, probably only ten by ten inches.

Mom always threatened to board it up permanently if she ever caught me peering out during the daytime.

Infinity

I promise that the only reason I was a prisoner was because she was always so nervous that if a human saw me watching him or her, then I would be totally toast in her mind.

I thought the opposite. I figured that I was the last zombie on Earth. I could possibly get some great attention, like a celebrity, at least for a short time.

What's a zombie girl to do? Fantasies were about all that I actually possessed. The television that sat on the corner of my faded blue jean-colored dresser could only pick up two stations: news and sports.

My mom found an old VCR and three ancient movies at a thrift store one day. I cannot tell you how many times I've watched *Pretty in Pink* and *Some Kind of Wonderful*.

I daydreamed about a guy, a human guy, falling in love with me like the characters in those two movies.

Daydreaming… my reality forever.

A human guy wouldn't have even wanted to look at me. I was repulsive… just ugly. I stared in the grey dingy mirror some mornings and nights, trying to find a trace of my humanity left.

All I saw was crater-filled pale lime skin. My hair was super dull and dusty brown. I'd become lifeless, to say the least. Whenever a flower blew into my window every once in a while, I picked it up with my hands, which had skin that resembled that of an alligator, and it trembled and wilted instantly. It was as if it sensed death, and that was its finale.

Trying to make my days go by faster, I flipped through old country cooking or celebrity magazines. Some of them became art for my four empty walls, mostly the pictures of models.

I admired those girls, dressed in their pretty don't-bend-over-too-much dresses, with their smooth perfect skin and bodies and hair full of life and bounce. I knew that I would never experience a life like they did in those pictures.

To pass the time, I played games on my phone, but my mind always

Almost Extinct

drifted back to my awful reality.

Mom tried to entertain me the best way she could and always prepared tasteful meals for me that met my dietary requirements, but my appetite was leaving.

You could say that I was actually and purposely starving myself.

Heck, my life was over when I first contracted the disease.

Now *that* was a day I'd never forget.

I remember it all. It replays in my mind like one of those stupid tape recorders from the 70s that I saw in an old movie once.

Mom told me not to go out that night because of the HZW and mandatory curfew.

Did I listen? I think you know the answer to that question.

So, I threw on my favorite hooded grape-colored jacket, zipped it all the way up, and snuck out of my window that night to go to Portia Howell's party for a few hours.

Portia was the girl that we all wanted to be like. She was beyond perfect, from her head to her feet, you know.

If you thought Snow White or Belle were beautiful, try combining those two together—then you had Portia, with Tink's feisty attitude, but without the sparkle dust.

She was smart, rich, and surprisingly kind. At first, I thought she was super fake. I met her in the sixth grade, and we hit it off automatically, despite my worries about her being shallow.

She lived in the suburbs, and to get to her home from mine, I had to catch the train.

I walked a few blocks, and then the wind picked up pretty high. I pulled my hood over my head, tucking my long hair inside.

The moon shimmered a golden glow that lit up my path.

That night was really different. I heard gunshots sounding over my head, and fires decorated the city. The scent of burning wood and flesh filled the night breeze.

When I arrived at the train station, I peered through the window

InFinity

and noticed the trains were stationary. No people were in sight inside or outside the station.

Plan B… I paced up and down the sidewalk, always glancing over my shoulder.

Out of nowhere, I saw a strange guy, leaning against a brick wall. He was scruffy-looking and dressed in a dark trench coat with unlaced black combat boots and loose camouflage pants. He wore wide-rimmed eyeglasses, and his hands constantly shook.

He yelled out, "Hey, kid! You trying to get somewhere?"

I acted like I didn't hear what he said.

"Hey, I'm talking to you!"

He pushed away from the wall and started walking towards me.

My hand flopped around in my jacket, searching for my cell phone. I recalled that I left it under my pillow.

"Hey, are you deaf, or something?" he asked, continuing to approach me.

I turned around and tried to play it cool.

"I didn't know you were talking to me."

"Yeah, I think you did, unless you see some ghosts around here."

I barely smiled and quickened my steps.

"Well, I'm meeting someone soon. Gotta go."

"Look, kid, I saw you earlier at the station. You were hoping to catch the train, right?" I shook my head. "Where you headed?"

Right then and there, I remembered my mom always drilling it into my head when I was a little girl—never talk to strangers.

Mom had raised me by herself. My dad left her when he found out she was pregnant with me. I give my mom a hard time and all, but she's really okay. She went to school at night to make life better for us. Eventually, she became a research scientist, one with a lot of respect in her field, probably way more than I give her.

All of those drills somehow vanished from my mind because Portia's party was all I could think about. Besides, I promised her that

Almost Extinct

I would be there.

"Yeah, I'm trying to get to 456 Riverbend. It's in the—"

"Kid, I know exactly where that fancy place is. What's your business there?"

"Why you wanna know?"

"Oh… I get it. Well, tell you what. I can take you there if you want. I'm a cab driver. That's my girl over there, parked two cars up."

"Thanks, but no, thanks."

"All right, have it your way."

He started towards his cab and stepped to the driver's side.

I walked in the opposite direction and picked up the pace.

Loud sirens circled around me. A throng of zombies, military men, and gunshots were headed right for me.

I ducked behind a metal trashcan just in time. The horde was maybe five feet away from me.

Think, Zoey! No time to freak out now.

I saw drooling mouths, outstretched hands, and beady eyes staring at me. I popped up and tipped the trashcan over, kicking it towards the zombies. I then ran for the guy's cab and banged on his window for him to let me in.

He was reading something on his phone and smoking a cigarette. He looked up at me.

I banged my fist harder against his window. The gunshots were becoming louder, and the zombies looked like they were about to reach out and touch me any second.

"Oh, it's you. So, you want my help now?"

"Please, please help me, mister. Let me in!" I screamed.

"I don't know. I'm this strange guy and all. Sure Mama taught you not to get in the cars with strangers, right?"

"Yes, she did, but I think that she would make an exception here!"

My banging grew even more frantic.

He slowly reached over to the passenger side to unlock the door.

Infinity

It was five seconds too late. As I placed my hand on the handle and began to open the door, a zombie grabbed my jacket sleeve. A single gunshot fired straight towards its head, and a shower of nasty stuff splattered all over me. I closed my eyes and mouth and turned my head away just in time.

The blood was cold, and pink clusters of brains decorated my hair, face, and chest. I shook and wiped off most of it. The zombie fell facedown, as I jumped into the front seat of the cab and shut the door as fast as I could.

Zombies were like flies all over the cab before the guy could start the engine. Gunshots continued to be fired.

The man yelled out and pushed my head towards the floor, as he screamed, "Get down! Incoming!"

He started the engine up with one rotation, placed it in drive, and took off like a rocket.

Before I knew it, the horde from before was fading behind us and falling down one by one from gunshots.

"Kid, you okay?"

"I think so."

"Did you get scratched, or get any zombie gunk or brains in your eyes or mouth?"

I pulled down the visor above me, which had lights on the sides, to examine myself. I didn't see any blood or brains in my eyes or mouth, but blood and brains saturated my hair and jacket.

I looked awful. I couldn't go to Portia's party with all the zombie gunk covering me.

"Mister, don't worry about driving me to where I told you earlier. I'm not party material."

"You look pretty bad, that's for sure, but I think your friend, Por…"

"Portia."

"Yeah, Portia will understand. It's not like the HZW just started."

"Yeah, maybe, but I'm not up for a party now."

Almost Extinct

"You sure, kid?"

"Yeah, I'm pretty sure."

He drove me back to my neighborhood and dropped me off a block away from my house.

"Thanks. What do I owe you?"

"Nothing. Glad I could help you out. Stay off these streets at night, especially now. The HZW is going to end soon."

"Yeah, no kidding. Thanks again."

"Sure, promise me that you will stay put."

"Gotcha."

I scooted out of the cab, with blood and brains following me and dropping to the dark ground.

"Sorry about your seat and floor, mister."

"Don't worry about it. It can always be washed out, right?"

I shrugged my shoulders, as he drove off slowly. I walked towards the side of the house and crawled through my window. The light came on.

"Where in the heck...? What happened?" Mom asked. Her eyes began to tear up, and she jumped to my aid. "Were you shot or bitten?"

"No, I'm okay, Mom. Just want to get these icky clothes off and shower."

"You know I'll have to perform a head to toe examination on you right after."

"Yes, Mom, I know."

"We have very little time to detect if you'll be infected or not. Make sure you shower with that special soap I made up a few months ago and take those pills in the red bottle as prescribed on the label."

"I know, Mom. I know the protocol. We've reviewed them a thousand times over the last few months."

"Zoey, how many times do I have to tell you that it's just not safe out there? It hasn't been safe for years. Do you think you're invincible?"

I stood there, listening to her, drenched in blood and brains.

Infinity

"Mom, I'll be done soon."

I went into the bathroom, shut and locked the door behind me, and peeled off all the wet clothes. I placed them in the red plastic biohazard bag in the spare clothes basket and sealed it up.

When the water was ready, I got into the shower and used the special soap all over my hair and body.

After I stepped out of the tub and into my house shoes, I walked over to the vanity and found the bottle of pills Mom ordered me to take. The label read:

Take only if you've been exposed to zombie hazardous fluids, such as blood, brains, saliva, etc. Take three pills every six hours, until a full assessment can be done, and call the number below to report.

Once you ingest this medication, side effects may begin immediately, such as vomiting, acne, hair loss, and/or weight gain.
There is also a risk of developing certain cancers and permanent infertility.

I looked up at the mirror at my thick flowing hair, long eyelashes, and decently clear skin. My body definitely didn't need any more help with weight gain, and the rest…

After I took off the top and shook out three pills into the palm of my wet hands, I stared down at them. I went over to the toilet, dropped them into the bowl, and flushed. I tightened my robe and walked outside.

Mom was waiting to examine me with her medical bag and special equipment.

"Sit here in this chair. I already disinfected your bedroom and will do the bathroom next."

I sat down. My palms were sweaty.

"You took the medication as instructed, right?"

Almost Extinct

"Yep, sure did." I stared at her computer.

"Good."

Mom started the exam with a special warm purple light that was connected to her laptop, which could detect the smallest traces of *Zinfection* within minutes of exposure.

The program shared my results in a female robotic voice. "*Subject is free of any traces of Zinfection and may be allowed to interact in normal affairs. Please retest within 24 hours to confirm final result. Thank you.*"

"Okay, Mom, all clear, right?"

"It appears that way, Zoey, but we'll need to retest. Remember to continue to take the medication as advised because if you're infected and it didn't show up on the test, then the meds may help destroy some of the *Z-antibodies* fast. This test is not perfect." She cupped my face. "You know I would go crazy if anything ever happened to you, right?"

"Yeah, Mom, I know."

She hugged me, her plastic biohazard jacket crinkling loudly, as we made contact.

"Get some rest. I'll retest you tomorrow, okay?"

She patted my back with her gloved hand and began to take the special gear off, revealing her scrubs beneath.

I walked down the hallway to my bedroom and flopped down on my bed as if I was performing a cannonball into a pool. I bounced a little and heard my cell phone buzzing from under my pillow. Twenty missed calls and texts from Portia about what happened to me earlier that night.

I texted her back and explained why I was a no-show. I told her how I attempted to attend her party, but met that strange cab guy, and before I knew it, a horde of zombies and cops were headed my way. I did leave out the part where a zombie grabbed me, and my arm could've been gnawed on like corn on the cob, and boom! Her best friend could've been part of *Zombie Race*.

Infinity

Portia didn't respond all night. I kept texting and calling her, all the way until I fell asleep, but nothing.

The next morning, I woke up, and I was extremely tired. I sat on the side of the bed. Everything around me looked super fuzzy, and my head felt like someone was slamming it against a concrete floor. I was really hungry, but not for bacon, eggs, or milk. I wanted something different; I couldn't put my finger on it.

I placed my house shoes on and shuffled into the kitchen. I yanked the fridge door open, then kneeled down to rummage through each shelf, but I saw nothing that would meet my craving.

I wanted something wet, slimy… and really raw.

What's going on with me?

After slamming the fridge shut, I ran into the bathroom. I closed the door behind me, flicked the light switch on, and leaned towards the mirror. My skin tone was fading from its natural color to a more milky hue like I was losing blood fast. I looked at my hair, and it had also transformed from its lustrous wavy bounce to lifeless, and grey strands were sprouting from my once-ebony head.

My nailbeds looked like dried coffee stains. I tried to rub it away, but instead, I pulled a nail up and off. It didn't even faze me.

No! No! It can't be!

Though it seemed impossible, I was transforming into the most hated species in every city and state. I was becoming man's worst fear—a zombie.

I hadn't even started thinking about a bucket list yet. I had too much more to do.

How could this be happening to me?

Why me? I had never hurt anyone deliberately. I should have listened to Mom, but I didn't. It was all my fault. I did it to myself. She had warned me over and over again to not be out at night, especially with the HZW rampaging through the world.

I dropped my head, and the tears followed.

Almost Extinct

Mom must have heard me walking around early, and all the other noises that I was making because she was knocking on the door.

Though I tried to pull myself together, I looked pretty awful. I jerked a towel off the counter and used it to pat my face dry. My eyes were red and a little milky, too. My heart skipped beats whenever I took deep breaths.

As I opened the door slowly, she was standing right there. I hugged her tight and burrowed my head into her plastic-covered chest.

"Zoey, I know. I knew last night."

With tears flowing, I looked up at her and said, "What do you mean, you knew? How? My results were negative."

"Like I told you before, that test doesn't pick everything up, especially right away. Your potential infection was fresh, and the program may not have read it correctly at that time. Plus, it just takes a speck of zombie material to ignite the *Zinfection*."

"Mom, what am I going to do? They won't allow me to survive. I'll be slaughtered, just like they do when they find a stray Z or a horde."

The process was always the same. Slaughtered zombies gathered up into a huge semi-truck, driven outside the city limits, dumped into a prepared 12-foot hole and lit it up like a bouquet of fireworks.

Mom stared at me. "Did you take the first round of medication?"

My eyes veered away from hers.

"You didn't. Why?"

"Have you read those side effects on the bottle?"

"I know them very well. Are you prepared for your side effects from the *Zinfection*?"

"The pills won't stop it."

"How do you know?"

"Once you're infected, that's it, Mom!" I stared across the room towards a picture from when I was just born; Mom was holding me in her arms.

"I have a temporary solution."

Infinity

"What?"

Mom walked into her bedroom and returned with a syringe full of an orange creamy substance. "Zoey, I've been working on an anti-z vaccine for a while now. I've been testing a few z-subjects over the last few months."

"You never told me you were working with zombies!"

"I had to keep it to myself, Zoey."

"I guess I get it, so good results?"

"Sort of. What's strange is you're exhibiting initial z-signs, but you haven't changed completely. The z-transformation usually takes less than 24 hours, if not sooner. I'll run your blood chemistries once we get to our new place."

"New place?"

"We have to. It's the only way to keep you safe and give me time to figure out what's going on with you."

I shook my head up and down.

"Ready for the injection?"

"I guess so." My eyes closed and I stuck out my arm.

"No, silly, I must inject it in your temple area."

She did, and I needed to sit down. It felt like a maximum brain freeze after you drink a frozen Slurpee in 60 seconds.

"I'll be monitoring you at our new home. I believe this injection will suppress your z-transformation for a few more days, until your next treatment. At least, it gives me time to work on something permanent, I hope."

I looked up at her and said, "Thanks, Mom, even if it doesn't stop it."

Mom started tearing up. "Now, go pack yourself a small bag of necessities and meet me in the garage in 20 minutes, okay?"

I pulled away from her and walked to my room. I took a yellow duffle bag out from under my bed. I opened up my drawers and threw in some jeans, t-shirts, undies, bras, shorts, and socks. My cell phone

Almost Extinct

was thrown in last.

I then went to the bathroom and grabbed my toothbrush, toothpaste, deodorant, and body spray. I tossed it all in the same bag. I wrapped it twice around my body with its long straps. Don't know why I gathered up so much stuff. Guess I just wanted to remind myself what it was like to be human.

Mom had done the same, and we went out into the garage together. She jumped into the driver's side of the SUV, and I slowly climbed into the passenger's side. As soon as she let the door open and placed the car in *Reverse*, we noticed a guy standing in the middle of the driveway, dressed like the cab guy who saved me the night before.

Heck, it *was* the cab guy!

Mom backed out and stopped before she hit him. He came out from behind the car and walked towards Mom's side. Mom let her window down with one touch from her finger as if she knew him.

He leaned against her side of the SUV and said, "Good morning, Mrs. Hunter."

Mom remained quiet.

"Mom, you know him? He saved me last night from the zombie horde."

She raised her eyebrows and gasped, and then she started to cry.

"Mom, what is it?"

"Zoey, she'll be okay," he said.

"Hey, wait a minute. I never told you my name, so how do you know it, mister?"

"Zoey, I want you to meet Tanner Hunter… your dad. He's a *Z-Special Agent.* He usually works undercover all around the world, but he somehow found his way into our city."

"Mom, are you serious? Cab guy is my dad? The man who ran out on you when you were pregnant?"

"Yes, yes, and yes, Zoey."

"I always thought that he was dead, or something."

Infinity

"Sorry, baby, your mom thought that was for the best at the time."

"I'm not your baby and never will be, so don't call me that."

Mom's tears started up again, as she said, "Zoey, it's okay. You have every right to be angry."

"Mom, I'm super pissed at him."

"Look, Tanner, we don't have enough time. We need to go," Mom said.

"Yeah, I know that. That's why I'm here. I have directions for you to go to a good hideout, where no one will think to look for you both."

"Thanks, Tanner."

"Wait, you know about me?" I asked. "Why didn't you tell me last night who you were?"

"I didn't want to force you to go anywhere, and you would've resisted. I didn't want to cause a scene."

"You allowed those monsters to almost get me last night, and because of you opening the door so slowly, I could've been eaten!"

I crossed my arms over my chest tightly and jerked my head away from him.

"Tanner, is that true?"

"No, not completely. I opened the door just in time. I didn't think that was going to happen to Zoey. Plus, the HZW ended last night. Zombies are history."

Mom looked at me, and I looked at her.

"Wow, Tanner. You've really got some nerve. You're the same as you were back then: selfish and always playing games. Keep your directions and special place. I have my own."

Mom placed her foot on the gas and backed out of the driveway, while looking behind her, and then she put the car in *Drive*. She sped off faster than I'd ever seen her go before.

I looked back in the rearview mirror to see Tanner standing in the middle of the road, with his hands on his hips, shaking his head.

We traveled for almost three hours, before reaching Mom's place. It

Almost Extinct

looked like an abandoned old school building. We unpacked all of our stuff from the SUV and stepped into the lower section. Mom punched a code into a keypad. It looked pretty shabby on the outside, but as soon as we walked through the doorway, the shabby exterior gave way to a polished white lab area.

"Mom, is this your workplace?"

"Yes, a secret one off the radar where I perform and keep my special experiments."

"What do you do here?"

"Various experiments to better mankind, since the HZW started. My focus now will be to find a cure for you."

"Mom, you really believe there's one?"

"Yes, I have to. You are my inspiration, and I'll find it."

I started crying again.

She grabbed me and held me in a deep embrace.

"Zoey, now, I'm pretty sure this place is off the radar, but your dad may have different intentions. Sure sounded like it last night. I had no idea."

"*You* had no idea!" I scoffed.

"So sorry, baby."

"As long as I have you rooting for me, that's all I need, Mom."

"Good. Now, back to Tanner. I don't trust him and never did. I need you to stay out of sight for a while until I can figure things out, okay? There's another level with a secret passageway and a small room."

"You need me to stay there."

"Yes, Zoey. You okay with that? It'll be just for a bit. Need to keep you out of sight, due to any cameras or mini drones."

"I understand."

Mom escorted me down to the secret passageway, which was beneath the lab area. It was very discreet, almost impossible to find unless you knew where it was.

She showed me my new room, which was not like the one back

home. It was much smaller and dark. I had one tiny window, and Mom instructed me to only look out at nighttime.

There was a TV, a small fridge, a VCR, magazines, a few old video tapes, and a radio.

It was my new home. I had a feeling it was not going to just be a few days or weeks. It was going to be until a cure was found—*if* a cure was ever found.

That was where I would be. It would never be safe for me to do the simple things that most of us forget. I wouldn't be able to roam the streets, go to the movies, walk through the zoo, or hang out at the mall.

I was no longer human Zoey. I was *Zombie Zoey*, who became infected on the night she met the man she had never known or would ever want to know. I had no desire to build a relationship with Tanner or use the "Dad" label.

Flipping through the magazines, I began to tear pictures out that I liked. I was planning to post them on the walls with some tape I found in one of the dresser drawers.

As I was placing the last picture up on the wall, I heard my cell phone ringing in my duffle bag. I walked over and dug it out, only to see that the number was unknown. I answered it after only a moment of hesitation.

"Zoey, it's Portia. What happened to you last night wasn't an accident!"

The phone call dropped, and a loud buzzing sound sprayed into my ears, just before the phone slid from my face, out of my hand, and fell to the concrete floor with a crash. I ran to my door and banged on it so hard that my thin skin began to slough off.

I yelled out as loud as I could, "Mom!"

The End

Almost Extinct

Creep

If a *Most Likely to Commit Suicide* award existed, then it would be issued to Zacharie Verstein.

Zacharie was 5'1" and roughly 200 pounds in the seventh grade. He had no friends in real life or online, including a whopping total of zero social media followers.

The kids in school gave him his nickname, *The Creep*, when he was in the fifth grade, after Clarissa Silver's party.

Of course, Zacharie wasn't invited, so he climbed up a tree in his backyard to watch them laugh and dance and see Clarissa open up her gifts. He had collected pictures of her since they were in the third grade and just about anything she threw in her trash. His eyes focused in only on her curly locks blowing in the wind and her orange ruffled halter top.

Someone happened to look up and noticed him staring and yelled out, "Hey, y'all! Look at Zacharie, *The Creep*. Run, before he catches you and drools all over you!"

All the kids looked up, screamed, laughed, and ran off in different directions. Ever since that day, Zacharie was not known by his real name, but only by *The Creep*, the name gifted to him.

No matter what he tried to do, the kids always reminded him he could never be part of their group.

One evening, a tattered envelope with no return address arrived for him in the mail. He flipped it over a few times and ripped it open. An iridescent pin with a strip of paper wrapped around it rested in the corner.

He jerked the slip of paper off the pin and read: *Prick your finger twice and become...*

Perfect was Zacharie's immediate assumption, so he didn't read to the end before pricking his finger.

He collapsed to the floor, and his body transformed within sixty seconds. He rose up, unsure of what just happened.

The computer screen captured his reflection and exploded as his glowing onyx eyes, shooting flaming golden sparks, rolled in the direction of Clarissa's house.

Creep

Sweet
Secrets

H ell found me at Brimstone Junior High School on Halloween, a day I would never forget!

I showered and hid in a basement bathroom stall, awaiting the last earsplitting ring of the bell, while crying over the latest nasty shenanigan performed by Tempest Pierce. I prayed that no one would find me, especially her.

Colorful gang symbols, love messages, creepy drawings, and a dozen phone numbers decorated the once boring walls surrounding me.

I sat on the toilet seat, with my spidery legs pulled up against my chest, while my elbows rested on my bony knees. My hands cupped my acne-riddled face. I could feel the cold wind seeping through the small picture-framed window above me, which invited a temporary slumber.

The last ring of the bell vibrated the loose metal toilet, so violently that I jumped up and stood on the top of the seat.

I peeped out the window and noticed Tempest, strutting toward the school bus loading area. Out of nowhere, a whirlwind of brown and burnt orange leaves swarmed around her and her flunkies. The leaves vanished before she took her last step onto the bus.

That was my cue to escape. I ran all the way home. I stopped to catch my breath near Mr. Grady's farm and ran my trembling hands through the dry rustling cornstalks. I wished that place could be my permanent hiding place until 3:30 p.m. every day.

Infinity

Upon my arrival home, my Aunt Ivy greeted me on the open porch. The body-hugging hot pink leather jumper she wore lifted everything up extra high. The matching highlights in her hair sparkled in the sun. I hugged her around her tiny waist, jingling the belt she wore that had decorative little bells that rang with every movement.

"Aunt Ivy, what are you doing here?" I asked cheerfully, with a huge grin painted on my face. I temporarily forgot about the worst day of my life. "It's been a long time since you've visited."

"I know, honey. I came on out to help your momma and all, since your dad will be out of the country for a while and it's Halloween. Remember how we used to celebrate Halloween together when y'all lived closer?" she asked, smiling.

"I've really missed you."

"I've missed you too, Copper."

"A lot has been going on."

"I know. I want to hear about everything," she said.

Aunt Ivy didn't think I knew that Mom and Dad were considering getting a divorce, for all the reasons adults did such a thing.

Before I started upstairs to visit Mom, she said, "Wait, Copper! Your mom received some sad news from the doctor today. She's resting."

"Oh, what did he tell her?"

"She'll be up in a while, and she can share with you. Now, go wash up, so you can eat dinner and help me get ready for the trick-or-treaters."

I took a long shower and thought about what happened earlier, as I pulled a t-shirt over my head and tugged up my favorite cut-off sweatpants shorts. The tears wanted to explode, but I fought my leaky tear ducts, so my face remained dry.

I left my room and walked down the hall. I noticed Mom's door cracked open. She was sleeping. I pulled it shut, headed toward the stairs, and climbed down each step as slowly as I could. I noticed Aunt Ivy, moving like a dragonfly from one end of the kitchen to the other, preparing dinner.

Sweet Secrets

"Copper, how long are you going to watch me?"

She giggled, her back towards me still.

"Uh… sorry. I was just thinking."

"Yes, I can sense that. Come on down and sit, so you can eat, before we start the Halloween fun."

I walked down the last step and into the kitchen, which was decorated in earth tones. I pulled a chair up and scooted myself closer to the tall wooden table.

Aunt Ivy placed a plate of hot spaghetti with her famous sauce in front of me. I gobbled it up in no time, having not eaten much that day. She sat in front of me and ate a bowl, as well.

"Now, Copper, tell me all 'bout your day," she said.

I hesitated for several seconds before spilling.

"Aunt Ivy, have you ever had someone hate you—really hate you—for no reason?"

"I've had my share, but nothing that I couldn't handle. Is someone bullying you at school?"

"It depends on what you mean."

"Tell me all, and don't leave one detail out," she said, as she twirled a perfect bite of spaghetti onto her fork.

"Well, there's this really mean girl at my school, Tempest Pierce. She's been making my life just awful, ever since the third grade, when she pranced into Mrs. Patterson's classroom on the first day. I didn't know then that she would become my worst nightmare."

"So, you're telling me that this Tempest chick has been tormenting you since the third grade?"

"Yes, off and on. Some years are better than others."

"Copper, why haven't you told your parents, teachers, or me before now?"

"Just figured it would get better one day, and she would leave me alone."

"Doesn't sound like it, and it usually doesn't happen until someone

InFinity

does something to put out those vicious flames."

"Last year, Tempest told everyone that I was having a sex change because of my short haircut. She's bleached my clothes, tripped me in hallways, and kissed my crush, Kodak Stevens." Aunt Ivy turned several shades of red. "Today was the worst."

"What could top what you've told me already?"

"First, I've gotta tell you what led up to the worst day of my life."

Aunt Ivy breathed in and out for several seconds with her head tilted back.

"Okay, shoot."

"I was in volleyball class early last week. I began to feel really bad to my stomach. I suddenly felt something warm run down my inner thigh. Tempest and her friends started pointing at me and laughing."

"Oh, no! Ms. Peabody came to see you?"

"Not that. Worse."

"What?"

Aunt Ivy climbed out of her chair and started pacing around the island.

"I looked down and noticed a small muddy-looking puddle, and I knew. I ran as fast as I could to the bathroom. I was on the toilet for over 30 minutes."

"Oh, Copper," she said, placing her hands over her mouth, as she leaned against the counter.

"Well, I then began to vomit violently. I saw a few flashes out of the corner of my eye. I didn't care about where they were coming from then."

"No! Someone was taking pictures of you?"

"Yes. The coach came in and called the school nurse immediately. Mom picked me up and drove me to the ER. The doctor told me that I had a bad bug and was dehydrated. I was in the ER for a few hours before going home."

"Copper, I'm so sorry."

Sweet Secrets

Aunt Ivy grabbed and hugged me tight.

Tears began to fall, as I asked, "Ready for the rest of it?"

"There's more?"

She pulled away and sat down on the floor to look up into my wet face.

"I went back to school today. As I walked down the hall, I noticed how everyone was whispering and laughing. I thought I had something on me. So, I dashed into the bathroom to stare in the full-length mirror for a few minutes. I turned around in a full circle, but I saw nothing."

"Oh, no, Tempest."

"Before I left the bathroom, I saw pictures pasted on the doors, spelling my name. They were all of me, from when I was sick in the bathroom last week."

"Did you go to the principal?"

"No, I yanked those awful things down, ripped them to shreds, and threw them into the trash. I pulled the bathroom door open so hard that it almost came off its hinges. I wanted Tempest. This was it. I had enough."

"I wish that you had just gone to the principal's office, but then again, did you find her?"

"Oh, did I find her? She was in the hallway. She had a fake and nasty grin painted on her plastic face. I threw my backpack at her, which caused her to stumble backwards. I stormed towards her."

Aunt Ivy raised both her hands up as if she was catching a football in midair.

"No applause yet. Before I reached her, I smelled something that reminded me of raw sewage. I noticed a note on my locker door. It read, '*Open with great care, Stinky Bessie.*' The odor became stronger and stronger."

"Please don't tell me what I'm thinking you're telling me."

She leaned back and tuned in to every word that came out of my quivering mouth.

Infinity

"As I completed my combination, I felt a lot of pressure on the door. When I opened it, a large plastic bag fell out, and its smelly contents splattered on the floor and all over me. It was cow manure!"

"Copper, where were the adults during all of this?"

"I don't know, but the bag must've had a leak in it because the manure saturated everything in my locker. All of my books and pictures were ruined. Tempest whispered, 'Look up, Stinky Bessie.' I stood there with cow waste dripping from me. Everyone laughed."

"Come here, honey."

I crawled down to the floor and into Aunt Ivy's open arms as tears raced faster down my face.

"As I slowly looked up at the ceiling, guess what was there for all to see?"

She gazed into my eyes and whispered, "What?"

"A life-sized poster of me at my worst. The same photos I destroyed in the bathroom covered the ceiling for everyone to gawk at. I tried to walk away, but I slipped in the pile of manure and fell on my bottom. Tempest led the crowd to *moo* at me and call me Stinky Bessie, in some kind of twisted chant."

"I'm so sorry, Copper. Just so sorry," she said, as she rocked me back and forth in her arms.

"The principal and teachers finally huddled around me to help, but I just wanted to get out of there. Once I was able to stand without falling, I ran down the hall and found myself in the school basement bathroom. I showered and luckily found a shirt and shorts that barely fit me in a box."

"You should've just called the house. I would've picked you up. Given that principal and Tempest's parents a piece of my mind, too. I'm going to make everything all better."

She kissed me on the forehead and wiped away all of my tears with her hand. Aunt Ivy stood, helped me up, walked towards the cabinet, and pulled out a large mixing bowl and spoon.

Sweet Secrets

"Copper, hand me the eggs, sugar, flour, and milk." She broke several eggs into the bowl, then poured sugar, flour, and milk in, as well. "Start mixing, girlfriend," she instructed before she walked out of the kitchen.

When she returned from the living room, it was with a glass bottle in one hand. Shimmering purple liquid with a glowing effect danced inside the bottle. She poured a few drops in the sugar mixture, as I stirred.

Sparkly, iridescent, smoky flames burst into the air and vanished. I stepped back with my mouth wide open.

Aunt Ivy baked a few dozen cookies. The aroma was intoxicating. She placed them onto platters to cool and then into small Halloween-themed plastic bags.

She put a few on a separate plate. I couldn't resist eating a few of the mouthwatering treats.

"Carry these up to your mom with a glass of milk," she said, as she laid them on a tray.

I did as she instructed, and then the doorbell began to ring repeatedly by early trick-or-treaters, dressed in their most prized costumes. As I walked back downstairs, I saw Tempest standing in the doorway, chatting with Aunt Ivy.

My knees buckled, and my hands grew clammy. Tempest was dressed as a gothic witch.

Perfect outfit for her all year 'round, I whispered to myself.

"Hey, you guys, Stinky Bessie's in the house. *Moooo! Moooo!*" Tempest shouted, as her evil posse followed.

"I'll have none of that!" Aunt Ivy yelled as she clapped her hands together violently.

Tempest terminated her nasty chant, pinching her lips together quickly.

"Copper, why don't you fetch Tempest and her friends some of those yummy sugar cookies, so they can be on their way?" she asked.

Infinity

I grabbed a few of the bags and handed them to Tempest and the rest of her clique.

They jerked them from my hands and ran off. I could see them from a distance, searching through their bags and eating the cookies uncontrollably, like a pack of wild hyenas—especially Tempest.

Dreadful Monday arrived sooner than I anticipated. I felt as if I was coughing up butterflies. When I walked into the school, I noticed Tempest in a huddle with her posse in front of my locker.

I sighed and thought, *Here we go. Dead girl walking*.

A note was posted on my locker door. I pulled it off and opened it up.

Copper, I'm so sorry for everything. I want you to have my locker, and I'll take yours. I replaced everything for you, including your backpack. I hope we can be friends.
Tempest

She walked over to hug me, but I pulled back. Her presence felt a little different. I wasn't sure what it was, but I finally believed that Tempest was being sincere for the first time in her life.

After school, I ran home.

I flung the front door open and yelled out, "Aunty Ivy, you'll never believe what happened at school today!"

"You'll never believe what happened here," she said, all curled up in an oversized chair in the living room.

"What?"

"Your mom's four weeks pregnant. The doctor's office called and shared that someone made a mistake with her test results yesterday."

"I'm going to have a baby sister or brother soon?" I smiled.

"Looks that way." Aunt Ivy smiled, looking up at me. "So, what happened to you at school?"

She placed the cooking magazine she was reading on her lap.

Sweet Secrets

"Tempest wrote me this crazy apology note, gave me her locker, and replaced everything that was ruined in mine. She wants to be friends with me. Can you believe that?"

"Wow, now, that's a surprise!"

"Do you notice anything different about me?" I asked.

Aunt Ivy paused for a while, not saying anything.

"Hmm... Are you wearing eye shadow?" she asked jokingly.

"No! No more acne! When I woke up this morning, my face was clear and smooth! I've had pimple craters so bad over this last year. Nothing worked from the stores or doctors."

"I would say that's pretty amazing, Copper."

"Mom's good news and mine. All in one day, almost like it happened overnight. What are the odds? How? Wait. Those cookies you made..."

I squinted, as I kneeled down to stare into Aunt Ivy's face, waiting for a secret to be revealed.

"My lips are sealed, and yours should be, too. Do let me know if you ever want me to teach you to make my special cookies—or anything else."

Her eyeglasses teetered off her nose, as they suspended themselves in midair. She laughed softly and the magazine floated up from her lap, back into her open hands.

The End

Infinity

Stalker

Paces the lonely halls, her feathery sable train dragging across the
dusty floors
Crawls up walls with her twelve-inch nails
Rides in backseats
Swims dark seas
Dances in the wind like an angry hornet
Flies faster than *Supergirl*, in and out of windows
Never sleeps
Constantly watches and solicits everyone
Now, she perches on a swaying tree branch outside a window, only
waiting to collect her next soul…

Stalker

2ⁿᵈ Annual
Z-Run

O uch!" Hillarie screamed out.

Something bit her on the ankle, as she was pulling up her bloodstained, shredded wedding dress. She raised it up to uncover her right leg, and she noticed a huge cockroach, maybe five inches long, shoot off towards an open crack in the wall.

Her ankle began to puff up and transform into a deep red and purple bruise. Her hands sped down to the inflamed area, and she scratched it for several minutes until she drew blood and found loose skin swinging from under her nails. She shook it off onto the floor.

"Hillarie, what's taking you so long? We're about to go to the starting line. Come on!" Daisy, her classmate, shouted.

"Look, a nasty cockroach just bit me here!"

Hillarie pointed out her swollen and mangled ankle.

"Eeww, gross! Cockroaches don't bite. You sure that's what it was?"

"Yes, I'm sure!"

"Well, cover it up. Let's go, already. You worry about everything, anyway. It's probably nothing Nurse Frankie can't cure. Let her check it out after we run."

Hillarie took a few deep breaths, but the last one felt as if someone plunged the claw of a hammer inside her chest."

She walked out of the room and down the stairs after Daisy. She heard roaring, rumbling sounds emerging from her stomach. Sweat beads covered her forehead and hairline. Her breathing was slowing.

Hillarie dragged herself to the starting line, standing beside all the other hyper runners in zombie costumes. Some were dressed in modern dirty clothes that looked like a team of mad razor blades performed a few quickstep dance rounds across their bodies.

An insatiable hunger came over Hillarie at the same time as pea-soup-colored drool flowed from the cracked corners of her mouth.

"You look really awful," Daisy whispered, as she popped her knuckles.

Hillarie lifted her head and barfed up a thick chunky lime-green liquid into Daisy's face. Some of the splashes of vomit flew towards three or four of the other runners—spurts dunked down their open mouths and splattered into their eyes.

The End

2nd Annual Z-Run

Lights
Out

Forest Wiseman never slept without her nightlight, affectionately known as Mr. Wigglesworth, an iridescent worm with an open-mouthed smile.

She woke up one morning, and Mr. Wigglesworth had vanished from his home, the outlet in the wall parallel to the bed. Forest hurled the heavy covers back, jumped onto the coarse carpeted floor, and ran into the kitchen to find her best friend Gabe, who was leaning against the island.

"Gabe, how did you get in, and where's Mr. Wigglesworth?"

She panted heavily, as she paced up and down the violet linoleum floor, with her arms crossed tightly across her chest.

"Your weird roomie... the nightlight? You're 19 years old. Calm down. You don't need that sort of stuff anymore. You got me. I'm stronger than any stupid nightlight."

He flexed his muscles like a weightlifter after winning an event.

"What did you do?"

She scowled, multiple beads of sweat outlining her fiery red hairline.

"I put him and some other junk you've been holding on to in the garage sale across the street earlier," he spurted out, as he stuffed an oversized blueberry bagel into his mouth.

"Mr. Wigglesworth was our protection."

"From what?"

Infinity

Forest snatched her cell phone from the table, opened the front door, ran outside, and sprinted across the street towards the garage sale in her flannel sea-turtle patterned pajamas. She began rummaging through all the items on the tables.

Nothing.

Mr. Wigglesworth was officially missing.

She felt the hairs on the back of her neck rise.

Mrs. Humphrey, an 88-year-old retired junior high school hall monitor and the nosiest neighbor on the block asked, "Honey, what are you searching for?"

Her hands rested on her rounded hips.

"Hey, there, Mrs. Humphrey," Forest said, as she pulled out her cell phone from her back pajama pocket without any eye contact.

She scrolled through her photographs.

"Did you notice if anyone purchased a nightlight that resembles this picture?"

A plastic worm wearing squared eyeglasses, holding a blue cane and dressed in a black and white polka-dot vest popped up on her brightly lit cellphone screen.

"Oh, yes. A gentleman purchased that one and a few other things. He was in a hurry, too. Never seen him around here before. He was some serious eye candy, though. He caught my attention immediately," she said, fluttering her eyelashes with a smile.

"Thanks."

Forest staggered to the side a little but caught herself before falling.

"Honey, you want some water or something? You're sweating terribly! Come here and sit down for a bit."

"No, I'll be okay. Thank you, Mrs. Humphrey."

She turned away from her, only to find Gabe rushing over from her house across the street.

"Man, you're fast. What's all the fuss, Forest? It's just a nightlight. I mean, you know that, right?"

Lights Out

He tilted his head to the side while scratching the side of his bearded face. Forest took his hand and pulled him under a large oak tree, away from Mrs. Humphrey, who was trying to listen in with her large spying ears.

The sun had been out when she started her search for Mr. Wigglesworth, but titanic black clouds were rolling in, ushering darkness in early.

"They'll come for us tonight," she uttered slowly, as a tear dropped in unison with the first raindrop.

"Forest, you're really making me nervous. Who's coming?"

He pulled her close to him and wrapped his arms around her, wiping more tears from her face with the palm of his hand.

"Dim Feeders," she whispered, as she looked up into his wide eyes and stared at his painted-on smirk.

"Dim… what? You really need to stop reading those horror books."

"Stop it, Gabe! Listen to me!"

She stomped her feet and pulled away from him.

"All right… all right," he sighed while trying to look at her seriously, as he pulled her close to him again. Forest appreciated the effort, but it wasn't enough.

"They're vengeful shape-shifting ghosts. They travel everywhere to rip out and absorb the souls of their enemies. Each time a Dim Feeder snatches a human soul, its power increases."

"Okay, I'll go along with you for a moment," he said, shoulders shaking with silent giggles.

"Gabe, this is really serious. Listen!" she huffed.

"Okay, this is my serious face. Please continue."

He pointed his finger towards his stern expression, fighting back laughter.

"A Dim Feeder can then break out of his or her chaotic world in order to enter ours to cause more havoc. Eventually, it will lead to total destruction."

"Now, why would these so-called… Dim Feeders… be coming for you? I mean, us?"

"When they were human, they were brutally murdered."

"What does that have to do with you, Forest?"

"Mr. Wigglesworth wasn't really a nightlight. He was a Protector, like the ultimate Guardian Angel. He prevented any Dim Feeder from trespassing into our world."

More disbelief bloomed into his eyes.

"How do you know so much about them, and why would you need protection from them?"

"Gabe, I'm not who you think I am. I did things in my teen years… things that had to be done," she said, as she squeezed him tighter.

"Excuse me," Mrs. Humphrey said, as she cleared her throat and tapped Forest on her shoulder.

She turned around slowly, assuming that Mrs. Humphrey was going to ask for their help in putting everything away before the rain became heavier.

"Mr. Eye Candy returned, and he really wants to meet you."

Mrs. Humphrey whistled him on over, waving her hands back and forth in the air as if she was guiding an airplane in to park.

Forest looked over and immediately locked eyes with him. His were sinister, and they flickered like an unpredictable, untamed candle flame.

She knew that her finale was near—over a thousand goosebumps populated her arms. Her entire life flashed before her, and then he was standing right there, in front of her.

The eye candy that Mrs. Humphrey claimed to see wasn't visible before Forest's eyes. He was larger than any she had ever encountered, almost ten feet tall. Long white stringy and knotted hair rested in the middle of his puffed-up chest. An oversized scarlet fedora tilted down to conceal half of his transparent skeletal face. His opaque nails were long and curled. A ring bearing a large glistening golden-red black

Lights Out

widow squeezed his right index finger.

Forest's entire body shuddered, as he placed the tip of his index finger against her lips, which felt like they had been super-glued together. She couldn't speak.

Gabe grabbed her hand with his trembling hand and closed his eyes.

He whispered, close to her ear, "Please, forgive…"

Before he could utter his last word, an umbrella of darkness swallowed the entire block and everything in it.

The End

Infinity

InFinity

Full moon last night, so was I…
I stared in the smeared mirror with broken edges.
I wiped it with my wet sleeve.
The bathroom's dim sapphire light flickered off and on, as flies
swarmed above me.
I could feel my arms touching both sides of the filthy walls.
Small droplets of sewage oozed out of the broken faucet
No fresh water there, or in the dark stained toilet
My shirt and pants were both saturated from earlier.
I peeled them off and buried them deep into the overflowing trash
behind me.
I wiped down my wet footprints with the coarse paper towels.
My claws finally retracted, as well as my bloodstained fangs.
I opened up the window with one glance.
As my arms rested close by my side, I flew back into the maroon sky.
I soared effortlessly with my glistening black wings spread wide open
and eagle eyes on my next prize…

Infinity

Snow's
Secrets

The sequined raspberry gown pulled Red deeper into the icy abyss. Her BFL, *Best Friend for Life*, Snow, loved the werewolf she'd beheaded.
Snow murdered Red tonight.

Double
Trouble

Dynasty Peters: 10-year-old girl, missing since 1979
Geneva Uptmore: 8-month-old baby girl, missing since 1986
Jimmie Vanguard: 22-year-old man, missing since 1999
Isaac Sanchez: 86-year-old man, missing since 2018
Bobbie Adams: 12-year-old boy; Queen Travellie: 16-year-old teen
girl;
Ozzie Hanes: 57-year-old man; Mattie Stone: 23-year-old pregnant
young lady; and
Mystery White: 17-year-old teen girl—all missing, since July 2,
2020…

**Fireworks at Wraw River Park have been cancelled. Curfew rules
effective immediately, until further notice.**
*100 people were reported missing yesterday in our town of Wraw,
Texas,
population of 5,200.
Despite the advancements in technology of law enforcement and
private investigators across the country today, those reported missing
have yet to be found.
Everyone is at risk.
Return to your home by 5:00 p.m.
Lock all your doors and windows.*

Double Trouble

Stay in your attics or basements.
Terminate all noises and movements until dawn.

(*Wraw Chronicle* front page, July 3, 2020)

Mystery's hands were handcuffed to the side of a table with IV tubes dangling from puffed and bruised arteries in each of her arms. Her eyes remained closed, but she felt that she was lying on a cold reclining gurney.

She slowly opened her eyes, only to find her vision extremely blurry. Bright lights found in operating rooms shined down on her. She shivered from head to toe.

She tried to scream, but not a sound was released from her mouth. After a few minutes, her vision was completely restored. She looked around the room and noticed the glistening floors, an oversized steel door, and large slabs of meat hanging on enormous hooks from the ceiling in the foggy distance.

She wasn't alone. There were others strapped down on the gurneys, as well.

They weren't in a room, but an enormous walk-in freezer, judging by the fog rolling out of her mouth with each heaving breath.

Mystery slammed her blistered handcuffed hands against the table repeatedly.

"Ssshhh… be quiet. Before he comes back," a young lady whispered, blowing her bangs up in the cold air.

Tight jeans and a rock band t-shirt hugged her small frame. Colorful tattoos of daggers, bullets, and several butterflies decorated her arms and neck.

"Who?"

"The hooded man."

"Come again?"

"You don't remember, do you?"

Infinity

"No… no. Remember what?"

"Last night, when we were all taken."

"Huh?"

"He came for each of us last night. You were the last one. You really struggled. He gave you more medicine to make you sleep."

"My head is killing me," Mystery moaned out.

"I bet. You resisted. I never believed what they said about redheads until I saw you in action. Listen, just be quiet and do what he says. If you do, then it'll be over quick."

"What will be over?"

"The ritual. Ssshhh. I think he's coming back. Pretend you're asleep."

"Wait, ritual? What the hell are you talking about? Who are you?" Mystery demanded.

"Be quiet. Do what I told you. My name is Queen. What's yours?"

"Mystery."

"Now, Mystery, close your eyes," Queen whispered, as her lids lowered.

The door opened in slow motion. The hooded man floated into the room, and the door shut automatically behind him, as he waved one finger in its direction.

Mystery sneaked a tiny peek to watch his movements.

With a quick motion of that same digit, the barrier was raised once more, and then out rolled the next table from the freezer, one with a little boy on it, as the man floated behind it. Mystery saw tears racing from the boy's eyes. His muffled cries echoed down the hall, as the door slowly closed.

"Queen, what just happened? Where's the boy going?"

"He won't be back. He'll be drained before his heart stops beating, just like the old man who was wheeled out before him."

"Please don't say what I think you're about to say."

"The hooded man isn't one of us. He's… vampire, vamp,

Double Trouble

bloodsucker, creature of the night, blood snatcher, dark knight... Whatever you want to call him."

"That can't be. The vampire tribes were eradicated almost two years ago here in the U.S. and internationally. I know this because I was part of the special medical team, Vampire Annihilation Squad, V.A.S., 0900."

"I guess your team missed a few."

"No, they were all rounded up!" Mystery screamed out.

"Listen, you don't have to believe me. We're here in a big freezer, waiting to be drained... for their ritual. It won't be long. You, me, and the pregnant lady over there, who hasn't said a word since our capture—we're the only ones left. The old man and the boy are gone and probably dead. We'll die tonight."

Queen's large green catlike eyes began to well up with tears.

"Tell me, how do you know so much? V.A.S. was top secret."

"My dad used to tell me old stories about my great, great granddad. He knew about rituals like this that these blood snatchers practiced in the old world. He was known as one of the best vampire hunters."

"What was his name?" Mystery asked.

"Amistad Travellie. He studied the diaries of his distant cousin, the incomparable Van Helsing."

"Yes, I read about him. He was one of the best. Look, Queen, we have to come up with a way to get out of here together and maybe rescue the others."

"There's no use. This isn't a coincidence, us being captured together. It was all planned, as it always has been."

Queen sighed and turned her head away from her.

"We have to try."

"You just don't get it yet, do you?"

"Get what?"

"Did you really think your team could destroy a creature that has been surviving since sin? They have always found creative ways to adapt. Mystery, you know those photos of the missing kids on the back of milk cartons in the late 70s, photos posted all over those Big-Marts and S3000 Hologram pads?"

"Yeah."

"I bet you probably thought strangers, the next door neighbor, crazy family members, child molesters, rapists, or serial killers were behind the missing."

"Of course. Right?"

"Nope, it's always been those filthy blood snatchers. Late granddad Amistad left my dad his diaries. In them, he wrote how the government made a pact with prominent vampire leaders centuries ago in order to prevent human overpopulation," Queen said.

"I can't believe what you're telling me. It's too much."

"Sorry. The truth isn't always so pretty. Want me to continue, or not?"

Mystery paused and then said, "Yes, go on."

"As I was saying, the government allowed those filthy parasites to feed on people with rules in order to prevent the vampire virus from spreading throughout the world."

"You're telling me that the government allowed vampires to herd us for their scheduled feedings?" Mystery asked.

"Yes, you're finally catching on. Once corruption starts, it can never stop."

"What was the purpose of the missing persons organizations being created?"

"They allow humans to retain hope that maybe their loved ones will be found one day from a posted photo. Once in a while, a family member is released back into general population to keep faith in that twisted system."

The heavy steel door opened again. The hooded beast strolled up to the pregnant woman. Her arms propelled up in the air. For the first time, she opened her mouth, and bloodcurdling screams saturated the

Double Trouble

cold room until he touched her mouth with his lips. He then carried her out.

After a few hours, the hooded beast reappeared and floated toward them.

"Greetings. Do you know why you two are here?"

Both Mystery and Queen remained silent, staring at him.

"I've brought you here for similar reasons and outcomes. Let's start with you, Queen. You and your family have been hunting my people for a very long time. You're the last descendant of your vampire hunting family."

She spat in his face.

He immediately pulled off his white satin hood and scooped the warm saliva onto his finger. He smelled it, opened his mouth, and sucked it off.

"Yum. You taste like raspberries and brown sugar. Simply divine. I can only imagine what your blood will taste like," he whispered.

His well-groomed beard and goatee outlined his perfect creamy mocha skin. Large chocolate curly locks draped down his back and shifted constantly in the air. The sheer shirt he wore hugged his tall fit body. His shimmering silver eyes glowed, accentuating the specks of red in his irises; they pierced his victims' souls immediately.

His mouth opened, and lion fangs climbed out of his abyss, aiming for Queen's pulsating neck.

"Go ahead, you, filthy blood snatcher. I'm ready to meet my maker," Queen hissed.

He retracted his fangs slowly and licked his full ruby-red lips.

His nails were hypodermic and dug into her jaw, as he whispered, "Patience, my sweet. I'll have you soon enough, soon enough."

His black fork-like tongue licked the side of her face, leaving a trail of transparent slime. He then turned to his other remaining captive.

"As for you, Mystery, it's just as personal, if not more. Does Zavier Ellington #015068 ring a bell for you?"

Infinity

"No," she said, shaking her head.

"Let me help you out. November 5th, 2018."

"Yes, that was the last roundup."

"Bingo! Give the girl three points. I'm Zavier's twin. A group of us planned on rescuing him and the others that night, but we were forced to go underground because of the advanced weapons your group possessed."

"Why are you telling me all of this?" she asked, as she squirmed around on the table.

"I want you to understand why."

"Understand why what?"

"Everything. May I continue without further interruption?" Mystery didn't utter a word, but only nodded for him to finish. "Now, where was I? Oh, we figured we needed to keep the few alive safe and out of destructive human hands. Humans have always participated in enslaving those who are different and conducted genocidal roundings, ever since the beginning of time. *They* are the ruthless ones!"

"You're such a liar! Y'all are the ruthless ones!" Queen yelled out.

He grabbed her throat, squeezed it tight, and whispered, "Not all of us are the filthy animals you humans perceive us as."

Queen couldn't move or speak. She was temporarily paralyzed for several seconds.

"Please, please, let her go and continue on with your story," Mystery implored.

He lifted his head up and looked into Mystery's eyes. His grip loosened, and Queen attempted to catch her breath.

"My late brother loved humans. He never participated in our snatching rituals of women, men, and children from their homes, cars, or parking garages, which were all arranged by your government."

"I'm sorry about your brother," Mystery said.

"He was in love with one of your kind. For what? I'll never understand. He was a stupid fool, but my blood, nonetheless. Your kind

Double Trouble

took him from me."

"I was only following orders."

"You killed many of my innocent brothers and sisters, just like Queen and her damn family for centuries, which is why a new plan will be pursued without any government assistance."

"You want us to say we're sorry?" Queen asked with a slight smirk. She lifted up as much as she could. "I don't regret staking any of your kind! If I had a stake right now, I would use it on you and any other nasty vamp in my way. Hunting vampires has always and will always run through my veins."

His laughs shook the floors and cracked the walls. He dug his long nails into his full chest until black blood bubbled up. He looked down and jerked his nails out of his flesh, which healed instantly.

"Well, we're about to celebrate, ladies."

"What?" Queen asked.

"Celebrations call for the proper attire and food," he stated without elaboration.

He pushed a large button on the wall, and the door opened quickly.

The young pregnant woman rolled in two gorgeous ball gowns—one sky blue, with rhinestones decorating the bodice; and the other onyx, with strips of red velvet flowing toward the mermaid-style skirt.

"Ladies, choose. Don't fight, now." They were speechless. "Oh, you both are so indecisive. I'll choose for you, then. Mystery, you'll wear the onyx, because it'll hug all those amazing curves you possess. Queen, the blue one for you, to enhance something on that boyish figure."

Before they could utter a word, they were given a sedative cocktail solution. Two helpers dressed them from head to toe.

When they woke up, they found themselves on a stage with the beautiful dresses and dramatic makeup on. Their breathtaking runway model-like hair designs were embedded with colorful rhinestones. They looked like pageant contestants, except for their arms being handcuffed to chairs.

"Mystery, what's all this?"

"I don't have any idea."

The red velvet curtains in front of them were sealed shut. They couldn't see anything beyond them. All of a sudden, they began to hear eerie classical music playing in the background. The curtains began to retract slowly.

The beast was dressed in an early 1900s tuxedo, with a top hat and a cane made of marcasite and rubies.

"Ladies and gentleman, welcome to this very special celebration. My name is Rabanus Ellington. I'll be your MC for the evening."

When Mystery and Queen looked out into the audience, they observed a crowded room full of dressed and polished men, women, and children, maybe a thousand people—scratch that, vampires—in total. They were all pale, with piercing iridescent black eyes and wore formal attire.

"Mystery, they're going to drain us on stage," Queen whispered.

Rabanus kneeled in front of them.

"Ladies, please be patient. Your curiosity will soon be relieved. You both do have reasons to be nervous. I would be if I was in your shoes. Hmm, size seven and eight, hardly would fit, though."

"Why are we here?" Mystery asked, stomping her rhinestone stilettos onto the wooden floor.

"You two still haven't figured everything out?" Rabanus asked with a wink.

"No!" Queen cried out.

Rabanus stood up, turned around quickly, and reappeared behind them.

"Can someone from the audience please come up to the stage to help these beautiful ladies?"

A ten-year-old girl in a sapphire chiffon dress floated from the aisle, up the stairs toward the stage.

Double Trouble

"What's your name, princess?" Rabanus asked.

"Dynasty Peters."

"May I call you Dy?"

"Yes," she said with a nod.

"Dy, would you please explain to these two ladies what their celebration is all about?"

"This is your homecoming," she said to them, as she giggled, covering her baby fangs with her tiny hands.

"Homecoming? For what?" Queen and Mystery asked simultaneously.

"To become part of our family," Dy stated.

She floated off the stage and back into her cushioned seat.

Queen's and Mystery's faces turned several shades of pale, as sweat began to drip down heavily from them.

"Okay, who wants to be bitten first?" Rabanus asked with a smirk decorating his sharp face, as he folded his long arms behind his neck. "Wow, no volunteers again. I guess I'll bite both of you together."

He smashed their faces together with one of his long hands and planted his poisonous fangs, which resembled long jagged fishhooks, into both of their throats. Blood gushed out of their necks like a broken water faucet. He slurped it all up in seconds.

They fell into unconsciousness.

When they finally came to, they felt stronger, lighter, faster, but most of all... thirstier.

He rolled out the little boy and the old man. They were both still alive.

Queen and Mystery fed on both without hesitation. He pulled them off before the last heartbeats echoed in the auditorium.

"Guests, please welcome the newest members of our family."

The audience gave them a floating ovation.

"Now, everyone, please exit to the dining room for bloody cocktails, before our main human courses are served cold or warm."

InFinity

He handed Mystery and Queen handkerchiefs and commanded, "Ladies, ladies… please wipe your mouths. This is, of course, a formal affair."

They stood up, and he floated with them, arm-in-arm, towards the reception hall.

Rabanus laughed under his breath and whispered in their ears, "We'll soon become the majority. You are now part of *MY SPECIAL TEAM…*"

The End

Birthday Surprise

Dear Nixon,
You'll find dinner in the fridge. Don't eat any of my
birthday cake.
Love,
Mom

After Nixon gobbled up dinner, his eyes drifted to the forbidden, only two slices missing. He leaned over and took in a big whiff. He fell asleep after six servings.

Mom woke him.

"Nixon, please tell me that you didn't!"

"What?"

"Eat half the cake!"

"Yeah… it was so delicious. Crunchy, too."

"Son, I wanted to throw it out when I first saw it, but Cassie was here and so proud of her creation and gift to me."

"What's the big freakin' deal, Mom?"

"It was infested with cockroaches. That's where the crunch came from, and that was the big freakin' deal."

Infinity

Last
Pass

Decapitated head found.

PM 6969 claimed another victim, Michael discovered on the front page of the newspaper. His iPhone vibrated on the table in his dorm room.

"Speak."

"Michael, please come home," Wichita, his sister, cried out.

"What's wrong?"

"It's Big Mama Rose. She had another heart attack."

He packed up and jumped into his cranberry Mustang with JD riding shotgun and a few of his friends secured in an ice-packed cooler behind his seat.

Driving up to Wraw, Texas, he thought about how Big Mama Rose raised him and his little sis after their mom left them watching *The Bugaloos* one Saturday morning.

She never returned.

In no time, he found himself pulling into the hospital parking lot and walking down the cold white halls to room 711.

Big Mama Rose looked like a shriveled-up dandelion, once so proud and strong.

"It's me. Michael." She opened her eyes and reached for his face but fell back onto the pillow. "My boy," she whispered, "I've been waiting for you."

Last Pass

"I rushed to get to you as soon as I could."

"Ssshhh. I know."

"I'm so sorry for being out of touch all this time. You forgive me?"

Tears ran down his face, as he kneeled down on one knee next to her bedside.

"I did that a long time ago, son."

"Thank you. I don't deserve it."

"Nonsense. Give me a sugar."

He kissed her cheek, making sure he didn't disturb her oxygen headgear.

"Can I get you something?"

"No, I have all I need now—you. I know all about your troubles, DWIs, and arrest."

"I shouldn't be surprised since Wichita loves to run her fat trap!"

A dozen frown wrinkles popped out on his forehead, as he stared down at the polished floor.

"Look, I don't want to see you end up with a bowl of regrets. It's time for you to change, son. I want to share something with you."

"Mama Rose, you need your rest," he said, looking up at her.

"No, I don't."

Using all the strength she possessed, she pushed the button on her bed's remote control to raise herself up.

"I came here to see about you, not for one of your stories."

"You, sit down right there. You need to hear this."

"All right."

He stood up and walked over to the flimsy plastic chair in the corner. He dragged it to her bedside and sat down in front of her.

"It was October 31, 1942, 100 degrees, a record scorcher for Halloween. My older brother Coop planned on proposing to Madison, his high school steady. She could've passed for Dorothy Dandridge's double."

"You told me that Coop never married, enlisted in the army, and later died in combat."

"I know."

"Why is this so important for you to tell me now? You need to rest, not talk."

"I don't have much time left. I need you to just listen to what I have to tell you."

The hospital gown swallowed her worn body.

"I really wish you would listen to me for a change," he said, but it was as though she didn't hear him.

"Now, where was I? Oh… Coop worked three jobs that summer and sold his red Ford truck, so he could get her an engagement ring from a fancy mail order catalog in New York. Madison drove up FM 6969 to meet him at the lake."

Mama Rose coughed several times, and Michael stood up to stroke her warm skeletal back.

"See, you need to rest. You're pushing yourself too much for something that's not important."

"I'll rest soon enough. Let me finish—and this *is* important!"

He poured her some water from the plastic pitcher, into a paper cup, and placed a straw into it. He held it for her to sip from before she started back up again.

"It came out later that the town butcher, Baker, owner of plenty white hoods, confessed he had been drinking that day. He walked away with a temporary limp and a few scratches, while Madison's family planned her funeral."

"Look, I don't need a reminder about what happened. I didn't kill anyone. Besides, I'm going to Alcoholics Anonymous meetings now."

"I'm not telling you this to make you feel guilty, son."

"Sorry, Mama Rose, I get a little defensive when reminded. So, what happened to Baker?"

"He went to trial several months later, and old Judge Merriweather, his best friend and part of the good ol' boys' club, slapped him with just

Last Pass

90 days of community service."

"So, he got away with murder?"

"Pretty much. Coop withdrew for a long time. There was something different about my brother after that. He wasn't a loving person anymore. I didn't understand right then."

Michael folded his hands behind his neck.

"Maybe he just needed some time. He just lost the love of his life."

"No, he craved a darkness… Demona Stone."

"Who?"

"Demona. She was a Boo-Hag."

"A Boo-what?"

Michael massaged his perfect goatee with a fifth grader's puzzled look on his face.

"A Boo-Hag is an evil witch and shape-shifter. The elders told stories every Saturday night around the bar halls about her. I fetched them longnecks, taking a sip or two, while soaking up their tales."

"All this sounds far-fetched."

He looked into Mama Rose's lazy eyes, then watched her lilac lips move in slow motion.

"Listen, if anyone saw her reflection, that person would be left with a permanent mark to serve as a reminder of the evil vision witnessed."

"You look so tired. Why don't you take a nap and finish telling me later?"

"I need to finish now, Michael!"

He took a deep breath while standing up beside her and holding her cold hands.

"Go ahead."

"When I was 13 and attended the Wraw Fair, my best friend double-dared me to look at Demona in a mirror. I lifted up his shiny pocketknife and pointed it towards where Demona had a palm-reading booth. Once I saw her image in it, I felt my hand burning from the end of the wooden handle. I dropped it to the ground, almost stabbing my right foot."

Mama Rose's hands trembled in Michael's.

"You okay? Do I need to get the nurse?"

"No, it always gets to me when I talk about her."

"Maybe this is a sign for you to stop talking about her and rest like you should've been doing."

"Nonsense. Let me finish, son. My body shook all over until I collapsed. My eyes rolled back. After a few shakes and some water splashed onto my face, I woke up."

"Honestly, this is too much for me to take in, Mama Rose," he said, as he sat back down.

"It's all true."

"Okay, whatever you say."

Michael cupped his chin in one hand, resting his elbow on his lap.

"I saw Demona for the last time in Baker's store a few months later. I was standing in the checkout line, holding a paper sack of red-hot suckers. She wrapped her long hand around my neck. Demona dug her grey hypodermic-needle-like nails, with red tips, deep into my throat. Drops of blood splashed onto my white Keds."

"Did she hurt you?"

"Yes, but what she whispered in my ear was worse than her death grip around my neck."

Mama Rose paused for several seconds, staring down at her tired and shriveled hands.

"What... what did she say?"

"I thought you weren't interested in my story, Michael."

"I'm not."

He shrugged his shoulders and glanced away from her, before quickly looking into her eyes, secretly craving more of her tale.

"Well..."

"Come on, Mama Rose, tell me. I want to know."

"Okay. Demona whispered, 'You caught me off guard once, but

Last Pass

never again. That was your free and only pass. Watch yourself, little girl! Keep your doors and windows locked, too. Tell Coop that I'll be waiting for him.' "

Michael stared into Mama Rose's eyes.

"I never told anyone, and my once-auburn hair turned snow-white that same day. My mama dyed it several times, but the color never held. That's how it remained, even to this day."

Mama Rose pulled her wig off, and white curls sprang straight up.

Michael stood to get a closer look, then ran his fingers through her hair.

"This doesn't really prove all that happened."

"You're right."

She nodded her head slowly and began to cough again, louder. She attempted to pick up her cup, but she spilled it all over herself.

"I told you that you needed your rest."

Michael called the nurse in to change her. He stepped out into the hall, until the nurse finished, then reentered.

"It just slipped out of my hands."

"Please rest."

"Don't you want to know what happened to Coop, Michael?"

"No. I'm more worried about you."

"Son, no sense worrying about me. I know where I'm going. I'm worried about you. That's why I need you to hear all of this."

"Don't worry about me."

"I do."

"I'm going to call Sis to sit with you, while I go and clean up."

"No. Please stay. I just have a little more to tell you. Please."

He walked back over to her bedside and sat down.

"So, how does Coop fit in with this Demona chick?" he asked, looking up at the ceiling.

"I begged him not to even think about trying to find her, but he ended up doing it, anyhow. He wanted Baker to pay. So, Demona cast

Infinity

a twisted spell for him. A week later, Baker went missing."

Mama Rose closed her eyes.

"You okay?"

She touched his hand, opened her heavy lids, and nodded. Her breathing began to slow down. She continued with more pauses between each word.

"Baker's wife and son found his bloody mangled body hanging in the middle of his store, as large vultures fed on it. I heard his wife lost her mind, and the son threw himself into a tree shredder on their farm."

"That's awful. I bet Coop left town after that."

"Nope. He jumped off the sharp lake cliff near FM 6969 six months later, on Halloween night, landing headfirst. Folks around here say Coop's restless spirit haunts that spot to this day, causing fatal accidents to careless drivers on that road, where Madison died."

"I didn't know that about Coop," he said, as he covered his mouth and stood up to stare out the window.

"Some claimed to have seen his old red Ford with a shiny bent-up grill and two tall black horns on the sides of the truck near the windows, with glowing, flaming tips. I saw it once and only then. I've steered as far as possible from FM 6969. So should you. Avoid it at all costs!"

Michael turned around to face her and leaned against the window with his arms crossed.

"Okay, I'm gonna call Sis."

He walked back to her and kissed her bony hand, and then he headed towards the door.

"Here, take this crucifix, my boy, and wear it always. I prayed a very powerful prayer over it."

He turned around and went to her bedside.

"You know I don't believe in stuff like this. I never have."

"Please, Michael, take it. Promise me that you will keep it close to you at all times."

"Give it here."

Last Pass

He rolled his eyes and frowned, as she dropped it into his baby-soft hands. He buried it in the back pocket of his *Gucci* jeans.

He bent over to hug her, and then she was gone.

Michael stayed until a caretaker from Wraw & Son's Funeral Home arrived to transport her. He attended the memorial service and stayed a few extra days to help Wichita out with Mama Rose's estate.

On Halloween night, he packed, loaded his vehicle, and backed out of her driveway. Wichita waved him on, as she pulled her heavy multi-colored shawl tighter around her shoulders.

Michael waved back to her, as he turned to a jazz channel on his satellite radio while positioning JD closer to him. He stared at the crucifix; it rested in the passenger's seat. He threw it into his immaculate glove compartment without a second thought.

After driving a few miles from Mama Rose's house, which was then his sister's, and passing the hospital, he noticed a work convoy with flashing signs: ENTRY RAMP CLOSED FOR CONSTRUCTION.

Alternate routes were entered into his GPS—Cedar Lane or FM 6969.

He looked up through his sunroof and whispered, "Mama Rose, wherever you are, I love you."

He made a left turn onto FM 6969.

Within seconds, he heard loud noises coming up fast behind him. His heart raced like a rabbit being chased by a pack of wolves. His eyes twitched, and his hands trembled on the steering wheel. In his rearview mirror, he saw only young kids packed in a neon yellow convertible.

Michael sighed and lifted up JD. He screwed the cap off and pressed his lips to its glass mouth and tilted it back, as he kept his eyes on the road. He then secured the bottle between his legs.

Just then, an old truck with flaming horn tips appeared ahead of the convertible. The driver of the car blew the horn constantly and flashed his high beams. The car passed the truck with loud laughter filling the chilly night air, accompanied by *Pour Some Sugar on Me,* blaring from the speakers.

The kids threw bottles at the truck, which picked up unbelievable speed. The flaming horns lowered and rammed the convertible on both of its sides and raised it off the road, tossing it up almost a hundred feet in the air. The horns retracted back into their original position, as the convertible exploded before it hit the asphalt.

Michael pulled over onto the side of the road to catch his breath while resting his sweaty palms and head on the steering wheel.

He tore his glove compartment door off its hinges to find the crucifix. Once he got his hands around it, he held onto it tight as if it was going to fly away. His pants were soaked with more than just the JD spill.

Before Michael could grab something from the back to dry himself off, he heard a loud etching sound from his windshield.

He looked up and read the bloody, sooty message:

YOU'RE REAL LUCKY. CONSIDER THIS YOUR LAST PASS.

Last Pass

Monster

Millions of cold and hairy tentacles flopped under the *Holly Hobbie*-dressed canopy bed, as Morgan positioned herself back into a forgotten corner

Odors constantly stung her swollen black and blue eyes

No one heard the screams behind the sound-proof walls...

Solitude became her temporary fix with makeup to conceal the visible marks

Terror started again after cheerleader practice every day

Events too appalling to rewind—only permanent, stained memories replaying in her mind

Red x-ray eyes burned holes to unlock every door she hid behind, until Morgan never ran again....

927
Ghost Trails

The Ghost Hunter Protection Program, the *G.H.P.P.*, relocated me and my parents from our hometown in California to a little dot way down South… Croak, Texas.

My parents testified against Hammer Bartholomew, a colleague of theirs, about his unethical ghost-capturing techniques. All in all, it caused the removal of his ghost-hunting license, a year in jail, and over $100,000 in restitution to his victims.

Hammer had a huge following, which placed my parents on his unpopular list.

My mom and I drove over 13 hours straight. Dad flew out a week before. I couldn't believe that I had to leave the city I grew up in to end up in the *Old West*.

We pulled up behind the moving truck, which appeared to tilt towards the left, with all our crap stuffed inside. A few suitcases and computers were pushing against the back of my seat, to the point where I couldn't wait to get out of there. My legs were cramped.

As soon as I opened my door, I nearly stumbled to the ground. I noticed a young girl with straight black hair, crooked bangs, and heavy freckles on her face, arms, and legs. She wore bright yellow square glasses. She walked up to me, as a large grape-colored bubble burst over most of her face. She quickly reclaimed the gum back into her mouth and started smacking it, while pulling away spider web-like bubblegum traces from around her lips.

"Hey, you know you just moved to one of the most haunted towns in Texas?" I shook my head and turned around to start unloading stuff from the backseat of the car. She tapped me on my shoulder. "Didn't you hear what I just told you?"

She stomped her red tennis shoes on the pavement while popping her gum about 20 times.

"Yeah, yeah, I heard you. Ghosts don't scare me one bit. I've been around them all my life. Big deal."

"What's your name?"

"What's yours?"

I grinned, pulling my suitcase out.

"Gertrude Waters, thank you very much."

"Interesting name, Gertrude. I'm Jo... Joanna Cooperstein."

"You mean like the famous Cooperstein Ghost Hunters?"

"Yep, they're my parents."

"So, that's why you aren't afraid of our ghost town?"

"Probably."

"Well, you'll see soon enough. By the way, keep your closet door closed at all times, and leave a light on inside at night."

"Whatever."

I stared at her and then rolled my eyes.

"Well, I'd better be going. It's almost dinner time, and I don't want my crazy brother hunting for me. Remember what I told you."

"The closet?"

She bobbed her head up and down.

"I'll make sure to send myself a text reminder."

Gertrude turned around and ran off towards the road.

"Jo, who were you talking to?" Mom asked, carrying a box almost half her size.

"Just some girl in the neighborhood."

"Nice! You're making new friends already."

InFinity

"I wouldn't quite call it that. She caught me and started blabbing."

"Still a good start. This will be a fresh start for all of us."

"Hey, Mom, that girl was mouthing off about Croak being one of the most haunted towns. Is that true?"

"Oh, honey, she's just exaggerating. Haunted towns exist everywhere. You know your dad and I'll be exploring soon."

"So, our house is ghost-free?"

"Absolutely. Dad ran his new ghost locator app a few days ago, and our new home is clean."

She sat the box down and pulled me into her.

"You have nothing to worry about. We're safe from Hammer and his evil pet ghosts. G.H.P.P. knows what they're doing. Come on in. I have some cold water bottles from the cooler and some sandwiches."

I nodded my head slowly, as she lifted the box again and headed towards the house. I pulled my suitcase handle up and dragged it along the pavement to follow Mom.

I could feel sweat dripping down my back, and my t-shirt soon grew saturated. I took my cell out from my back jeans pocket. The weather app showed that it was 104 degrees.

Before I could reach the door, a gust of cold wind hit me, which felt like icicles raking over my face and arms. My entire body shivered. I looked up and noticed a swinging curtain in one of the windows, but within seconds, it stopped moving. I continued on towards the entryway.

The house possessed dark wood flooring and was spacious with a fireplace in the living room. Oversized lights hung throughout. I peeked out the back and saw that the yard was a decent size with a wooden fence.

"Mom, where's Dad? Oh, and which one is my room?"

She was setting the table with napkins and paper plates from one of the boxes.

"Dad is on his way. Your room is on the opposite end of the house.

927 Ghost Trails

Go down the hall and turn left, and it's the last door on the right."

I marched down the long hallway, pulling my suitcase behind me. The chill returned, and I shivered a few times. Before I could figure out where the cold air was originating from, it vanished, same as before.

A twin bedframe and mattress sat in the middle of the room. There was a large window adjacent to my bed, covered by sheer baby-blue curtains, with miniature yellow dots decorating the top and bottom.

Noticing a bathroom to my right, I went in to check it out. There was a tub with my safari-themed shower curtain already hanging in front of it. Two cream-colored bath towels with matching washcloths, a pink toothbrush, a bottle of liquid soap, and a grey hair dryer decorated the counter. A large oval mirror hung above the center of the sink.

As I stepped back into my room, I saw the closet door half-open, and I crept over to it. The knob was glass with small floral designs adorning its surface. I opened the door to find that it was pretty spacious. A light with a yellow braided ribbon swayed back and forth. I turned it on to get a better look. A few shelves lined each side, which I assumed were for shoes and whatever else. A switch on the outside also controlled the light, so I flicked it off when I left.

The door was still slightly open, so I walked backwards and nudged it with one push of my hand, until I heard it seal shut.

"Joanna, come on, it's lunchtime," Mom yelled out in a gentle tone.

Before I stepped out of my bedroom, I glanced back and saw that the closet door was ajar, though I knew I'd shut it. I pushed it closed, listening for it to catch. I started out, but then I turned around one more time to make sure it remained closed. That time, it did.

I gobbled up the sandwich, chips, and room-temperature cherry cola. I surveyed the kitchen with tiny wagon wheels on the cabinet doorknobs and mini Western pictures dressing the walls.

Dad walked in and bent down to kiss me on my forehead, as he slipped off his backpack, which had been secured by both straps.

He slid into the chair next to me and said, "Joanna, your mom

InFinity

mentioned what you asked about earlier. I want you to know that our house is ghost-free. I made sure of that before you both arrived."

"So, did Mom also share that a neighbor girl was telling me that this is one of the most haunted towns in Texas? Is that true?"

"Nonsense. There are stories about every town. I would know if that was true, right?"

I blinked a few times, shrugged my shoulders, and whispered, "I hope so, Dad."

He leaned in closer to me and said, "Jo, I'll protect you and your mom at all costs. This is one reason why I decided to agree with the recommendations of the G.H.P.P."

I nodded and headed back towards my room. As soon as I walked in, I noticed my closet door slightly open and a note sticking halfway out from underneath it. I crept over, stooped down, and picked it up.

It read: *Leave and don't return.*

I gasped, and a cold sensation ran through my body. I fell backwards onto the floor. When I opened my eyes, I found myself tucked in my bed. I saw Mom and Dad talking in the hallway.

"Jo, you're up," Mom said when she turned around to face me.

She came in and sat at the foot of my bed.

I looked around and saw that it was almost night, judging from the last remnants of sunset pouring in from my window.

"How long have I been asleep?"

"At least six hours or so," Mom said.

Dad leaned against the wall parallel to my bed, facing Mom and me while cleaning his glasses with the hem of his shirt.

"You really had us worried."

I sat up and leaned my back against the headboard. I looked around the room and noticed the closet door was closed again.

"The note... Did you find the creepy message?"

"Jo, what are you talking about?" Mom asked.

"There was a note. I remember reading it, feeling strange, and falling backwards."

"Honey, there was nothing like that near you when we found you on the floor. I figured that you were just so exhausted that you drifted off to sleep. I placed clean sheets and a comforter on your bed. Your dad picked you up and tucked you in."

"Mom, that door was open a little, and I found a message just inside the closet, which, by the way, I know that I shut before eating lunch."

"What did this note say?" Dad asked as he moved closer to me.

Rubbing my head with my left hand, I said, "I don't really remember."

"Honey, I think exhaustion is playing a big role in all of this. Rest," Mom said.

As they headed toward the door, I said, "You don't believe me, really?"

Mom turned around and walked back over to me.

"Jo, let's talk about this more tomorrow. We've been on the road for a long time, and your body and mind need to rest. When our bodies and minds are tired, we tend to see things that aren't there sometimes."

I looked at her and then turned around onto my side. I stared out the window, as the thin blue curtains blew back and forth.

My parents whispered, "Good night," and left my room.

With an uneasy feeling, I stared at the closet door again—it was still closed. I pushed the covers back and placed my bare feet on the floor. I tiptoed to the closet and shoved on the door to confirm that it was latched. I bent down and looked under it to make sure the light was on, as Gertrude instructed earlier. It wasn't, so I hit the switch and checked again.

Before I could turn around to head back to my bed, I heard a tapping at my window. I walked over and saw Gertrude standing outside. I opened the window a crack, so I could talk to her.

"Are you just going to stand there, or invite me in?" she asked, setting both hands on her hips.

Infinity

"What are you doing here so late?"

"I came by earlier to deliver you some homemade snickerdoodle cookies that Mom made for you and your family, but your mom told me you were resting."

"Oh, she didn't mention that to me."

"Yeah, I'm sure they were busy."

New window screens were being added to the entire house, and mine hadn't been installed yet, so I opened my window wider. Gertrude crawled in and flopped onto the floor and sat down with her freckled legs stretched out.

"Did you leave those cookies?"

"Oh, I left them on the porch in a covered container," she said.

"Hold on, let me go check the kitchen."

I went to the kitchen and hunted for the cookies. I looked on the counters, table, and fridge. Nothing. I did find two cold black-cherry colas and a bag of white cheddar popcorn. I grabbed them and zipped back to my bedroom. I found Gertrude standing near the closet. She turned around like a mini tornado and flopped back down, where she was when I left her.

"You okay?" I asked.

"Yeah. You didn't find the cookies?"

"Nope, but look what I did find."

I held up the goodies and sat down on my bed to face her. I opened the bag, scooped up a handful of popcorn, and threw it into my mouth. My jaws were stuffed. I offered her some, but she pushed it away.

"Popcorn isn't my favorite."

While I continued to eat, I opened up my drink and gulped it down. I handed Gertrude the extra one, but she declined. I placed my empty bottle and the bag of popcorn on my nightstand.

"Gertrude, what do you know about this house?"

"It was built back in the early 60s, and something awful happened right in there," she whispered, pointing towards the closet.

927 Ghost Trails

I scooted down to the floor to be closer to her.

"What?"

"There's a…"

We heard footsteps coming from down the hall.

Gertrude stood up, tapping her thighs with her hands, and said, "Listen, I'll tell you more another time. I gotta go."

She climbed out my window and before she was fully over the fence, she looked back and whispered, "Remember, keep your closet closed and a light on every night."

Lickety-split, she was gone as if someone was chasing her.

Mom opened my door to find my body half out the window.

"Jo, what in the world are you doing?"

I pulled myself back in and said, "Oh, nothing. Gertrude stopped by for a bit and had to run."

"Why didn't she use the door?"

"I guess she didn't want to bother you again," I said, walking back towards my bed.

"Bother me again?"

"She came by earlier, but I was asleep, remember?"

I picked up the bag of popcorn and poured a mouthful into my hand.

"Jo, I don't recall anyone stopping by for you."

"Well, maybe she talked to Dad," I said, shrugging my shoulders.

"That's possible."

"I guess so."

"Get some rest, Jo. By the way, I want to talk more with you in the morning about the note, okay?"

"So, you believe me?"

She nodded and said, "Rest."

She shut the door, and I picked up a YA paranormal book, *Doll,* off my nightstand near the half-empty popcorn bag and read almost to the end. I looked at my watch and saw that it was 2:00 a.m. Still not sleepy,

I decided to jump into the shower.

As I flipped the switch in the bathroom, the light flickered a few times, before it settled into a full off-yellow tint. I tossed my clothes into the hamper and turned the water faucet on to allow it to reach a comfortable temperature.

I brushed my teeth and looked around the tiny bathroom with white walls and daisies painted as a border above me. The water was steaming up, so I grabbed my liquid apple-scented soap and turned on the spray. I stepped into the tub and pulled the shower curtain shut.

After about ten minutes, I heard something drop to the floor. I was all lathered up, and I wiped the soap from my face with my hand, so I could see.

I noticed that my blow dryer was on the floor, even though it was resting on the counter before I stepped into the shower. I rinsed off, grabbed my towel and wrapped it around my body, and stepped out onto the rug.

A message was written in the condensation on my mirror: *EVAEL*

I studied it for a few seconds and knew immediately what it was.

I dried off at lightning speed, threw on some pajamas, and ran out of my room, towards the hall. I knocked on my parents' door. I tapped a little louder because I didn't hear any response. It was open partially, and I could see that they were sleeping. I walked in and went over to Mom.

As I shook her, she mumbled, "Jo, what time is it?"

"Close to 3:00 a.m."

"What are you doing up?"

"Mom, I gotta show you something."

"Right now?"

"Yes."

Dad rolled over and said, "Go back to bed, Jo."

"No! You didn't believe the note, and I need to show you both something right now. It can't wait. Come now!"

They looked at each other and then at me, and both rolled out of bed.

I directed Mom and Dad back to my bathroom. When I walked in, the mirror was sparkling clear... with nothing written on it.

"It was just here!"

"What, Jo?" Mom asked, as she yawned and rubbed her eyes.

"There was a message written backwards—LEAVE—on the mirror when I got out of the shower."

Dad looked closer. He held his phone up to the spot and turned on his ghost locator. It scanned the space with a blue beam, and he checked the reading.

"Just like I thought. This area is clean. No traces of ghost presence."

"Dad, I promise it was just there, like the note earlier."

"Jo, there's nothing here and nothing to be worried about," Dad said with a long sigh.

Mom walked up behind me and stroked my back.

"Something just doesn't feel right in my room."

"Jo, I've checked this entire house thoroughly more than once," Dad said with a slight frown.

"Dad, something happened here a long time ago."

"Who told you that?" he asked.

"The neighbor girl down the road, Gertrude."

"What did she tell you, exactly?"

"Nothing yet, Dad, but that something awful happened here in the 60s... in my closet."

"Jo, this house isn't haunted. What will convince you?" He stomped quickly towards my closet door. He grabbed the glass knob and twisted it. The door swung open. It was empty. "You see? Nothing, Jo!"

He walked inside the closet and held up his phone app, scanning the entire area.

"Negative, just like in there. You're safe."

He walked out, and his arm swiped the light off. He stood at the

Infinity

threshold with his back towards the closet, rocking on his heels.

"Dad, close the door and turn the light back on!" I screamed.

The hairs on my arms rose up and waved.

"Jo, you're not six anymore. You outgrew nightlights a long time ago, and definitely no lights will be on all night. They're staying off, young lady! Time for everyone to finally get back to bed."

Glowing neon orange eyes appeared, darting back and forth inside the closet.

"Dad, behind you!" I screamed.

Long arms with huge claws pulled him into the darkness.

Mom screamed, and we both ran towards Dad. She stood at the opening and yelled out his name. The same thing started tugging her in there. I grabbed her arm and tried to keep her from being yanked away.

Yet, I was getting dragged into the blackness. Mom looked into my eyes and shook her head. She pried each of my fingers from around her arm. I lost my grip and landed outside the closet on my back, while she disappeared inside.

I screamed out several times. I turned the light switch on, ran into the closet, and pushed against the walls, calling out their names. No one responded. My parents were really gone. Walking back into my bedroom, I slowly shut the door and left the light on. I cried the rest of the night.

When I was able to think clearly enough, I called the local law enforcement and my aunt in Los Angeles; she booked the next flight out. Two cop cars showed up after I finished talking to her. One of the officers interviewed me. I answered all of his questions. My eyes were puffy and red.

Before wrapping up, the sheriff said, "One of my officers will stay parked outside your house. This town breathes a lot of history. You're real lucky."

"I don't understand how this place was haunted. My dad checked it thoroughly with his ghost-finder equipment."

927 Ghost Trails

"Not all fancy gadgets work on every kind of ghost. Take care, Miss. It's a good thing that you're leaving here."

As he turned and was about to walk out the door, I said, "Wait." He turned around and looked at me. "What happened here?"

He paused for a few seconds and then said, "Twin teen sisters hanged themselves in your closet many years ago."

"What were their names?"

"Helen and Gertrude Waters."

My blood ran cold in my veins.

"No, that can't be right. I met Gertrude Waters and talked to her yesterday," I said, shaking my head.

"Well, Miss, I believe you've had yourself a ghost encounter." He grinned, tipped his cowboy hat at me, and said, "Do yourself a favor and don't come back."

He left and shut the door behind him.

I pulled the curtain back and saw the other officer in his car, parked outside. I stayed in the living room with all the lights on. I continued to cry and stare down the hall.

My cell phone buzzed. It was a text from my aunt, saying that her plane would be arriving in about three hours.

When I went to my room to gather up a few essentials in a backpack, my cell dropped to the floor from my pocket. When I stooped down to pick it up, I noticed red tennis shoes in my peripheral view. I stood up and turned around.

"Why didn't you tell me?"

"I was about to." Gertrude sighed. "I'm so glad you're leaving here. Sorry about your parents."

Tears filled Jo's eyes. "I'll never see them again or be able to tell them things, you know."

Gertrude remained silent.

"Do you ever regret committing suicide with your sister?"

She shook her head and whispered, "Sometimes."

Infinity

"Why did y'all do it? You two had a choice to live." Teardrops rolled down Jo's face.

She paused and then said, "Something really bad happened to us, and we made a pact. I don't like to talk about it."

"Understand. Can I ask you another question, not related to your death?"

"Sure."

"Why the spooky messages?"

"I was trying to warn you and your parents."

"About what?"

"The bad ghost in your closet, Jo."

"What?" I said with a frown.

"Someone placed a *Lemur* in your closet."

"Like the monkey, lemur?"

"No. A hostile wandering type of ghost that craves darkness and steals lives. Your closet was the perfect ground."

"Who would do that?"

"I think you know. Jo, I know that I cannot follow you, but the *Lemur* may try. So, wherever you go, promise me that you'll always keep your closet door closed and the light on, especially at night. *Lemurs* like to finish the job they were summoned for."

Gertrude went into the closet and touched the yellow braided ribbon. Her twin appeared in a brown smoke-like form. Gertrude grabbed her hand, and then she turned into a silver figure in the same form as her sister. They turned around and walked through the wall, vanishing entirely.

I sighed, wiped my face with my hands, and finished packing. My aunt arrived shortly, and a taxi drove us to the airport.

As I was zipping my bag up, I noticed the yellow braided ribbon from the closet sticking out from under some clothes.

The End

927 Ghost Trails

Zeke:
The Un-Freak

My junior year at Polaris North High erased all the previous years of being known as *Zeke: The Scary Freak*.

I know, I know. I get it… being the one and only successful zombie transfer.

Unlike my predecessors, I wasn't the stalker-biter type. You can pretty much figure out what happened to them, without me repeating those gory details. If you've watched one of those zombie apocalypse movies, then you already know the conclusion for most of my kind.

So, let's move on to the late fall.

It was nearing homecoming, only a week away. Let me tell you that the homecoming football game and dance were huge at Polaris High, almost bigger than prom. It was a day for the jocks, cheerleaders, and whoever else was on a team to strut their egos big time.

Even before Polaris, I always sat in the back of the classroom. No one ever talked to me. I was pretty much the loner. None of the girls ever looked my way. I thought about what it would be like to be popular, part of the team, and just normal. I knew that I wouldn't ever be any of those things, especially normal, so I tried my best to stay away from others.

I took a part-time janitorial job, and the boiler room became my sanctuary. The rusty smell of the pipes, the strange noises, and whatever stale odor was festering down there gave me peace and company. I didn't even mind a few rats roaming my place.

Don't even think it. I'll have you know that I've never craved a rat. I had my own special diet and medications that kept any human and animal cravings from creeping up.

Okay, back to the story.

Late one evening, a few days before homecoming, I was cleaning up the jocks' locker room.

Oh, I forgot to tell you that I always had to have my cool tunes in my ears whenever I was working. Dancing kept me sane, and I was pretty darn good at it.

As I was mopping the muddy floor and moonwalking sideways, I felt a heavy tap on my shoulder.

My earbuds flew up in the air, as I fell backwards with the mop in my hand. All of a sudden, two large hands grabbed me by the collar and caught me before I went down.

My body quivered from head to toe, and I screamed out, "Please, don't hurt me, man," as I kept my eyes staring down towards the ground.

"Dude, I'm not going to hurt you," he bellowed out in a husky, desperate tone.

Crimson Stuart was not only the most popular guy at Polaris North High, but he was also the captain and quarterback. He was super good on the football field and the other playing fields, too, if you know what I mean. *Wink, wink.*

"Crimson, what's up?"

"I've been watching you the last few nights after practice."

"Hey, and y'all think *I'm* the creepy one. That sounds pretty creepy, dude."

"Man, I'm talking about those freaking smooth dance moves of yours. Can you teach me?"

"You don't even notice me. Why would I want to teach you?"

"Come on, Zeke. Man, you know how it is."

"No, I don't. Why don't you tell me?"

Zeke: The Un-Freak

I crisscrossed my arms over my chest.

"All right. Whatcha want?"

I paced for a few seconds, giving it some thought.

"Okay, if I show you some of my moves, then you have to hook me up with Frankie Fox."

"Man, Frankie. She's almost hotter than my girl."

He massaged his smooth wide chin while staring at me.

"Crimson, my man, is it a deal, or what?" I asked, patting him on his back.

"All right, you got it, but only if you teach me how to dance in the next three days."

"Okay, deal."

We shook on it. He pulled his hand away and wiped it on his back jeans pocket as if I had slimed him, or something. I was used to it.

"Crim, let me explain something. You cannot become a Z unless I stop taking my special preventive injections, which I take every morning. I'll never become an Un-Z, but it protects humans if I'm ever triggered and bite someone involuntarily or my bodily fluids get on them—both super rare."

He nodded.

"Sorry, can never be too careful, you know."

"Meet me here tomorrow night, and we'll get started."

The next day came fast. I just knew that I failed my physics quiz that morning. Newton's Laws of Motion and angular acceleration weren't my focus. My mind was on dance lessons and Frankie Fox, which was probably why I bombed it.

The halls cleared, and I got all my cleaning done in a hurry. I rushed to the locker room and plugged my iPhone into a speaker dock the coach kept there for after practices and home games. I scrolled down to my favorite jams, pressed pause, and waited for Crimson.

As I stared at my slender pale face in a mirror, he walked in and slammed his bag on the bench.

Infinity

"Okay, let's do this, Zeke."

We practiced for two nights. I showed him countless dance steps, even in slow motion. When it came down to it, though, we weren't getting anywhere. He possessed no rhythm or balance.

Homecoming was around the corner, the following day. Crimson was pacing the floor.

"Crim, I mean, Crimson, I've done all I can for you."

"Yeah, yeah, I know, man. Thanks. You tried. I'm just lousy at this one thing. Sorry about wasting your time."

"Nah, it's okay. It was nice, hanging out with you. As you can tell, I don't have a lot of friends. Shoot, I don't have any. At least, for a few nights, I kinda got to see what it's like to have someone to kick it with, even if it was only temporary. Thanks."

"You're not that bad, Zeke. See you around," he said in a soft tone.

He grabbed his bag off the bench, tossed it over his shoulder, and started walking out.

Before he could reach the door, I yelled, "Crim, there's one way you could absorb my moves."

"What? I'll do anything!"

His bag slipped off his shoulder and fell to the concrete floor. We had about seven hours before the bell.

"Really?"

"Yeah."

Crimson followed me down to my sanctuary.

That homecoming night, I hid behind the bleachers and watched Crimson from the sidelines. Polaris North Bears beat the Cleveland Pythons 55 to 10. Right after the game, I headed towards the gym for the dance.

Crimson slid in through the draping black and gold streamers that were hanging down like wild ivy in the gymnasium, as hip-hop music vibrated the floors and bleachers. Multi-colored lights bounced off the walls.

Zeke: The Un-Freak

He looked really cool on the floor. He was locking, popping, floating, jerking, and krumping simultaneously. He then took it to another level and moonwalked sideways toward the wall, up it, and onto the ceiling. The entire school body stared with their mouths open while clapping and jumping. His name was chanted over and over again.

I must say, Crimson's dance steps were almost superior to mine.

As he walked down the wall, to the center of the floor, to grab his girl, he twirled around really fast, and his left ear flew off and landed in Ms. Oliver's punch glass.

He stopped and touched the side of his head. Nothing was there. Everyone stopped, stood silently, and just stared at him.

I dug into my deep pocket and pulled out some special super-glue—I always kept that on me—and tossed it to him. He caught it in midair with one hand from almost 30 feet away. He knew exactly what to do with it. He walked over to Ms. Oliver and removed his ear from her glass.

"Sorry."

Using the side of his shirtsleeve, he dried it off, dabbed on a few drops of glue, and placed it back where it belonged.

He looked around, and as he moonwalked towards me, he yelled, "I owe all of this to you, Zeke! You the man!"

The crowd's screams roared and followed with higher-pitched clapping and laughter.

He slapped me on my shoulder and whistled, and then Frankie Fox pranced towards me. My knees wobbled. She reminded me of a hottie fairytale princess in her sparkling silver mini dress.

Crimson resumed dancing with his girl, and the whole class joined in.

Frankie whispered, "Hey, Zeke. Crim told me all about you."

My eyes bulged, and my vocal cords were temporarily frozen.

When I could finally speak, I said, "For real?"

I sounded like a pre-adolescent boy, going through the voice transformation thing.

"Oh, yeah," Frankie said.

She grabbed me by my arm and pulled me towards her. She pressed her full ruby-glossed lips on my cheek. She smelled like cinnamon, apples, and strawberries.

I felt warm, just for that moment. Man, I was in Heaven.

We walked towards the steel doors, and I pushed them apart and allowed her to go out first. I looked back and saw Crim, killing it on the dance floor. He looked up and saluted me, and I reciprocated the gesture.

Yep, a skipped injection with a consensual Z-bite and a drop of vampy blood will do the trick, every time.

The End

Zeke: The Un-Freak

Damaged II

*One concussion with a black eye last Halloween because I didn't
wear the right costume...
Two broken ribs for hugging a friend on my 16th birthday
Three visits to the ER within six months and a web of lies rotating in
my mind,
ready to be unleashed
Four new part-time jobs in the last year, while
Nightmares chased my fractured shadows...*

My name is Riley James, and I once dated a monster.
Every time I ran, J.C. Bleu—a basketball celebrity I was engaged to for almost a year—found me.

No one saw what I saw; they only saw perfection and power. J.C. had the ability to influence anyone.

I knew J.C. would never set me free, so I traveled to a special place that I read about online—my last hope. I met the Roadrunner, a middle-aged bald cowboy, with a golden six-inch double-braided beard.

Roadrunner gave me a possible solution and explained to me what I had to do. My late aunt left me a small inheritance, and I used some of it to pay him up front. I met him at an outside shooting range every evening for almost two weeks.

On our final night, Roadrunner placed a worn leather pouch in my hand. Before I made it to my car, I dropped my keys from my rickety hand. I picked them up and caught my reflection in the side mirror. I didn't look 18 years old; many fighting grey hairs dominated my brunette mane.

Roadrunner shouted out in a gruff tone, "Remember what I told ya. Drink the juice in the vial, load her up like I showed ya, aim, and shoot."

I nodded.

He walked over to me and bent down to my height with his large hands resting on his full hips.

"Ya sure ya up for this?"

"I gotta be. This is the only thing that will solve my J.C. problem."

I opened the door, got in, and started my car.

As I began to back out, Roadrunner yelled, "Call me when it's done, and I'll take care of the rest for ya."

He watched, as I drove off.

One of my headlight beams was dim, but it didn't matter because the moon made up for what was lacking.

With one thing on my mind, I traveled to J.C.'s favorite place: the basketball court at J.C.'s old high school. J.C. loved to practice there before a game when the team was in town.

After turning my car off about a quarter of a mile out, I allowed it to coast into the parking lot. I opened my door slowly, scooped up the pouch, and left the door ajar. I took the vial out and pulled the cap off. A twirl of turquoise smoke climbed up my nostrils—the scent reminded me of tropical Kool-Aid. I closed my eyes, placed the vial on my lips, and tilted my head back, drinking the shimmering liquid. It was bitter, and it felt like a flame, scorching down my throat.

I loaded up my Springfield XDM handgun with a silencer attachment, as Roadrunner had instructed, while my vision transformed into an extreme 3D multi-layer format. With a bright lime-green glow, I could see the tiniest spider buried deep in a bush. Roadrunner told me

Damaged II

that it could come in handy if J.C. turned the lights off. It also slowed down my breathing and heart rate.

Walking in the back, towards the gym, I heard a basketball bouncing on the floor. I placed the gun in my waistband at the small of my back. I opened the door and found J.C., sitting on top of the backboard with the ball in hand.

"I knew you couldn't stay away from me," J.C. barked with a half-grin.

Shaking my head, I said, "You're not going to hurt me anymore!"

J.C. jumped off the backboard, and I noticed the gym floor shake with ripples, as J.C. landed. J.C. bounced the ball up and down, which made large indentations with each impact.

"You can't stop me. I'm going to make each day of your life Hell until I get tired of you! I could've killed you when I slaughtered your parents that night."

"What are you talking about? They died at camp from a bear attack."

J.C. roared out a sickening laugh and said, "You were naive when I first met you, and you're still the same. So pathetic. You really shouldn't have interrupted my practice. You know how much I hate that. Remember when I slammed your face into the dining room table for butting in during my friend's visit?"

✳ ✳ ✳

J.C. walked closer to Riley and threw the basketball at Riley's face.

Riley fell backwards, and J.C. leapt on top of Riley. Streams of thick saliva flowed from J.C.'s protruding long and curved fangs, as fur started to emerge all over J.C.'s face, chest, and arms.

In a growling voice, J.C. asked, "Who's going to save you now?
"Me!"

Riley's hips thrust upwards. Riley reached back with one hand, pulled the gun from the shorts' waistband, and pointed it at J.C.'s face.

Infinity

J.C. roared in a deep laughter, which vibrated the entire gym, causing the backboards' glass to shatter and the rims to fall to the floor.

"Your gun is no match for me!"

"What about a gun loaded with silver bullets, a-hole?"

J.C.'s piercing yellowish-scarlet eyes widened, as Riley pulled the trigger and shot J.C. in the mouth.

Fur, blood, thick saliva, and broken fangs decorated Riley's face and t-shirt. Riley pushed J.C. off and ran towards the car. Riley took out a phone and placed the call.

"Roadrunner, it's done."

"I'll be there in 30 minutes or less."

"Please hurry!" Riley's hands began to tremble.

Using some paper towel in the backseat, Riley wiped off as much gunk as possible.

Roadrunner pulled up in his truck, turned it off, and jumped out with a chocolate-colored mammoth duffle bag.

Walking over to Riley, he said, "Are ya ok?"

"I think so."

"Show me the scene, so I can get rid of the evidence."

Riley and Roadrunner went to the gym and opened the doors. They stepped inside, and Roadrunner circled the body twice, staring for several seconds without a word.

"Ready?" Riley asked as he wiped the sweat off his thick brunette eyebrows with the back of his hand.

"I really thought you were crazy when we first met and you told me your story. I just went with it."

"Why?"

"Nothing. Let me get started so we can get out of here."

"Say it!" Riley shouted.

"I never would've thought your monster would really be a *She-Werewolf*. Thought you were pulling my chain."

"That just goes to show you... *A monster can be what we least*

Damaged II

expect, living inside of anyone. Jacquelynne Constance Bleu turned out to be mine."

The End

One-Way

Terrie's plane landed at LAX Airport, and she found that no rental cars were available. She was co-hosting the 45th annual *Howling Halloween Ball* with her celebrity bestie. She thought about calling a taxicab, but instead, she called PULSE, a luxury transportation service.

A short time later, a 2017 silver Mercedes E63 with charcoal-tinted windows pulled up, and the door opened. Terrie slid in and sat in the backseat with her small carry-on next to her; she was dressed as Elvira.

"Wow, I love your costume," she whispered to the driver, as she took mascara and silver shimmery lip-gloss out of her purse. "It looks so real. Jack the Ripper, right? You attending the ball?"

He nodded and looked up in the rearview mirror, staring at Terrie with glowing red eyes.

"I'm not attending the ball. I'm transporting my next victim to her final destination."

App

Have you ever wished that you could have one do-over in your life?

You're probably familiar with this saying: Whatever happens in Vegas stays in Vegas...

I wish that I had stayed out of Vegas 24 hours ago.

My name is Milo Falcon.

What I'm about to share with you is my true story, and I so wish that I could have my do-over right now. My time is running out, so I'll tell you the quick version.

Four years ago, I attended Gunter College, a place for the upper crust. The campus was nestled perfectly in a hidden spot in Northern Delaware, under a canopy of white birch trees.

That was where I met my best friend Benji Wilson. We didn't start off that way. In fact, we never hung out together at all until my sophomore year, when I dated Benji's sister Hickory. Our relationship was very short-term. Basically, I promised her a few things and broke her heart.

Benji knocked on my dorm door soon after and challenged me to an actual duel, like in the Old West, to defend Hickory's honor. I ended up squashing that pretty fast. I invited him out for some drinks at Yellow Tails, a local pub. I learned a lot about Benji that night, as he did with me.

That conversation went something like this:

"My sis really liked you. Why did you have to mess with her, out of all the girls on campus?"

"I don't know. I thought I wanted someone different," I said, as I shrugged my shoulders and wiggled a bit in the straw barstool, staring down into the bottom of my empty glass.

Waving the bartender over, I asked for my sixth drink.

"You'll never be the committing type."

"Nope. C'mon, look at this. I'm young, fit, good-looking, and rich. No girl could ever resist me. I've got it all. I'm beyond the triple threat. I'm perfection on fire! Guess I'm the kind of guy who wants what he wants when he wants it, and when he doesn't... Oh, well!"

"Yeah, I suppose you are."

Benji lifted his rootbeer bottle to his quivering lips and took a long swallow while staring into my eyes as if he was downloading everything about me.

"We good now, Benji?" I asked, patting him firmly on his back.

"Yeah, I guess we are."

"Tell me more about your interests, Benji. Hey, I'm going to call you Benj from here on out. Sounds cooler, right?"

He smiled, and we talked all night.

As the semesters flew by, I tried to hook Benj up with girls, but he never pursued my gifts that I offered him, yet he did enjoy hanging out with me.

My coolness must've attracted him, and no one ever gave him a hard time when I was around. If I heard someone did, I made sure he never messed with Benj again. He helped me out a lot, too.

If it hadn't been for Benj, I wouldn't have graduated. His IQ and patience were off the charts. I could always find him in the library, with a pile of science books—especially those about viruses—or in the research lab, running tests. He was constantly finding new solutions to biological problems that no one else could figure out. He had several

App

articles published in science and medical journals.

High government officials and scientists kept a close eye on Benj, especially the DVD1—Deadly Virus Division 1—a special task force created by the military for extreme epidemics.

Many things happened during our senior year at Gunter. The worst was the horrific virus outbreak, which infected over 85,000 people in Littlebean, Texas. DVD1 sent in a special team several miles outside the area to set up a lab, and Benj's services were requested. He texted me updates—well, as much as he was allowed to, since everything was highly classified.

The entire city and surrounding suburbs were quarantined until further notice. More than half of those residents perished from the Dand-Virus.

Luckily, Benj helped the DVD1 develop a vaccine within weeks and saved the remaining people in Littlebean. If he hadn't been on their team, then I really think that I wouldn't be telling you this story.

I'm jumping ahead of myself.

The Dand-Virus—or the name no one will ever forget, *The Dandelion Virus*—would've wiped us all out if it hadn't been for Benj's crazy smarts.

The Dand-Virus was one of the worst that had ever entered the U.S. Once someone was infected, severe flu-like symptoms developed within 15 minutes. It was one of the most contagious viruses—DVD1 ranked it a level 10, 11 is the highest, especially since an infected person died soon after contracting the disease.

Upon death of the host, the virus automatically released its lethal cells, like the white puffball of the dandelion flower dispersing its seeds into the air, where they could span out over miles. Anyone in the vicinity who breathed in those cells was automatically infected and only had a short time to live, maybe two hours.

Survivors in Littlebean, Texas were given the vaccine by qualified DVD1 medical staff, as were all the inhabitants of the U.S. and surrounding countries, as a precaution.

InFinity

I recall that date because it was exactly a week before our graduation. Swarms of helicopters decorated the sky like bees, chasing prey from their hive. They were dropping off cases of the vaccine to every city in the U.S. and beyond. All the news media outlets covered the activities of that day and those that followed. Social media blew up like crazy, as well.

So, upon graduation, Benj ended up leaving the U.S. at 20 years old to pursue special research in Japan, while I played up and down the coastline, having several encounters with ex-girlfriends and one-night stands.

I had my share of bar fights and trips to the doctor's office for my indecent choices, which led to some painful consequences, but those were only temporary for me.

A few years passed by, and I received a call from Benj.

"*Konnichiwa watashi no yujin?*"

"What?" I paused for a second and instantly knew. "Benj! How long has it been?"

"Too long, friend."

"How have you been?"

"Pretty good."

"So, you still in Japan?"

"Yeah, I am. You still getting into trouble?"

Laughs echoed into the cell phone receiver.

"When you coming back home, Benj? New Years is in two weeks. I was thinking about celebrating Vegas-style with some buddies. I'd love for you to join us. Plus, it'll be your big 25th birthday!"

"Thanks. I would like that. There's something I need to ask you."

"Anything, Benj."

"I'm getting this special award for something that I designed, and I want you to share the occasion with me."

"No problem. You know that I'm there for you. You've been there for me. When do you need me?"

"It's December 29th at 7 p.m. here at the Silver Dragon Hotel in

App

Osaka. All of your expenses will be taken care of by the company, of course."

"Count on me. By the way, how's Hickory doing? I heard that she went to see you a while back." There was a long pause. "Benj, can you hear me?"

I pulled my cell from my ear to see if the call had been dropped.

"Yeah… Hickory was murdered several months ago."

I rubbed the back of my head with my left hand and paced the patio, as snow began to fall.

"Man, Benj, no one told me. Why didn't you contact me?"

"I'm dealing with it. Each day gets a little easier, but I still have those bad days. You can say she's the inspiration behind my new invention, in a way."

"I bet. Man, what happened?"

"No need to discuss it now. We'll discuss it face-to-face, when I see you, okay?"

"I understand."

"I'll forward you your ticket with itinerary tomorrow."

"Good. Can't wait to see you, Benj."

"Same here. See you soon."

I clicked the *End* button on my cell and slid it into my back pocket. I walked over to a patio chair in a covered spot, sat down, and stared out into the moonlight.

The days flew by, and before I knew it, it was the early morning of December 28th. I had my one carry-on bag packed.

A taxicab arrived at my apartment several hours before the flight. The driver placed the car in *Park* and popped the trunk. I tossed my bag inside and pushed the lid down to shut it.

A young lady wrapped in my hunter green plush robe walked out to give me a leather satchel, where my passport rested inside. She pressed her warm mouth against my almost frosty lips.

"Thanks. I wouldn't be going anywhere without my passport. Jessie, right?"

Infinity

I squinted my eyes, as the brisk cold wind slapped me on my face.

She threw my satchel into my chest and said, "Milo, everyone told me about you. You don't even know my name. It's Tabitha!"

"Oops! Sorry. Don't get all worked up for nothing. Just make sure you're gone, before I return after the first of the year. I've got surveillance."

I opened the door to slide in, just as she threw her slipper towards my face. Instead, it slammed against the icy window.

"Let's go!" I shouted to the driver.

After we drove a few feet away from her, I rolled down the window with the push of a button, held my head halfway out, and yelled, "Don't catch cold, honey. Get back inside!"

Tabitha yelled back at me, but I never knew what she said, due to the snow from the road slushing up against the tires and light Christmas music playing up front. I knew it was nothing nice, though.

I readjusted my jacket and closed my eyes until I arrived at the airport. I paid the fare, collected my bag, and closed the trunk. As I walked into the terminal, pulling my carry-on behind me, I checked my cell. There were 20 missed calls from several ladies. I smiled and turned my phone off.

My gate was close, so I had plenty of time to grab some breakfast at one of the cafés. I ate, while I watched the news. After an hour, it was time to board my flight.

I arrived at the check-in counter, turned on my cell, and showed my flight information listed in the email. I then switched my phone off again. In no time, I was boarding the plane, entering the first class section, and was on my way to see my friend. A few movies were played during the flight, but I didn't pay much attention to those... only the stewardesses.

"Please fasten your seatbelts. We'll be landing in Osaka momentarily. It's been a pleasure having you fly *Jade Airlines*. Please remember us again when you are booking your next international flight," one attendant said while maintaining eye contact with me.

App

Before I stepped off the plane, the same woman whispered in my ear, "I'll be in Osaka for one night."

After we exchanged numbers quickly and discreetly, I walked towards the exit of the immaculate airport and immediately saw Benj, standing in the center of the crowd.

He threw his arms up, and we hugged for a moment.

"Can't believe it, Benj! It's been so long!"

"Yeah, it has."

"Look like you've been working out. You were always so scrawny back in school."

He smiled, as we walked out the automatic glass doors, towards the parking lot.

"Benj, this is my first time in Osaka. It's colder than I imagined."

"Yes, it reminds me of the East Coast."

"Too much. Thought I would escape that for a bit."

Once we arrived at the car, I threw my bag in the trunk, ran back to the passenger side, and jumped into an unexpected heated leather seat. Benj was already inside, with the engine running.

"Nice, Benj. It's all toasty inside," I said, rubbing my hands together.

"Yep, I turned the heat on once I knew you were landing. Figured you would like that."

Before he shifted into first gear, I couldn't resist any longer; I had to ask.

"If you don't mind, Benj, what happened to Hickory?"

He gripped his steering wheel with both hands and lowered his forehead onto it with a slight turn towards me.

"All I know is that she was keeping bad company. One night, she never returned to her apartment. I received a visit from the police a few days later. They told me that her purse was found a few miles away from the Osaka Castle."

"Man, I'm so sorry, Benj."

"Thanks. The funeral was private, and it was a closed casket because of the disturbing condition of her body."

Infinity

"What do you mean by 'the condition of her body'? Like an animal attack, or something?"

"The police are still trying to solve it."

"Benj, anything I can do?" I asked, resting my hand on his shoulder.

"Just you being here is some comfort for me."

"How long has it been since Hickory's death?"

"Almost six months now. Milo, did you know that Hickory always talked about you? She never could get over you. She really changed after that."

"No, I didn't. We just dated a little while. Nothing serious, Benj."

"Yeah, guess that's all it took for her. She told me what you did, Milo," Benj said, glaring at me.

"What did she tell you?"

"You know... it's not even relevant now. She's gone. Let's get going."

Benj put the car in gear and drove towards the highway. We passed by endless rows of cherry trees dressed in snow.

"Milo. I thought about you staying in the hotel after I talked to you and figured, why not stay with me?"

"Right on. You know that I'm down."

"It's not huge, but it's mine. I want to share something with you before tonight's ceremony."

"Sounds good to me, Benj. Do you think you'll ever return to the U.S.?"

"I don't know. This company has been really good to me, and Osaka is growing on me."

"I get it."

Benj drove for several miles until we arrived at his home on the waterfront, which was located on the outskirts of Osaka. It was a modest house with Japanese architecture and culture on the outside and the inside.

"Looks like you're doing pretty good here. Nice."

"Thanks. You know I'll never be a suave as you, Milo."

App

I placed my bag on the island, and then Benj gave me a tour of the upstairs and showed me where I would be staying.

As he rolled my suitcase through the long hallway, I noticed a bright blue door to my right.

"What's in there?"

"Oh, that's my lab."

"Do I get a tour of that also?"

"Sure. Why don't you get settled in and meet me there when you're done. I'll make us some snacks and drinks."

I placed my bag on the bed, unzipped it, and laid my suit out for the evening event. I then walked down the hall to find the blue door open.

"Benj, you in there?"

"Yeah, join me."

After descending the spiral wooden staircase, I surveyed the entire room full of computers and strange gadgets, all perfectly snug in their cubbyholes.

"I'm impressed, Benj. I bet you live down here." He smiled and pointed over his shoulder. A twin bed and mini fridge rested in the corner. "So, what do you have to show me? I've been trying to figure it out since you mentioned it."

"You'll have to be the judge, Milo."

He stooped behind his lab table and removed a metallic cell phone from underneath.

"Okay, that's nice."

"Here, look closer."

Benj dropped it into my manicured hand. I turned it on, scrolled a few pages, and surfed the internet for several minutes.

"Okay, I guess I'm missing something. It's just like any regular cell."

"You're right about it being like any ordinary phone. Now, I want you to take a picture of me."

I positioned it to take his photo. Benj stood away from the lab table. I pushed the button, it flashed twice, and I looked down at the screen.

InFinity

"Okay, a pic of you. So, what's the big surprise?"

Benj walked over to me and gave me more boring instructions.

"Now, press the H-App button, under the camera icon."

I followed his directions, and Benj's photo popped up with a detailed profile of his past and current makeup. I mean, it listed his age, height, weight, lack of criminal history, body temperature, and that he was clear of any infections.

"What the...?" I asked, almost dropping the device.

"Don't panic, Milo. It profiled me. It can inform you of crimes anyone has committed, their vitals, chemical imbalances, substance use, traces of diseases or viruses that may be lurking in one's bloodstream, and more."

"Man, you've really outdone yourself this time, Benj. I mean, I knew that you were a brain and all back at Gunter, but I can now classify you as a genuine genius, with crazy skills."

"I invented this, Milo, because of the past Dand-Virus scare and Hickory's unsolved murder. I wanted to create something to save others from a possible outbreak and equip them with the ability to find out someone's potential risk to cause them harm."

"Is that why it's called the H-App, in memory of Hickory?"

"Yeah," Benj said, wiping tears from his face with the back of his hand.

"Man, I didn't mean to..."

"I know. I'm okay."

"So, can I ask you a personal question?"

"Sure, Milo."

"Remember that one summer when I traveled to Costa Rica, and how I told you I had the time of my life with those hottie triplets?"

"Yeah, couldn't forget those details."

"All right. Now, remember how I also came back with a very uncomfortable friend, and I had to use that annoying ointment and take those awful antibiotics for a month?"

"Oh, yeah. Almost forgot about that."

App

Benj laughed out loud for several minutes.

"You done?"

"Yeah, that was pretty awful for you. You were out of commission for a bit."

"One of the worst times of my life. Anyhow, can this app detect... you know?"

"What?"

"C'mon, Benj. You know..."

"Oh! Of course. It can detect just about anything under the sun, from A to Z and then some."

A huge smile appeared on my face like I was a little boy who just scored his first homerun.

"Wait, I already know what you're thinking, Milo. This prototype has to pass several tests first, and a few things still need to be added. Plus, it wasn't created for that."

"What?"

"I know you. Don't even go there."

"I wasn't."

"Really... really?"

I gave him a mini smirk.

"Let's go get dressed. A car will be here in two hours to pick us up."

As we walked up the staircase to prepare for the awards ceremony, I looked back at the special device, resting on the table.

"Benj, is that the one you're debuting tonight?"

"No, I'm debuting an advanced prototype."

We dressed in record time.

"Look at you, Benj, in your tux. Not bad, my friend. Here, let me straighten your bowtie."

I stepped closer to him, untied it, and redid it.

I was dressed in a fashionable charcoal silk suit, without a tie.

"You look stylish, as always," he said.

"Thank you very much. Hey, I see the limo pulling up," I said, as I looked over his shoulder in the kitchen.

Infinity

As we left, Benj set his security system, and we walked down the stairs, towards the limo. The driver stepped out of the car and opened the door for us. When we arrived at the front of the hotel, the man opened our doors once more and then ushered us towards the red carpet.

Mammoth crystal chandeliers with shimmering green lights decorated the conference room, which was jam-packed with scientists, law enforcement, physicians, military, and government officials.

We took our seats, and an exquisite four-course seafood dinner was served. I winked at two young ladies at our table.

An Army colonel spoke about Benj's impressive accomplishments and noted that he was the one who saved millions from the Dand-Virus a few years ago. When he finished, a standing ovation overtook the room for several minutes.

Benj smiled and rested his eyes on me, as he stood beside the colonel.

Once the applause and chattering ceased, Benj made his moving speech. He ended on the note of his new invention, the H-App. He showed an impressive PowerPoint presentation on it and demonstrated how it worked with selected audience members.

All jaws dropped. They were in awe. Benj was given a tall glass cherry blossom tree award for his multiple talents as a researcher and inventor, as tears ran down his cheeks. The clapping continued until he returned to his seat.

I hugged him and said, "Benj, I'm so proud of you. You're a man of change."

"Thank you, Milo. I'm so glad that you could be here to share this moment with me."

"Wouldn't have missed it."

The evening continued with cocktails and several guests approaching Benj for pictures and autographs. He was happy to accommodate them.

My cell vibrated in my pocket. I pulled it out and saw it was a message from the cute flight attendant Hisako I had met earlier on the plane. We texted about hooking up at her hotel.

App

As he was talking to someone, I tapped Benj on his shoulder and whispered into his ear, "Man, I'm going to excuse myself and head out for a while. I wanna slip into something a little more comfortable."

"Milo, there's a private reception later, where I'll be sharing more information about the H-App."

"You got your audience for that. You don't need me anymore tonight. You can tell me all about it later, but I really need to get out of here."

Benj blew out a long sigh with his head down, staring at the golden carpet.

"Okay. I'll text you the code once I get a free moment."

"Thanks."

It didn't take long to wave down a cab. I opened the door, slid into the seat, and gave the driver Benj's address. He texted the security code to me and shared via text that he would be at the private reception a little longer and would see me the following morning. He knew I wouldn't be home, anyhow.

I laughed under my breath.

Once I arrived at the house and got inside, I went into the bedroom and peeled off my suit. I slipped on some jeans, a sweater, and a platinum leather coat. I grabbed a few goodies out of the bottom of my suitcase and slipped them into my satchel.

After splashing on some *Armani,* I stared at myself in the mirror.

"Dang, I'm one good-looking…"

Something clicked inside of me, as I moonwalked out of the bathroom. I placed the satchel around my waist. I texted Hisako to ask if she could assist me in booking an earlier flight. She messaged back that a friend of hers could do that and only needed my flight information. I sent it to her, and it was done.

After packing all of my belongings into my carry-on, I called a cab to drive me to Hisako's hotel. I then sat down and wrote a note to Benj and left it on his kitchen table.

The taxi arrived in minutes.

Infinity

As I was about to close the door, I stopped and yelled to the driver, "Hold on! I forgot something. Need a quick minute."

I parked my carry-on at the bottom of the front steps and ran down the hallway, then opened the blue door, grabbed the prototype metallic phone off the lab table, and slid it into my back jeans pocket.

After closing the door, I entered the code, grabbed my carry-on, rushed out to the car, and placed it in the backseat with me.

"Okay. Thanks. I need to get to this hotel," I said to the driver, clumsily reciting the name Hisako gave me.

When I arrived, she greeted me in a black nightie, holding a bottle of champagne. I walked in and shut the door behind me.

"Thanks for the help with my flight."

"No problem. We have about five hours before we both have to be at the airport. What do you want to do?"

"Hmm, I don't know. I think we can come up with something. Hey, let me get your picture for a keepsake."

"Okay."

She climbed on the bed to pose for me. I pulled Benj's phone out of my pocket and took her photo. Her profile popped up. Let's just say that she passed her criminal background check with flying colors, but she failed with her personal data.

"Babe, you know what? Let's watch a movie. I really need to get some rest. I had a long flight in, and I've been up ever since. We gotta get up in a few hours for another long flight and all."

"What? Are you serious? Look at me!"

"Yeah, I know. You look fantastic, but let's take things a little slow. I've been in that fast driver seat too many times."

"Wow, that's kind of sweet." She slid closer to him. "So, what you wanna watch?"

"You choose."

"Really?"

"Absolutely. Why don't you go put something on that's really comfortable? Don't want you to catch a cold. It's pretty nippy in here,"

App

I said, rubbing my hands together.

"Okay. I'll be back. I have some cute kitten pajamas that I've been dying to jump into. This thing crawls everywhere."

"Yeah, I bet," I mumbled.

As she was getting dressed in the bathroom, Benj texted me. I called him and had a whispered conversation.

"Are you having fun yet?" he asked.

"Haha! Listen, I'm taking an earlier flight to get things ready for us in Vegas. I left you a note at the house." Silence followed. "Benj, you there?"

"Yeah, I just thought we were flying to Vegas together later tomorrow night, Milo."

"Just want to get things ready. Plus, we'll have a blast tomorrow night, New Year's Eve. We'll bring in 2017 and your birthday together in style."

"All right, I'll see you then. Have a safe trip."

"Cool. Hey, Benj?"

"Yeah."

"You did good tonight with your speech. You're really going places."

"Thanks."

I attempted to get some sleep, but Hisako tossed and turned with arms and knees poking me. Finally, I got up and walked over to the chair to nap the remaining 30 minutes before my alarm went off.

She called a cab to transport us to the airport nearby. I slid out of my seat and closed the door, as she remained in the cab. She threw sharp daggers with her eyes into my chest.

"What?"

She pointed at her door with her chin, so I walked around, opened it, and grabbed her luggage.

"Thanks."

"Sure thing. After you, princess."

The glass doors opened. She went to kiss me on my lips, but I quickly turned my cheek to her.

"Appreciate everything," I shouted, as I walked towards my gate.

She waved at me and yelled out, "If you're ever in Osaka again, then look me up."

I turned around and gave a slight nod.

When first-class passengers boarded, I found my seat and fastened my belt. I slept until the plane landed in Vegas. A couple of my buddies were waiting for me, as I rode down the escalator. They hugged me, and we all loaded up in the van. They drove me to the hotel to check in.

After I took a shower and wrapped the towel around my waist, I noticed my cell phone glowing with several missed calls from Benj, so I gave him a ring.

"Hey, Benj, what's up? Our room is awesome. Got us the supreme suite."

"Milo, I think someone broke in and stole the first prototype device."

"What gives you that idea?"

"I can't find it. I searched in the lab everywhere. I know I didn't take it with me. The last time I had it is when I showed you."

"Yeah, I know."

"Wait. Please don't tell me…"

"Tell you what?"

"You didn't!"

"Didn't what?"

"Stop with your games!"

"I'm just borrowing it until you get here, Benj. Anyways, I'm doing you a big favor. I tested it out last night with that flight attendant chick. Let me just say, you saved me an ER visit!"

"That's not what it's for! Promise me that you won't use it anymore for your personal indiscretions." I said nothing. "Promise me, Milo," Benj said.

"Okay… okay."

"Just don't do anything stupid until I get there, okay? I should be there after 6 p.m. tomorrow night."

App

"C'mon, you know me, Benj."

"Exactly. There's something I need to tell you."

"Tell me now."

"Not over the phone. Just promise me you'll wait for me before you go out."

"All right, I promise. I'll just tell the guys to party without me tonight, and I'll do some gambling instead."

I played several games of Blackjack and Roulette. Quite a few hot ladies passed by my table, and I stared down at my pocket, where the device rested. My hand glided over it a few times, but I never used it. At least, not that night.

New Year's Eve arrived fast. Hundreds of parties were being held all over the city. I received a call from Benj around 4 p.m.

"Hey, my flight from Osaka to Vegas is delayed. I should be there sometime after 8 p.m. We can still bring in the New Year and my birthday together."

"Okay. A driver will be at the airport to pick you up."

"Stay put. Give me your word, Milo."

"You got it. I'll be right here until then."

Time flew by, and it was 8 p.m. The driver called me to report that Benj's flight wouldn't be in until after 10 p.m., so I decided to just wait around.

I texted him.

M: *Benj, the driver will be there to pick you up. He'll then take you to the Naughty Blue Iguana, where me and the guys will be waiting for you.*

I got no response from him, which made sense since he was on the plane.

We arrived at the club, where girls were painted on the walls and floors. I was in paradise. I found a nice secluded section on the top floor and ordered drinks for everyone. The rock music was playing loudly, as shiny lights danced on everything in the space, while my buddies circulated the room.

Infinity

Alone at our table, I felt my phone vibrate, and I answered.

"Hey, Benj!" I yelled into the phone.

"Milo, my plane is at the gate. A passenger fell ill during the flight, and he has to be escorted off first. I should be at the hotel in the next hour or so."

"Okay, but I'm at the club with the guys already. They were antsy and didn't want to wait for you. Can't blame them, you know."

"Just stay right there. See you as soon as I can."

"Sure."

The music grew louder and louder, as I scanned the room several times. My gazed landed on this one hottie. She was tall with long black curly hair. She reminded me of a Brazilian ballerina. I watched her every move.

She saw me staring at her, and our eyes locked onto each other's. After ordering a drink, I poured it down my throat quickly and slammed the glass down on the table. I stood up and walked towards her. I was on the hunt.

The club was extremely crowded. I lost her for a few seconds, but then I found her once more.

I softly pushed her over to the wall with my whole body pressed against hers.

"I've been watching you for a while."

"I know," she said.

"What's your name?"

"Tanja."

"Beautiful, just like you."

"Thank you."

She ran the tip of her hot pink nail down my chin to the middle of my chest. My heart felt like a ticking bomb.

"Can I buy you a drink?" I asked.

"Why don't we just go to my room, baby? It's not far from here."

"You don't beat around the bush, do ya?"

"Why play games? You know what you want, and I know what I

App

want. Ready?" I pulled back a little and glanced around. "You looking for someone else, baby?"

"Sort of. My best friend is at the airport and on his way. He'll be here in a bit. We're bringing in the New Year and his birthday together with some buddies of mine."

"Oh, that sounds like fun, but I know something else even more fun."

"I bet," I said with a smile.

Tanja pulled me in closer and guided my hands to rest on her curvy hips. I eyed her full cleavage and the short red dress that hugged every inch of her body; it might as well have been painted on.

I licked my lips, and she caught my tongue with her teeth softly.

"Wow, you're really something."

"Yes, I know. Let's go. I promise to have you back in time. He won't even know you left," Tanja whispered into my ear, and then she bit my right earlobe.

"Just let me tell one of my buddies that I'm leaving and will be back."

"I'll be downstairs. Don't make me wait too long."

"I won't."

I glided back into the ocean of dancers and found one of my buddies.

"A.J., I'm going to make a quick run, but I'll be back in an hour or so. Just let Benj know, okay?"

"All right, man. Do your thang," he said, bumping my fist.

I found my way downstairs, where Tanja was waiting for me in a limo with the door open. I stepped inside, and the driver shut the door.

"Where are you staying?" I asked.

"I'm at the Hunter's Casino."

"Nice. We're at the Broadway Casino at the end of the strip."

"Yes, I've stayed there before."

"So, Tanja, you from here?"

"Oh, no. I travel all over. I was in Osaka recently."

"Really? Me, too. Beautiful country."

Infinity

"Yes," she purred, running her hand through my hair with constant eye contact.

Before I could say another word, she pulled me towards her and planted a long kiss on my lips.

"Man, I don't think that anyone has ever kissed me to the point where I almost feel paralysis in my legs."

"That's a good thing, right?"

"Yes. Can I get a quick picture of you?"

"Sure."

I pulled Benj's phone out from my jeans pocket and pointed it towards Tanja. She leaned back and smiled. I quickly looked at the photo with her profile. The pic was blurry, but the information on her was good, with no issues for me.

"Let me see, baby."

"Oh, I didn't have the flash on. It's all blurry. Where were we?"

Before she could respond, the driver pulled up to the front of her hotel. As I jumped out and ran over to open the door for her, my phone vibrated. I pulled it out to check, and it was a missed call from Benj.

"Who's that?"

"My buddy."

As I was getting ready to call him, Tanja took my phone, turned it off, slid it into my pocket, and said, "He can wait a little bit, right?"

"Yeah, he can."

"My driver will take you back, okay?"

We entered the elevator, and Tanja pushed the button for the 45th floor.

"You're on the top."

"Yes, I like being on top of everything, baby."

I stared at her and whispered into her ear, "I've never met anyone like you."

"I know, and you never will again."

The elevators opened to her penthouse. Everything was hot pink, from the walls to the floors and furnishings.

App

"A lot of pink."

"Yes, my favorite color. I'm going to the bathroom. Why don't you get us some wine out of the fridge? Strange, I know, but I like mine cold."

"No problem."

After I leaned in and kissed her, I then watched her strut in her eight-inch black rhinestone stilettoes, until she got to the door.

She turned around and said, "I won't be long, baby. Know you want to get back to your buddies."

"They understand."

As I walked towards the kitchen, I noticed a couple of buttons on the wall. I pushed both; the light turned on dim, and jazz began to play. I opened the fridge and found several bottles of red wine. I pulled one out and set it on the island, where two black wineglasses stood.

I searched in the drawers and found a corkscrew. I put it to use and had no problem getting the bottle open. I poured both glasses almost full and took a sip. It was thick and odd-tasting. I quickly spat it out on the floor, dropping the glass.

"What the...?"

Wiping my mouth, I looked down and noticed that my fingers were stained with a thick reddish substance. I brought my hand to my tongue.

It tastes like blood.

I felt something dripping on top of my head and on my arms, and I wiped it away. It appeared to be more blood, but I knew I hadn't cut myself anywhere.

Why would blood be falling onto me?

Suddenly, I looked up, and there was Tanja, with her long nails embedded in the ceiling, acting as an anchor. I stepped into the splattered crimson liquid, slipped, and fell backwards.

Tanja was staring directly at me. Her eyes transformed into a series of colors, like a nervous chameleon. Her lips folded back, and long glistening fangs appeared.

My eyes grew wider.

Infinity

She dropped down and landed on my chest without a sound; her thighs clamped tightly around my waist. I couldn't breathe.

"Baby, what's the matter? You can't speak?" she asked, as she pulled me towards her face. "Do you really think you chose me tonight? Wrong. I selected you! In fact, I've been hunting you for a while. Guess I really got lucky tonight. You left Osaka before I could snatch you up. You remember Kelli Waters from your senior year at Gunter?"

I nodded.

"She was my daughter. She told me how you treated her. She was so hurt and heartbroken over you that she committed suicide! Someone gave me this gift, and I knew exactly how I would use it."

Tears ran down my face.

"Oh, you have feelings now? Well, I'm not buying it."

Before I could utter a word, she pulled me closer and plunged her long fangs into the side of my neck. They dug deeper into my carotid artery each time I tried to squirm out of her tight grip.

Lifting her head up, as blood trailed down the sides of her mouth, she said, "Baby, I'm not going to drain you dry. I want you to suffer."

She stood up, and before I could blink, she flew out the window, as the sheer pink curtains waved in the wind.

I barely managed to pull my phone out of my front pocket. My hand was growing numb. I texted Benj, as my finger missed letters and numbers.

M: *Hep n troub cal 91…*

Benj and the paramedics arrived at the penthouse in rocket speed because his cell had reverse-GPS tracking. They found me sprawled out on the kitchen floor, as my blood continued to seep out.

I heard Benj faintly whisper to one of the paramedics, "His color is fading. We've got to get him to the hospital quickly."

My body felt like a life-sized deflated doll, weightless.

The paramedics scooped me up, placed me onto the stretcher, guided me out of that penthouse to the elevator, rolled me out of the hotel lobby, and loaded me into the ambulance. One of the paramedics

App

started an I.V. with a saline drip, but I knew that I was a goner because I had lost too much blood already.

I was ushered into the O.R., where they repaired the lacerations to my neck and gave me a blood transfusion. I was then relocated to the ICU. After the nurse left the room, Benj sneaked in against hospital regulations.

He whispered, "Milo, I told you to stay put. Why didn't you listen to me?"

I couldn't talk. I could hardly look up at him. I attempted to blink my eyes with an oxygen mask covering the lower half of my face.

"Milo, you were always in such a hurry. I asked you to stay and hear what else I had to say after the ceremony with a select few, but you had to rush off, as you always have. I told the others that if the photo turns out blurry with the H-App, then that means it measured no body temperature, which meant... yep... immortal. Let me spell it out for you. V-a-m-p-i-r-e."

My eyes widened, and my lips began to quiver.

"Osaka has been infested with one of the oldest viruses on record. It's been around for centuries, and I've been studying it for a while now. That's why I was chosen to work in Osaka... to develop a detecting device and a vaccine. I just finished successful test trials on the serum, and I have it in my bag over there. It could possibly save your life, but..."

My eyes widened more, and I attempted to reach out my deflated hand towards Benj's arm.

Pushing my hand away, he turned his back to me and said, "You know what? I'm not going to give it to you. I bet you're wondering why. It's simple, Milo. You don't deserve to live. You're beyond vain. I should've killed you years ago when you lied to Hickory to snatch her innocence from her and so many others after. However, I waited... because I knew that it would be just a matter of time, as this virus has always been selective of its heartless prey. She finally found you all on her own."

Benj walked over to the table and picked up his bag. He tossed it over his shoulder, walked out, and shut the door behind him. I hoped and prayed he would have second thoughts and come back into my room and inject me.

He didn't.

I'm not going to make it.

So, I hope my story serves as a lesson for someone else. Don't be in a hurry all the time, and above all, don't be reckless with people's hearts.

You never know how it may come back to *bite* you.

The End

App

HIDDEN

Fantasy Tales

The
Gift

17 weeks
3 days
9 hours
36 seconds

Unemployment and Jasper Crawford remained constant enemies. Jasper stared up at the dark mocha-stained wet ceiling over his bunk bed. Razor-sharp mini springs and multiple bed bugs pierced his body constantly, that night more irritating than usual.

With the incessant tortures and powerful stench brewing from his roommate, Jasper jumped down from his bunk and paced the wobbly floor until morning.

After slipping on his boots, he grabbed his denim coat off the back of a chair, threw it over his shoulder, and walked three blocks to *Dr. Feelgood's Diner*. He had almost forgotten about his emergency two-dollar stash in his worn right boot.

He found a table, sat down, and ordered a coffee. As he sipped the warm drink, *Dust in the Wind* played softly on the jukebox, and he drifted back to a road trip he had taken almost two years before.

As he glanced around the room, Jasper noticed a bright orange flyer on the floor. He picked it up and read it.

Deckhands Wanted
$100,000 in four months. No experience necessary.
Interviews on 10/20 from 11 a.m. to 1 p.m.
234 W. Raven Road

On Tuesday morning, he arrived early, but the line was already a block long. It moved at a slow pace until he finally came to the office entrance. A young lady with curly ponytails, tied with red and white polka dot ribbons, handed him an application to fill out on a clipboard with a pen attached.

After he completed it, he handed it back to her, as she blew a large blue bubble with her gum. She retrieved his form while twirling a fallen strand of her hair with a ballpoint pen.

A tall older man stepped out of the office. The smell of cigars and dead fish exuded from him and went straight into Jasper's nostrils. Marty extended his long ghostly hand towards Jasper and placed it on his shoulder. He felt the cold wet sensation through his heavy flannel shirt.

"I'm Marty James," the man said, as he grabbed Jasper's hand and shook it. He then led him back to his office. "Please, have a seat. I'm the head of human resources."

He sat down in a lime-green cloth swivel chair that reminded him of the ones his late grandparents had covered up in plastic in their garage when he was a young boy in the late 90s.

"Today must be your lucky day, Jasper Crawford. You're the last one we're taking for interviews. I see you worked for Dave's Construction Company for almost a year."

"Yeah… I've been laid off for a while now."

"Any family?" he asked, wiping his sweaty forehead with the back of his hairy hand.

"No, my parents died in a house fire when I was 12 years old. I rotated a few times in the foster care system after my grandparents died

Hidden

when I turned 15."

Tears filled his eyes without falling.

"Sorry to hear that. No girlfriend, or...?"

"No, girls have never been interested in me much. Pretty much been jumping from shelter to shelter on the island after I dropped out of high school in the 11th grade." Jasper sighed while staring at the stack of papers on Marty's desk. "Just need to get back to work."

"You're almost 18?"

"In about two weeks."

Dropping his eyes down to the floor, Jasper rubbed his knees with his hands.

"This job is far from construction. It's rough. The weather can be brutal out at sea. How does that sound to you?"

"I'm a hard worker and really need the job, Mr. James. I have nothing waiting for me here. I'm up for anything and everything."

"Wait here."

Jasper rocked back and forth in the swivel chair, staring at the sea paintings on the wall. He noticed something unusual in one. He stood from his chair for a closer look, but before he reached it, Marty stormed in.

"Come back tomorrow morning at seven sharp for paperwork and introduction to your captain and crew."

"I'm hired?"

"Yep."

"Thank you!" he said, shaking Mr. James's hand.

As soon as Jasper laid his head down and drifted off to sleep that night, he heard his alarm clock chirping. He jumped up and threw his clothes on. He slid his dingy backpack, which contained all his belongings, over his right shoulder and walked towards Raven Road. He had a feeling that his life was about to change.

As he approached the dock, he saw Marty talking with a group of guys. He waved him over.

The Gift

"Hey, Jasper, come meet your crew. This is Joe, Hank, Teddy, Ben, Mario, and Steven."

"Hey, guys," he said, throwing his hand up.

The six-man crew responded by looking up at him, and then they continued to load the boat and check all the equipment. The captain slithered over to Jasper, while Marty exited like a field mouse barely escaping a feral cat's attack.

"Damn good to have you on *Stealth Lucy #13*, Jasper. They call me Cap Brutus," he said, as he slapped Jasper hard in the middle of his back.

Two cigars leaned halfway out both sides of his mouth, and his beard was matted with dried food and snuff.

"Good to be here, Cap Brutus. Thanks."

"So, what you waiting for? Climb on board, and let's get you acquainted with everything.".

"I need to complete some paperwork with Mr. James first."

"Nonsense, boy. I'll take care of all that when we get where we're going at sea."

The captain wiped his runny nose with the back of his puffy hand and twirled the cigars in his mouth.

After a few days, Jasper learned pretty fast that it wasn't crabs that were being captured in the deep dark waters of the Bering Sea and its unbearable elements.

He pulled up a heavy cage full of frightened creatures he'd read about in old comic books when he was younger: Screaming mermaids!

Hundreds of them were being caught in those rusted cages. They all had long curly locks, flowing over their iridescent voluptuous bodies and lengthy fish-like tails.

"Bloody marvelous, rookies!" Captain Brutus shouted.

"Unbelievable! My great granddad used to read me stories about these creatures on our camping trips. I thought he made them up. He was always sharing fantasy books about mermaids with me," Jasper

Hidden

said.

"No fairytales here, my boy. This is a great catch. They're worth almost half a million per pound."

"Per pound?"

"Mermaid meat is the cancer cure, and plenty of fat pockets are lining up to buy it for themselves. I like mine extra crispy!"

"Are you telling me they're slaughtered?"

"Nah… Yep, that's exactly what I'm saying. We're helping nature out. They breed like bloody cockroaches! You're not going soft on me, are you, boy? Maybe this isn't for you, after all."

"No, Cap. I… can do this."

As Jasper and his crewmates secured the cages, one of the mermaids grabbed his wrist tightly with her sharp glowing fuchsia nails and whispered, "Help us! Please!"

Heavy tears ran down her youthful face.

"I… I can't. I'm so sorry."

As Jasper pulled his arm back, Captain Brutus drew his machete from his side and chopped her hand off. Goosebumps popped up all over Jasper's body, as she let out a blood-curdling scream. A tear attempted to run from the corner of his eye, but he tilted his head back to prevent its escape.

"Watch out, boy. They'll try to trick you. They're evil beasts, every last one of them. I've seen one rip a man's heart out with her bare bony finned hand while slitting a man's throat with her tail. They're vicious monsters, I tell you! They're worse than the broads back home. I hate them all. No matter the breed!" Captain Brutus yelled, "All of them secured, mates?"

"Yes, sir," the crew said simultaneously.

"Now, all of you… Get in those cages to the left! Now!" Captain Brutus shouted. When no one moved, he said, "Guess I gotta play hardball with you fellas." He picked up his Winchester rifle from a corner and pointed it in their colorless faces. "March, dammit!"

The Gift

"Why are you doing this?" Jasper asked.

"You were all first draft pick—homeless and worthless. Nobody's gonna search for the likes of you. Each of you was chosen. That flyer is bait to drive the food in—the sacrifices. It's been working for centuries now. I have debts to pay on land and at sea."

"What do you mean, sacrifices?"

"Boy, I gotta say, you're a little slow. I gotta give the sea something in return for giving me those beasts. You'll find out soon enough."

Captain Brutus chuckled, as wet snuff accumulated around the sides of his mouth.

"Please!" Jasper begged.

The captain's gun poked the back of his head repeatedly. He and the deckhands walked into the empty cages, as Brutus prepared them to be lowered into subzero-degree waters.

Jasper dropped to his knees suddenly.

"Stop horsing around, boy. Get up!"

He noticed a deep scratch glowing bright fuchsia on his inner wrist. He collapsed, as his eyes rolled back, remembering the mermaid's tight clutch, while the deckhands huddled together at the end of the cage, shaking feverishly.

Iridescent scales covered his entire body within seconds. Wide multiple gill slits unzipped on the sides of his neck. His hands transformed into webbed talons, while his legs turned into a long tail with a razor-spiked sphere about the size of a bowling ball.

Captain Brutus froze in disbelief, yelping, "No, this can't be!"

He pointed his rifle at Jasper, shot at him, and fell back on his plump rear from the recoil, but the bullet only grazed the side of his face. Within seconds, the new scar vanished.

That was when Jasper's spiked tail slammed the locks off the mermaids' cages. They hurried to the side of the boat and dove into the water, without a splash, and waited for him in a circle, humming a tranquil song in unison.

Hidden

Jasper wrapped Captain Brutus in his massive tail and threw him up in the air, as a gargantuan harpy-serpent, with flaming red eyes, flew up from the depth of the ocean and devoured him.

The End

The Gift

Stormie's Birthday
Wish

Stormie's alarm clock jiggled off her table to the floor. She rolled her ratty blanket away from her face to look out her small window, as two seagulls paced up and down a tightrope-like rail while fluttering their wings at each other in the breeze.

She could hear Walter, her dad, walking above her, as dust from the ceiling snowed down onto her.

He yelled out, "Stormie, it's almost 7:30! You're going to be late again. I need to sail out soon. It's going to be a warm one today. You hear me?"

"Yes, Walter," she mumbled, pulling the blanket back over her head to avoid the falling dust.

A few minutes later, she climbed out of bed and scurried around her tight quarters to get dressed.

Stormie climbed up the narrow stairwell to find a small bowl of stale cereal soaked in milk. She took one whiff and pushed it aside.

"I know, Kitten. I've been going out, but very few salmon have been meeting with my nets. I hope today will be different."

"Sure, Walter."

"I'll see you this evening. If I'm lucky today, I'll hold on to a salmon for us to eat for dinner. By the way, I really wish you wouldn't call me that."

She sighed and swung her backpack onto her shoulder. A book fell

Hidden

out from a large hole in the bottom.

"Kitten, you dropped something."

"I'll hold on to it. Thanks."

"Looks like it's time to retire this."

She shook her head and grabbed the rope rail to pull up to the dock.

As she headed off to school, she whispered under her breath, "I can't believe Walter forgot today is my birthday."

The bell had already rung, when Stormie eased Mrs. Little's door open and crept inside, as the teacher was turned around, writing an assignment on the blackboard.

Veronica Chambers sneezed and shouted, "Loser's late again!"

The class snickered.

"Stormie, please take your seat."

In her fitted grey pencil skirt, Mrs. Little turned her model-like body around, clicking her red polished high heels against the floor.

She sat down behind Veronica, pulled her book out, and placed it on top of her desk.

Turning around in her seat, Veronica whispered, "Daddy's overalls again? Pew, you even smell like a dirty old fisherman. It must be really hard, being poor trash."

The teacher slapped her pointer stick on Veronica's desk, causing her to almost jump out of her seat. The entire class laughed except Stormie.

"Miss Chambers, since you have everyone's attention now, why don't you solve the word problem on the board?"

As Veronica stood up to walk towards the front of the room, she smirked at Stormie and bumped her desk, knocking her book to the floor.

"Oops! I'm sorry," she said with a smirk.

The end of the day didn't come soon enough for Stormie, but when she walked up to their boathouse, she was surprised to see colorful balloons tied to the shaky rails, swaying in the air.

Stormie's Birthday Wish

Her dad walked out, carrying a tiny birthday cake lit up with 13 small candles.

"Happy birthday, Kitten."

She jumped onto the boat and dropped her backpack.

"Walter, I thought you forgot."

She wasted no time blowing out the candles, but she forgot to make a wish.

"Never. Cake first, then dinner. Today was a good fishing day. I kept a large salmon out for us."

From his overall pocket, he dug out a tiny box with a hand-tied hot pink bow, while Stormie stuffed cake into her mouth.

"Here."

"What's this, Walter?"

"Just a little something for my favorite girl."

She opened it and found a sterling silver kitten necklace with emerald eyes. Walter walked up behind her, placed it around her neck, and fastened it for her.

"I love it, Walter. Thank you," she said, as she twirled it in her fingers.

"There's something on your bed, too."

She zipped down the stairs and found a backpack, a beautiful dress, and new shoes. She ran back up.

"We can't afford this."

"No worries. This is your special day. I know it's been hard for a while now, not just living like a sardine, but also at school."

She hugged him tight around his slender waist, and then they walked into the petite kitchen to prepare the salmon. They spoke not a word, but just smiled. The phone rang, and Walter went outside to answer it.

As Stormie was about to slice open the belly of the large fish, it levitated off the counter and hovered in front of her. She dropped her knife in the sink, as her eyes widened.

"Please, please don't kill me," the salmon begged. Stormie rubbed

Hidden

both eyes with the dishtowel. "I'm still here. Only you can hear me."

"What?"

"If you allow me my freedom, so I can find my family, then I'll grant you one wish."

"Like a genie?" she asked with both eyebrows raised.

"Yes. We don't have much more time before your dad returns."

"Okay. I wish for Walter's fishnets to always be full." A neon blue glass vial appeared in her hand. "What's this?"

"It's very special. Tell your dad to place one drop in the water where he anchors, and the fish will jump into his nets."

"Seriously?"

She twisted her mouth back and forth.

"Yes."

"What if he needs more? How would I find you again?"

"There'll be no need to search for me. Now, your wish has been granted. It's your turn to fulfill your end of the bargain."

Stormie opened up the small window above the sink, and the salmon flew out into the sunset.

"Okay, how's it coming with the fish, Kitten?" Walter asked as he walked back in.

"Dad, I have something to tell you."

She sat him down and explained everything that had happened and what the salmon had said.

He stood up and kissed her on the forehead, and he stepped out onto the deck without uttering a word and stared out at the rolling waves.

The fall drifted in quickly with a fleet of Walter's Flying Boats outlining the majority of the marina.

The End

Stormie's Birthday Wish

Rebirth

The frying sun baked Echo's deformed strawberry blisters, which decorated her body, as her long black hair stuck to her tearful face in matted clumps. She wished she had not sailed out to sea alone a few days ago, leaving Piper and a group of spring breakers.

She found Piper performing acrobatics earlier, with a heavily-accented Australian exchange student from their high school. She had sprinted from the scene, forgetting to pack the necessities, such as more bottled water, snacks, and sunblock. Most importantly, her cell phone was left sleeping on the nightstand, under an entertainment magazine in her hotel room.

She had drunk the last droplets of boiling water three hours ago, which burned her puffy lips, with tiny strips of flesh missing. She attempted to operate the boat radio, but she noticed that the wires had been mutilated somehow, and the fuel hand was flickering towards empty.

Echo realized that she was lost and stranded.

No one would find her. Even if Piper requested a search party for her, she knew that she would probably be dead by then.

Echo could feel her heart beating faster, as she pushed her tongue against her arid lips. Her legs became wobbly.

Objects began to swim around her head to the point that she slumped onto the bow to brace herself. Her shriveled lids attempted to close, beckoning her into an eternal slumber, as she slid to the floor.

A thundering noise woke her up. She slowly lifted herself and then fell back down. Her tiny eyes widened as soon as she noticed something fast approaching in the distance. She rubbed them to try to make them focus.

A huge wave carried the most magnificent horse-like creature towards her. It stood over 20 feet tall. Its perfect muscular snow-white body glistened like a bright star, as if diamonds and rubies were pasted down its immense head and luxurious ebony mane. The bottoms of its feet were decorated with fluffy rainbow feathers. Its tail resembled a dolphin's.

Echo opened her eyes even wider, as she looked down and noticed her light blue shorts turning darker. She tried to scoot herself away from the bow to find safety. She yelped out and buried herself in a corner of the boat.

"Don't be afraid," the creature said.

She lifted her head from her shivering knees.

"Here, drink this." A seashell floated towards her.

She grabbed it and looked at the liquid in the seashell; it was slimy and yellow.

Echo lifted it up to her torn lips. Her shaky hands spilled some of it.

As soon as she sipped a few drops, she noticed how her blistered skin healed. Her insatiable thirst from a few hours earlier had vanished. She stood with no trace of weakness and felt extremely refreshed.

"What did you give me?"

"A special tonic that my people have been making for a long time. It replenishes the body in seconds. From the looks of you, Echo, it served you well."

"Wait, how do you know my name?"

"We've been waiting for you. Please come with me, and I'll show you."

"Is this some kind of dream? I must be hallucinating. Yes… I'm delirious. You're not real. I just need to close my eyes and count

Rebirth

backwards from 10, then you'll be gone."

Echo lowered her lids and counted; she opened one eye and then the other.

"You're real."

"We need to go soon, so I can show you."

"Just leave me here. I was almost holding her hand until I saw you. I have nothing to return to."

"Are you sure that is what you desire?

"Yes. I thought my future would be a new beginning with Piper, away from my abusive stepdad, but I figured wrong."

"What if what I'm about to show you is your new beginning?"

Echo shook her head in frustration and stared down at the floor.

"Give me a chance to show you something."

"What's your name, anyway?"

"I'm known as Aban."

She smiled and said, "Beautiful, like you." She lifted her hand to stroke his thick, curly mane. "Aban, I know that you mean well, but please just leave me. This is my fate."

"No, I promise you that this is not your fate."

Aban kneeled his enormous body down onto the sea without sinking below the surface. Echo looked at him for several minutes. She then climbed out of the boat and mounted his back, and his mane instantly transformed into reins.

"Echo, do you trust me?"

"I think so."

"You'll need to wear something, so you can breathe and remain warm underwater. I promise, it'll be something beyond your human imagination."

"All right. What is it? Give it to me."

She reached her hands out in a grabbing motion. Suddenly, a luminous heart-shaped ruby necklace appeared on the top of Aban's crown. He tilted his massive head backwards, and the lovely piece of jewelry flopped into Echo's waiting hands. She studied its natural

Hidden

beauty for a moment, before putting it on.

Aban stood up on the water and dove in without any splash. As they descended toward their final destination, they passed hundreds of jellyfish, viperfish, giant squids, and gulper eels.

Tremendous gates opened up for them to pass through, and large shimmering metallic castles waved in the distance.

Before they could go any further, Aban's master, Zeton stopped them.

Zeton's long fiery red hair complimented his chiseled chest with accompanying multi-colored necklaces and a headdress. Glowing neon tattoos outlined his face and arms.

As she studied Zeton's attractive caramel body closer, she noticed that he didn't have legs. Instead, he had a lengthy iridescent shark tail, waving back and forth with the water rhythms.

"Echo, we've been waiting. Welcome to your tribe!" Zeton shouted.

The glowing necklace collapsed from around Echo's neck. Her heart sped up, and bubbles from her open mouth began to rise.

Zeton swam up to her and said, "Relax, Echo, and breathe in and out… in and out."

She did.

"You never needed the necklace," Aban said in a rustling tone, as he and a thousand others like him bowed their heads in her presence.

The End

Rebirth

Hidden

Caramel and orange leaves tossed in the cold fall wind, battering the dense rainbow leggings on Autumn Steele's crane legs, as she stared down at *Bartholomew's Ladder,* a deep pit.

Her long fiery red braids crisscrossed in the high blowing breeze. She felt the inverted six-inch scarlet snake birthmark throbbing on the back of her neck, as her hand slid across it.

She closed her wet eyes, and jumped down, falling nearly 200 feet.

Mrs. Steele peered out the window, wiped her floured hands on her apron, and wondered about Autumn and Tyler, as fried country steak with gravy and peas slowly simmered on the stove. They should've been home by now.

She'd instructed Autumn early that morning to go straight to the store and nowhere else right after school and pick up cornbread muffins before the first cold front ushered in.

Mrs. Steele paced the cement floor, with one hand resting on her waist and the other rubbing the back of her sweaty neck.

Panting like a racehorse, Tyler burst through the wooden door, almost falling.

"Mama, come! Hurry!"

Her pacing ceased. She sprinted towards him, kneeled down, and looked into his watery eyes.

"Tyler, w-w-where's Autumn?"

Hidden

He wiped his eyes with his corduroy sleeve and sniffled.

"Mama, Sissy did it again. I saw her bicycle and the flashing lights at that place, as the bus drove by."

She stood up quickly and stomped into the kitchen. She turned off the burners, snatched her purse and keys from the table, and grabbed Tyler's hand. She slammed the door behind them and scurried to the car.

After securing Tyler in his car seat, she jumped into the driver's seat and sped out of the gravel driveway.

"Mama, is she going to die this time?" he asked, as tears drizzled from his big brown eyes.

"Now, honey. What did we talk about last time?"

She looked up in the rearview mirror, back at Tyler.

"Yeah. Sissy will be okay because she's really, really special and strong!"

He flexed his little arms and grunted like a wrestler.

"Good boy. Now, remember, that's our secret, right?"

"Yeah, okay, Mama."

A smile began to curl up on his face, as he pulled out an action figure buried in the seat.

Mrs. Steele arrived at the hospital and parked near the ER. She unbuckled and grabbed Tyler and her purse and rushed to the entrance. The large sliding doors made whooshing sounds, as they opened to allow them inside. She marched to the check-in desk, with the boy snug on her hip.

A young woman asked, "May I help you, ma'am?"

"Yes, my daughter Autumn Steele was transported to the ER this evening."

"Hold on, please. May I see your ID?"

Mrs. Steele balanced Tyler on one hip to search for her driver's license. She found it and handed it over.

"Yes, she's in room six. You can both step through those doors."

Hidden

She buzzed them in, and they walked swiftly through to Autumn's room, where she lay asleep in the hospital bed, with an IV attached to her left arm and other vital machines beeping behind her.

Her charge nurse walked into the room and shared Autumn's x-ray results. She said, "No broken bones or bruises. The doctors are speechless, just as I am. Mrs. Steele, this is her second suicide attempt in the last eight months. What's going on?"

"I don't know. I hope she talks to me this time." She rubbed her hands together, staring at Tyler, who was playing with his action figure under Autumn's bed.

"I hope so, too. Even a cat's luck eventually runs out. She'll remain here tonight for observation and then be transferred to Doyle Psychiatric Hospital."

"I know."

She cupped her mouth with one hand and began to cry.

"I'm sorry," the nurse said, digging in her scrubs pocket to pull out a tissue packet. "Here, I'll give you some time. Please push the yellow call button if you need anything."

She grabbed her hand and gently squeezed it.

"Thank you."

The door closed behind her.

Mrs. Steele walked over to Autumn's bedside. She bent down and handed Tyler the television remote.

"Honey, go watch your cartoons, so Mama can talk to Sissy."

"Okay, Mommy."

She pulled a chair closer to her and sat down. As she began to stroke her hair and hand, Autumn woke up immediately.

"Mama, guess it didn't work."

"Don't say that. Autumn, why did you do that?"

She paused and then cried, "Mama, I'm so tired of being laughed at by everyone at school. They hate me. Look at me!"

Tears raced down her emaciated face.

"Honey, no one will ever laugh at you again. You don't know who you really are."

"I don't understand, Mama."

"You'll be 16 tomorrow."

"Big deal."

She turned away from her and lay on her side, staring at the white wall.

"Autumn, you remember the Medusa stories I used to read to you when you were Tyler's age?"

"Yeah, what about them?" She frowned, turned back to face her, and sat up a little.

"You're her great descendant and your mark has been activated," Mrs. Steele said, as she examined her birthmark on the back of her neck. "There's way more to those stories than you know."

The End

Hidden

WINGLESS

Awareness Tales ——————————————————————

Pens

Forgotten ones fill these streets...
They sit inside their caged porches.
Watching drive-by horror scenes...
Little broken girls ride their bikes in aimless circles.
Watch out!
I see an aqua 65 Chevelle flying from out of nowhere and speeding so
fast that
flames flicker from its tires.

Will the driver stop this time?

Keep on watching...
No rewind buttons.
Screams carry the leaves in the cold winds.
Delayed 9-1-1 responses over and over again

Gunshots
Stabbings
Suicide Sabrinas
Aborted Baby Janes tossed into dumpsters
Only to become lost souls

Pens

Tears rain down…
Skyscraper weeds conceal this world.
No fairy tales dreamt here.
Only nightmares…

Side Effects

Somebody warned me about
Immet's
Destructive charm, but those hazel
Eyes easily

Exterminated all those so-called *Big Bad Wolf* rumors
Forward I fell and tumbled into his massive cradling arms
Friends floated out of my life
Emptiness ruled my world, as he
Crossed out all my dreams, one by one
Trapped now in his cage of prickly poisonous thorns with dangling
        oleander all around me
Somebody warned me...

What
If

I woke up this morning
Peered out the window.
My vision was a bit fuzzy.
So, I wiped my eyes and refocused once more.
This is what I saw and heard:

Murky, oily skies
Countless bird wings blowing in the breeze
Motionless stallions under rotten willow trees
Butterflies flopping around in saturated sewage ponds
People roaming up and down the streets
No conversations, only hateful reactions
Police sirens twirling with empty cars
Acidic snowflakes falling and burning holes in the rooftops
Babies crying
The sun, moon, and stars all lassoed up, one by one
Total
Darkness

Then the music stopped…

Wingless

Faded
Dreams

Ones who need to see don't see, and because of that, they'll not mend the broken ones, who'll remain powerless behind their gates…

Faded Dreams

Waiting
Games

Constant mind pacing
Drives me to twisted
Exhaustion, until the
Finale
Is exposed…

Wingless

Haunting

Carmon
walked in and
signed the clipboard
She was called after she counted from 500 backwards, while her eyes
remained closed.
A nurse in cherry-colored scrubs escorted her to the room and showed
her the exit two-and-a-half hours later.
Ramon asked, "Did you take care of it?"
She nodded once and gave him one tear.
Days floated by
Nights soared
Every time Carmon looked in a mirror, she remembered.
Remembered that day she walked into that room with walls saturated
with silent screams, tears, and invisible blood waves…
She wishes she could forget.
Permanent triggers wait in dark corners to hold her hostage.
To push her
Push her to remember
Again
Again
Again…

Haunting

Atlanta

Aurora, a 13-year-old cheerleader and
Teen heartthrob admired by all in school, but
Life at home overflowed with hot boiling secrets, so
A plan to run away she made, to travel to
New York, maybe…No, California—where stars are made to shine.
Tall, dark, and handsome Dallas Ewing she met. He promised her a
      movie role. She took his hand and boarded his private jet.
After a six-week search, she was found naked in a shallow grave, not
      too far from the Hollywood Hills. Brutally tortured from head
      to toe—another unborn *star* gone…

Wingless

Trial

Testimonies of vicious and twisted lies, stirred and baked
Read out loud to four judges to absorb and assess
Ironic turn terminated the enemy's plan to toss her into the filthy grave
Action propelled only by One—who prevented the impending
    condemnation
Light destroyed her revolving mind-tsunamis and restored her
    innocence...

Trial

On and Off

You're up.
Then you're down.
Up again and down the next…
Which is it?
Do you even know?
I don't even know if you know what you're doing sometimes.
Your thundering emotions are like a light switch being turned off and on, constantly…

Wingless

Believe

Dreams fly in and out, day and night, like luminous fireflies bouncing
in the crisp November air…
It's up to you to lasso up the ones that matter, pull those babies in,
and store them in your special place…

Believe

Prisoner

Pacing back and forth in my cold birdcage of steel bars, without sunrays kissing my forgotten face

Remembering my once upon a time freedom—not having to ask permission to eat, urinate, or sleep...

Insomnia is my only and best friend that I can trust

Survival is now my hope

Over my shoulder, I watch constantly...

No one can be trusted

Endless enemies circling my territory with their hidden shanks to pierce one more part of my "Raggedy Andy" body

Running through the dark jungles daily, where countless wild boars, piranhas, and pit vipers wait in the lunchroom, the yard, showers, and corners, waiting to devour my existence...

Wingless

Heartless

There the weasel stood… peeping his stretched, splotchy neck around
the corner.
He sniffed the air with his crooked wet nose.
He beckoned Stella to follow him with his stringy finger.
His stench drifted in the air for several minutes.
He shut the door, as she sat in the old chair in his office, almost
catching his hairy long tail, swarming with flies.
30 minutes felt like hours…
I caught Stella walking out.
Her eyes were wet and puffy.
I held her without any verbal exchanges.
Only silence was the temporary solution.

Heartless

Damaged

Dear Diary, I met someone today
Absolutely gorgeous from head to toe
Mesmerizing turquoise eyes placed me under a dark spell and his touch
      set me on fire
Assassin of my heart, body, and soul daily with his verbal and physical
      swords
Gravestone chosen by my parents for me at sixteen-years-old…
Endless tears now for them and my infant daughter, who I left behind
Destroyed by his once upon a time hands of love, I thought… Should've
      known he would kill me the first time he punched me in my right
      eye for staying over fifteen minutes with my tutor in homeroom

Wingless

Tricks

Lies ignite fiery flames, bells, and a parade of mechanical dancing mini soldiers dressed in hot pink tutus with magical whistles to any story.

A
Glimpse

I was driving home one early afternoon and noticed an elementary
school playground to my right.
A car in front of me slowed down to make a turn, so I had to come to
a complete stop.
Something pushed me to pay more attention to the playground.

Out of nowhere, I saw her...
She was dressed in a bright peach t-shirt, dark jeans, and pink tennis
shoes.
Her dark long hair floated all around her, as she twirled 'round and
'round
I could almost hear her laughter spill out.

No worries
No sadness
No pain
No fears
Just for that moment, she gave me a priceless gift...

Freedom...

Wingless

One
Knock

He invited me there… a place where no one could witness…
He was stout and smelled like baking dog feces. His fingers looked
like stringy spaghetti with deep scratches. His droopy empty eyes
burned my eyes every time he stared at me.
His shadow crept towards the ceiling and hovered over me.
I felt suffocated there.
I couldn't scream.
He whispered something in my ear. His breath felt hot.
I stepped backwards and fell against the wall. His spaghetti fingers
reached out and flickered all over my face, leaving traces of wet
stinky goo, as he attempted to pull me towards him.
Footsteps approached the door, and someone knocked.
His eyes commanded me to hide behind the hamper. I did without
hesitation, like a robot being operated by a remote control.
The door cracked open, and a familiar voice yelled out, "Hey, I can't
find Charlie. Have you seen him?"
"Nah."
He scurried to the sink to wash his hands, looking back towards the
hamper cautiously.
After a few seconds, I crawled out from behind the hamper.
"What are you doing in here? Get over here, now!"
He said, "I didn't even know he was in here."

One Knock

My older teen sister told her guests that the party was over and later
tucked me back into bed once all had vanished.
She never spoke about that night to anyone or me.

I never saw him again, until I was a college freshman.
I came across an awful picture of him in the newspaper and read how
he was awaiting his sentencing for multiple accounts of molestation
of little girls and boys in my town and countless others.

I knew then that my sister's knock saved me from the
Monster…

Unbelievable

Indigo and sapphire skies with tangerine highlights
Phoenix in flight silhouettes
Tree canopies
Butterfly ballerinas
Rolling fields of daisies and sunflowers swaying
Honeysuckle aroma bombs exploding in the air
Millions of twinkling stars
Sparkling streams
Baby scents and heartbeats
Glistening double rainbows hanging over mountaintops
No charge from the
Unstoppable
Unbreakable
Unbelievable…

Unbelievable

Gone

I stopped by last Thursday.
No one present then.
You were sleeping.
My soft touch on your hand didn't wake you.
I watched you.
A ton of bricks were stacked on top of your paper-thin chest.
I could smell baby powder all over you, as I kneeled down to whisper
something in your ear…
Monday rolled in.
I opened up the paper to read the obituaries, and I knew your name
would be there.

Wingless

Buried

Blue tears saturate the shallow ground underneath me
Unbreakable windows encircle my forgotten world
Ravens pace across my shabby roof
Inspiration exited years ago
Eternal
Dark shadows follow me day and night…

Buried

Rushed

The Cancer Bandit tiptoed in one day and stole my best friend away.
I was told:
"Enough with the tears… Get over it, now!"
After all, I should be.
It's been a few months, right?
So, I walked down to the local thrift store.
I hunted through the entire store until I found my disguise… a dark mask.
Now, I could shield myself and no one would ever know who I was because of my secret identity.
I could go anywhere and no one would ever know my pain.

Wingless

Penelope

Alone in a crowded room, people walk up and down the aisles,
gazing at her.
No sweaty palms to be concerned with.
She knows that she will always share a stage.
She stares out, as large raindrops crash up against the window.
She recalls her twisted life.
Decorated with wicked smiles, countless lies, silent screams,
permanent scars, and shattered glass…
She daydreams of watching her daughter twirl in her glistening Vera
Wang wedding gown.
A dream to never unfold…

Attempted tears of regret, but impossible to shed now
Her body soon to be returned back to her box with the others…
Ether and pine are her familiar perfumes.
She waits for her next show.
She is lifted from her box again and positioned in her special place.
She stands among 145 red bodies…
Wooden silhouettes of other women and children

She finally remembers her finale:
Her boyfriend knew she couldn't swim, yet he pushed her off the boat

Penelope

during a trip last 4ᵗʰ of July.
Now, her downsized story is written on a tiny plaque glued to her red wooden chest for others to read.
Not only to remember her, but hopefully to empower the next 16-year-old *Penelope…*

Birthday
Candles

Curly bronze locks with hints of cinnamon highlights
Emerald eyes sparkling like six carats
Size 0
Perfect skin
Most popular girl at Semoa Valley High
Cheerleader Captain
Prom Queen
Honors Graduate
Accepted to Harvard in the fall
Traveled to Europe for a month with the *Mean Girls* the summer
before
Returned home a few weeks before college begins
Missed a period…
Purchased a pregnancy test
Positive…
Cried all night
Confessed to Mom
Mom made one call
They drove almost 150 miles for the procedure because of the laws in
her state.
Un-pregnant now with a prescription on 07-23-1990…
Not a worry in the world anymore!

Birthday Candles

Free as a red cardinal jumping from one tree branch to another during
the first winter's snowfall
Four years of college flew by with a soon-to-be *Mrs.* Degree…
Platinum wedding a year later
Married an up-and-coming attorney
Honeymooned in Japan, Barbados, and Australia
Two years later
Twin girls—Heaven and Trinity—born on 7-23-1997
As Daphne decorated the two tier birthday cake, it finally hit her.
There should have always been *three* sets of birthday candles…

Wingless

Hero

He could have chosen a different path easily
Eliminating all of the pain without a second thought, instead
Rejections, insults, and unbearable tortures endured…
Overflowing, unconditional love given in return—the ultimate
    sacrifice…

Sixty Minutes

If you had just one hour left, then what would you do?
Remember, only one could be chosen.
Would you…
Walk barefoot on the beach
Float down a river
Dance to your favorite song in your room
Watch the last sunset
Hang out with your friends
Stare into your boyfriend's or girlfriend's eyes without one whisper
Write a letter and place it in a cranberry-scented envelope
Call and apologize to the person you needed to most
Taste all the ice cream flavors at your favorite ice cream shop
Look through your photo albums on your phone
Make a video
Stare out the window
Finish the jigsaw puzzle you've been working on for months
Show those you adore how much you love them
Or
Pray and ask for forgiveness…

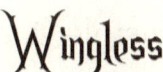

Invisible
Ones

The days are always long.
Nights worse
They walk by with empty expressions painted on their lonely faces.
I watch…
Yet, no one watches me.
I count the shadows on the ceilings, hoping time will move into the
next day faster.
It runs the same as any other ordinary day.
I sit…
365 days
I wonder: Will this year be different for me?
Probably not
It never is.
I stand in the middle of the room.
They always walk through me, as if I'm a ghost.
What if I am?
A ghost….
Am I real?
I just keep on watching day and night.
Maybe someone will see me tomorrow…

Invisible Ones

Wagon

Never owned one like most
No shiny silver wheels
Mine possessed two wheels, one oversized in the front and regular sized in the back
The wheels were wobbly and nearly corroded
Every time I tried to carry something in my wagon, it always seeped through
Its bed was full of large holes
A loose and constantly unraveling rope served as its handle
Eventually, my wagon collapsed
I tried to take it downtown for someone to repair, but I was told it was impossible to repair something that could never be…

Wingless

Hate

Historical examples of brutal murders and division
All because of someone's chosen beliefs
Today, the unimaginable continues in front of closed and opened eyes
Earsplitting screams haunt the utopian world that I build with my LEGO
    blocks, where unconditional love could live in everyone's
    hearts, without this virus's penetration…

Hate

Trip

Warm bath
Snow silk
Ballet slippers
Crimson Orchid
Sweet jasmine perfumes
Manicured nails
Soft piano concerto playing in the background
Rain showers ignited
Time stood still for a moment…
The driver pulled around back to take her on her final car ride.

Wingless

Poisonous Voices

Have you ever been surrounded by a swarm of negative bees?
Stinging you with those phrases that pierce your inner soul:
"You're not thin enough."
"You're not doing it right."
"You'll never be smart enough."
"You'll never make it."

Eventually, the soul retreats and empties itself into a dark pit to hide
from those constant stings…

Poisonous Voices

Rescue

I almost went there....
To that very dark place
You know, the one with the one-way ticket without the second
chance.

My eyes were opened, and I could feel the chlorine stinging them.
I felt as if someone was pushing me up to the surface before I took
my final breath.
Within seconds, my once-perfect plan extinguished, like a candle
flame no longer swaying due to a swift breeze.

Today, I know that my guardian angel saved me that night.
She placed her hands on my shoulder for only a moment to turn me
Away from an eternal darkness.

I see and taste everything differently now.
Amethyst ribbons in the sky are brighter and full of motion.
Strawberries are sweeter and juicier.
My once upon a time dark world unraveled into new hope and peace.

I was almost lost, but was found and dusted off...

Wingless

Venom

Vicious, vicious poisonous lies stitched in your filthy web
Every chance you have to build your layers of corruption
Now, you wait in the darkness
Of your wicked, wicked world for
More lethal lies to vomit up to your next prey…

Venom

UnFallen

I fell
I fell
Way, way down into a hollow pit
I yelled out
My echoes spiraled back down to me
My clothes were ripped and dangled off.
My body and mind decorated with multiple lacerations.
I stood up.
I remembered a lighter in my back pocket.
I dug it out.
I flicked it once, then twice.
Black mambas, lions, wild boars, and laughing hyenas surrounded
me.
Growls and hisses penetrated every inch of my frail body
I turned a thousand shades of grey.
Their tongues were like hovering daggers in the air, preparing to
shoot towards my rapid heartbeat.
I closed my eyes, whispered a prayer, and took my final breath.
I knew it was over.
I knew…
I would drown in their sticky venom.
I felt the earth move from under my feet…

Wingless

A golden winged unicorn swooped down and
I landed on her back within seconds of the ground caving in.

They fell
They fell
Way, way down...

UnFallen

My
Closet

1,013 secrets hide in there
They overwhelm me...
Should I confess to you?
I know that too many judgments would be stamped on my forehead
with your perceptions.
So, I keep it closed and locked.
The key is kept where you would never expect.
You pass by sometimes, hoping to comprehend the ongoing, muffled
whispers.
I command them to be quiet when you approach.
I dreamt of being open to you once, and I was a few times.
Big mistake!
To share my secrets with you
You didn't even notice my heart weeping.
Of course, not...
You only see what you want to see, so you can then label me as you
wish.
I know that I could never confess anything else to you.
Just too many judgments!
Too many...

Dark Place

Kimber's heavy cobwebbed world imprisons her.
She tries to tear them down, but her little broken
bloodstained hands are too weak.
Suddenly, she feels something heavy attach to her back.
Unable to detach, she scurries down the twisted halls to find a mirror
to discover a vulture carcass.
The rotting stench dominates the room, as it embeds deeper inside of
her skin.
She screams out.
Others walk past her, as her screams crackle and eventually fade
No one helps.
She refuses to close her eyes anymore.
Nightmares always find her
They crawl under doors or seep inside her windows.
So, she stumbles across a needle and thread.
She threads the needle, while pricking her finger several times, and
begins to sew each of her eyelids near her eyebrow.
Abused, *defeated*, and *loser* are the ongoing taunts she hears, as all the
choir-like voices linger inside of Kimber's displaced mind.

Dark Place

Choose

Do you ever just wish?
Just wish you could step into a magic time machine.
Set the month, day, year, and time a few days before an event
unraveled…
Zipping through time
You step out into that new world one more time.
It's yours to transform…
March 28, 1692: Salem Witch Trials
April 14, 1865: Abraham Lincoln assassination
March 8, 1965: Vietnam War
November 22, 1963: JFK assassination
August 11, 1965: Watts Riots in LA
June 17, 1972: Watergate
April 20, 1999: Columbine High School Massacre
September 11, 2001: Deadliest attack on American soil
August 29, 2005: Hurricane Katrina
July 20, 2012: Aurora movie theater shooting…
November 8, 2028: Election results in Austin, Texas…
The worst day of your life
or
You fill in the date: ___-___-_____
Would you do it?

Wingless

Would you step into that rocking time machine
to be zoomed back in time or forward?

Choose

Cherish

We travel this time just once, so…
Don't allow your life to be a repeat of yesterday, until you're empty.
Tell the ones you care for how much you love them right now—no
postponements.
Better yet… show them
A few hours from now and tomorrow are unknown.
Throw away those grudges… slam-dunk each one!
Shred all those hate files, too
Imagine a different world—a better world full of grace and
forgiveness
Breathe in the fresh first autumn rain
Taste honeysuckles
Hear all the music outside
Dance
Dance…
Rest under sparkly waterfalls
Watch the hummingbirds serenade
Play more… travel to local hot spots in your town or dreamy places
you only talked about
Dream in real time…
Do as much as you can, while you can.
We all have a one-way ticket, so
Make it count!

Wingless

~Warning~

This work was inspired after watching the true documentary, *"Bullying."* It is graphic and illustrates one of our society's many problems. It was written to serve as a form of **realistic awareness**.

Bullying is real and happens everywhere to many, and some remain silent for various reasons. I hope this piece will inspire someone to reach out for help or take a safe and positive stand. I wish that I had stood up more during my junior and high school years.

Broken

Broken

Friends don't exist in my world because I'm part of the "*Nobodies*."
You know us…
The **Bull Sharks** swarm around me daily, preparing to rip out pieces
of my flesh.
Their wicked giggles bounce down the hallways only in my direction.
Mr. Heart, sixth-grade science teacher, and Ms. Love, sixth-grade
history teacher, join in the party with their plastic smiles.
They slide on their dark shades, while I'm thrown up against lockers.
Extra on game nights…
Held under water, until I almost lose consciousness
Walking in the nude toward the gym teacher's office again because
they hid my clothes
Cutting another layer of hair because of a wad of gum or crazy-glue
cemented in my hair
Scooping dog feces out of my shoes for the 50th time
Arrows pierce my back daily—sometimes three or four at a time—as
if a large bulls-eye target was permanently painted on my back.
Ongoing visits to the ER for broken teeth, arms, and ribs…
The doctor questions me, but I continue to lie and share how clumsy I
am.
You don't know what they would really do to me if I ever told the
truth.

Wingless

So, please don't judge me.
Tearing me apart is their priority…
Last night I decided to help them out.
My parents found me the next morning, as my 60-pound limp body
swayed in the early sunrise, over their bedroom balcony.

Broken

If

To blow out all the candles on my *17th* birthday cake
To see a red-tailed hawk circling vacant ground for her next prey
To shop at *Mall of America*, while gift bags seesaw on both of my
arms, until I drop
To ski down the white glassy slopes of Aspen, while a million
fireworks
zigzag across the sky, and fly toward Jupiter's highway…
To sit front row at the Bellagio for the *O* experience
To hear the angelic voice of Jackie Evancho
To dance the Argentinian Tango on a chiseled diamond dance floor
with my soulmate
To walk a white sandy beach in Hawaii barefoot and feel the cool
sand between my toes
To watch a parade of blue and white dolphins dance on their liquid
stage, as I listen to *Think of Laura* on my iPod
To talk without yelling and to be understood
To not scare anyone because of my twisted, fetal appearance…

Instead, I lie in my hospital bed each day facing the same cold, brick
walls.
Unaware if it is day or night—Monday or Friday
Sleep is my best friend, while

Wingless

Silence and loneliness are my constant enemies.
I only dream of living outside this eternal cocoon
One day to be normal
My perpetual wish
I would give anything…

Wingless

We all make choices.
I made mine.
Dismissal of future consequences served
As my golden ticket to do what, when, and whom I wanted
Once upon a time, I defined myself as a free bird.
I flew in and out of countless bedroom windows from the West to the
East Coast, London, too.
I collected personal souvenirs along the way.
No cages could imprison me
I slipped through the tightest bars in masquerade balls with drizzled
lies
Until *the call* came…
On that day, when the first snowflake danced down my car's
windshield, as I was
told my life adventures would need to be postponed.
My extracurricular activities ushered in my *Finale* sooner than I
anticipated.
No more dates or
Dancing on stages, while lip-syncing to the 80s dance hits
Phone calls stopped
My so-called friends abandoned me without any hesitation, including
my best friend.

Wingless

Now, I wait all alone in children-sized PJs that would fit a ten-year-
old, while my hospital bed swallows me up.
Each night
I'm afraid to look at myself in the mirror because I don't know who's
staring back at me.
I smashed all the mirrors in the house with a hammer three months
ago, when I saw a frail creature painted with sores and fish scales all
over its face
and naked body.
Sometimes, I notice a feather or two on the floor, before my mother
sweeps them up.
Her cries echo through the halls each morning from
4:00 a.m. to 7:00 a.m.
I know this will be my last summer to watch
the ladybug family
play outside my window in their tree house.
The prison I swore that would never surround me found me…
Someone once asked me if I had my life to relive,
Then what would I have done differently?
I'll tell you everything.
EVERYTHING…

Wingless

Transformed
Restrictions

Within my tight cocoon,
I live in a dark world…
Locked windows and doors
They're all bolted down.
With rusty screws and tangled razor barbed wires
I dream of experiencing a cool breeze
dancing on my blank face…
My tight cocoon restricts my dreams.
I long to shatter my cocoon into a thousand pieces
with a sledgehammer.
Blowing them into an Oklahoma twister
Yet, I don't possess the strength to commit the act.
So, I retreat back into my dark chamber.
I don't know freedom there…

As time passed, I noticed a small ray of sunlight
reflecting off the ceiling.
Too afraid to follow
what was awaiting me outside
I closed my bloodshot, swollen eyes and ignored…

Sharp poisonous thorns encircle

my extinction, internally
The days grew longer, and the sunlight that I first noticed
off my dark ceiling grew larger—
To the point where my cocoon split in half.
Uncertain of what to do, I found myself sliding down and falling
out of my broken cocoon.
To the outside world of unfamiliarity
blues, yellows, sweet chocolate, cinnamon, and peppermint
decorated this new world.
So, I stretched my folded,
shredded wings and took off flying
before I reached
the busy ground.

From there on out,
I flew from one place
to another.

For the first time,
I chose my own paths
with no painful consequences.

I tell you,
I flew and flew…

The gentle winds carried me
whichever direction they wanted—high, low, left, right, sideways, and
upside down, like a Navy Blue Angel.

No complaints!

I breathe and taste everything.

Transformed Restrictions

I'm fearless to make any choice I wish.
I'm not willing to exchange or compromise
my freedom to anyone, again.

Ever!

This is my time to reclaim
who I once lost.

I thank you
for sharing what
I can *forever* do without…

Wingless

HEAVY EYES

Wounded Tales —————————————————————

Alone

I drove straight home that day.
I just knew I would find my *Happy* there.
So, I searched under the bed.

Nothing.

I flung my closet doors open and shoved the clothes back.

Nothing.

I stared outside and blew the fluffiest clouds away.

Nothing.

I saw **Cupid**.
I begged him to place me on one of his love arrows to shoot me up
into space.
He granted my wish.
Once I landed on one of Saturn's rings, I asked **Aphrodite** for advice.
I ended up falling back down and landed in a black rose garden,
covered with 1,000 thorns.
I realized that I had pushed her away.

Heavy Eyes

I poured oil all over her feathers of love.
I locked her up in a *Cage of Misery*.
I never made it right.

So, she figured out how to fly…

Alone

Crave

Calculating blood-shot eyes
Roam up and down with attempts to pierce the empty soul, while
Acidic whispers drift in and out to
Vibrate
Eternal wounds…

Heavy Eyes

Willow's
Dress

The tree's octopus-like arms swayed back and forth, tickling Willow's nose in the cool breeze, as she leaned her body against the open window.

She balanced herself on her tippy-toes like a ballerina before a performance.

"Willow, you sure you want to do this today?" Aunt Mercedes asked, knocking on her door decorated with frilly paraphernalia.

"Oh, yes," she said, opening the door halfway. "This is the day."

She giggled and shut the door softly.

"Now, you're just regaining your strength. I really think we should wait and go next weekend."

Willow flopped herself on the bed and buried her head in a pillow.

She lifted her head up after several seconds and said, "I really want to do this with you today. I'm jumping in the shower right now."

Aunt Mercedes shook her head, turned around, and walked downstairs with a dishtowel over her shoulder.

After her shower, Willow dried off and sprayed body spray all over herself, while singing into her hairbrush. She wiped the fogged mirror with a towel in order to begin her makeup ritual, while slipping on her favorite rock and roll t-shirt and shorts.

She bent down and scooped rainbow-colored flip-flops from underneath the bed with one hand, then skipped down the stairs towards

Willow's Dress

the garage door.

Willow opened the car door and slid into the warm seat. Aunt Mercedes backed her 98 Volvo out of the driveway. Willow's eyes were fixed on the dancing tree.

"You smell so pretty, Willow," Aunt Mercedes said. "What fragrance is that? It's so light and refreshing."

"Cherry Boom-Boom... I know, it was Mom's favorite. I'm so happy that you're helping me with this. I wish Mom was here, too. Aunt Mercedes, I miss her so much."

"I miss her too. These past seven years have been very hard."

"I just wish Mom had never stepped onto American Airlines Flight 11..."

Aunt Mercedes cleared her throat and tilted her head back to prevent the tears from falling. She'd made a promise to herself a few months ago not to cry, when Willow talked about her late baby sis, Sahara. Sahara would have stayed until the following weekend if the two of them hadn't argued that night.

They drove to at least 10 different stores before Willow found the perfect dress.

Couture and backless, it was made of purple chiffon and lace, and hundreds of miniature sequin butterflies danced around the mermaid-styled bottom of the dress, as she rotated it back and forth.

Once she put it on, it fit her tiny frame perfectly. The sunlight from the window and dust in the air collided together, resembling sparkly crystals, falling down on her.

She was simply breathtaking. Her long wavy scarlet hair bounced in the air, as she twirled around like a six-year-old little girl, wearing Mommy's highest heels.

Images of Willow as a newborn, all the way up to that moment, flashed in front of Aunt Mercedes's eyes. She wept.

Aunt Mercedes still remembered that tiny dimly lit waiting room. A team of doctors dressed in their stiff white coats entered, and all of

Heavy Eyes

them could barely fit.

They shared that Willow would need to be transferred to Benson's Children's Hospital immediately after Sahara delivered her. Willow remained in the ICU for several weeks before she could be discharged home.

Willow kneeled onto the floor, scooping up the bottom of the dress to comfort her. Aunt Mercedes's distant memory faded.

"Please don't cry."

"Oh, these are tears of joy. I'm just happy right now, Willow. I love you so much! Sahara should be here right now, not me."

"No, Aunt Mercedes. Mom would have wanted this. I want you to know that I really do appreciate all you've done for me."

"Sweetie, you're so welcome. It was the least I could do."

"You've stuck by my side, especially during this last year. I love you for that."

"I love you and will always be here for you, Willow."

"I know. You never gave up on me. I'll never forget that. Thank you."

She gently wiped her face with the back of her hand.

Aunt Mercedes shook her head, as tears dropped onto the wood floor.

"I just wish I'd had more time with Sahara, you know..."

Willow placed her arms around Aunt Mercedes's neck and whispered, "She knows... It's time to let go..."

The four seasons flew by.

The big day finally arrived.

Aunt Mercedes pinned her ivory and hot pink orchid corsage onto her silky mocha suit.

As she walked out and shut the door behind her, she looked over her right shoulder to capture the dancing willow tree in her mind. Purple flowers decorated its arms from top to bottom. She walked up under the magnificent giant designed only by God. She gently broke off one of its

Willow's Dress

branches to take with her.

The limo pulled up. The polished chauffeur stepped out and walked around to open the door for her and grab her hand to assist her to sit down. He ran around the car, jumped into the driver's seat, and they were off.

Before Aunt Mercedes stepped out, she noticed Stellie Mayweathers from the cleaners and Mrs. Davis, who taught Willow in kindergarten, march into the church's doors.

Some of these people she hadn't seen in years.

The usher escorted her towards the front pew.

The church was packed.

Before she reached her seat, a purple butterfly with white and golden-tipped wings landed on her shoulder for several seconds, fluttering its massive wings slowly back and forth.

She reached her hand up to touch this delicate creature, but it flew off her shoulder and out of the open church doors. The magical essence of Cherry Boom-Boom showered her nostrils immediately.

After the beautiful service, Aunt Mercedes walked up to Willow.

She stared at Willow in her mesmerizing dress with Shirley Temple curls hanging on the side of her soft and youthful caramel skin without any verbal exchange, placing the tree branch inside of Willow's perfectly French manicured hands.

She kissed her fuchsia full lips and watched Willow being rolled out in her glistening almond casket.

The End

Heavy Eyes

Rumors

Ripped
Up bloody lies
Milked by enemies
Only to
Rake one's
Soul over filthy tracks, over and over…

Rumors

Solo

I stood there, holding my rotten bouquet of white roses.
Dried petals abandoned me, into the dusty winds
until there were none…
I still stood there in the empty space.
A place I never knew.
Something whispered, "You're in *Nowhere*."
Sweat droplets dropped and fell into the loose sand below…
I screamed.
Still, that voice whispered once more
No one heard me
I begged.
I cried.
I tried to write S.O.S. in the sand, but the winds erased it.
Hope vanished, as fast as the moon ushered in the next sunrise
I felt myself sinking into the sand.
I looked down and saw cement shoes strapped to my feet.
I sunk farther and farther down… deeper
I looked all around
No one
No one
I vanished into *Nowhere*…

Heavy Eyes

Heavy
Eyes

Full of broken glass, dirt, and tumbleweeds
Unable to blink anymore…
They remain half-open, as if a boulder rested there, without ever
rolling down.
Tears of dark despair is her eternal song
Sunrises and sunsets conceal themselves
Only climbing shadows keep her company…
One day, she found some empty soda bottles, buried under some
smelly newspapers.
So, she filled them up with tears and mailed them in a box, off to the
"Land of Sadness."
Each time, she received the same box back with a message scribbled
on the outside:
"Return to Sender. These tears fail to meet our guidelines…"

Heavy Eyes

Dear Ms. Margaret

You throw your slimy, dripping poisonous darts at my chest
constantly.
You shout out sharp words and phrases that all destroy my inner soul
like exploding bloody pipe bombs.
How callous can you be?
Oh, very... Remember this one: "That's why God *didn't* bless you
with..."
You know my delicate situation, but you went there anyway. Lowest
blow yet!
No empathy from you.
Hell, Miss Sympathy flew out the window years ago. I can't blame
her for leaving, though.
Now, look at me... I'm a basket case of mess and heartache.
All because of you
Only you could succeed in making me break into a million little
pieces.
I'll never be glued back together like Humpty Dumpty.
Now, I wish that I had been the aborted...

Heavy Eyes

Lost
Beauty

Asia stood tall and proud with her branches stretched out and fuchsia
pom-poms dancing all around.
The winds played soft melodies through her heavy leaves.
Birds and butterflies adored her.
They always knew they could find rest and dip into her sweet
delights.
When the birds and butterflies heard the giant marching towards her,
they dashed away into the clouds.
Almost 12 feet, he was…
His deep bloodcurdling laughs echoed throughout the forest miles
away, as he chopped down her branches.
The birds flew in to wrap red ribbons around her amputee limbs.
He returned every autumn before the first snowfall to chip more away
from her until she was no more…

Lost Beauty

Dream
Thief

You ripped off my pretty sparkly forest-green wings with your wet
venomous whispers.
They floated down a dirty rapid stream, as they twirled down a
skeletal sewage gutter.
A world darker than *Gotham…*

Heavy Eyes

Hope's
Wishes

A real family, like those famous television sitcoms in the 70s and 80s...
Hope almost tumbled out of bed to realize that she was only dreaming again.
So, she closed her eyes, wishing for her dreams to come true.
She placed her wishes in a tiny rocket and sealed it tight with care and love.
It launched into space where she thought dreams came true.
Hope walked, and her heart skipped beats.
Hours passed
Days too
Eventually, several years flew by...
Nothing
Unlike Pinocchio, who finally received his wish to become a real boy, she never received her wishes, not even a single one.
So, last night, Hope couldn't get to sleep—she tossed and turned over 100 times.
She rolled out of bed and decided to pack her wishes up and try one more thing.
She secured her wishes to a toy boat and pushed it out into the open sea, towards the North Pole.
She waited, as her heart skipped beats.

Hope's Wishes

Hours passed
Days too
Eventually, several years flew by again…

Heavy Eyes

Crushed

Stabbing words…
Words that pierce your heart and soul—all the way through—with a
jagged sword.
I have always despised this ridiculous saying:
**Sticks and stones may break my bones, but words will never hurt
me.**
What a big, fat lie!
Evil words can ignite doubt, fear, pain, and endless tears.
Torment and shattered confidence are the effects of evil words.
These words can take you to a dreadful place that you never thought
you could find.
How could someone you trust and love say such terrible things?
Hate
Revenge
Spitefulness
Satisfaction
Victory
Truth
All of the above
Stop!
I don't want to believe.
I'm raped over and over again by your cruel words—the pain grows.

Crushed

Your thorns of deception wrap around my brittle and fragile heart.
Can you just be happy for me once?
No!
I'm tired of your bitter, nasty lies.
You push me away from you each time you say those awful things.
You ask me why we're not close like we used to be.
Why ask me?
You already know the answer.
You are acting selfishly again.
I can no longer confide in you.
You won.
Are you happy now?
You finally stripped me of my fairytale.
Who will be your next victim?
Then again, you are your own Victim
Who feeds off *Destruction* and *Misery* from others…

Heavy Eyes

Porcelain
Girl

Come on in…
Don't be shy or think that you're staring too much
Look at me!
Closer…
You'll see all my infinite cracks and imperfections.
My torn dress with permanent coffee stains.
Nothing to hide…
I'm pale without a trace of sunshine.
Day after day, I sit on my shelf, as dust rains down and accumulates
around me like dirty snow.
I'm never the chosen one to play with.
I'm too worn and broken.
I know that I'll never know what it means to be chosen by someone.
My vocal cords were stolen long ago.
So, here I'll remain, until I'm finally tossed away…

Porcelain Girl

Un-Goodbye

Large raindrops slammed against the windshield, as Chance drove away from his parents' mammoth Virginian estate.

Storie said, "Chance, you promised me that you were going to tell your parents that we're engaged this time."

He expelled a loud sigh.

"Listen, Storie, I thought it through and just didn't think it was the best time to tell them, all right? It was their 35th anniversary celebration."

"I know, but we've been engaged for almost a year now. Why do you always make me take my ring off when they're around? Do you need to tell me something?"

He quickly jerked the wheel and pulled off on a side road.

"Storie, can't you just drop this? I'll tell them when I want to tell them. What's the big deal? You know, I could have any girl I want. I chose you. You should be really happy about that."

"Chance, you honestly think I'm happy?"

"You got the 12-carat platinum ring. You won't ever have to work. What else is there? Why can't you just let me do this when I'm ready?"

"I don't know how much longer I can play this undercover game."

"So, what are you saying?"

"I don't know!" she shrieked, as a stream of tears raced down her heart-shaped face.

Heavy Eyes

"Every time we talk about this, you end up crying. Come on! It is what it is."

"That's just it. I don't know what it is, Chance."

"Listen, let's just drop this right now before you get on that flight back to school. I'll fly up in a few weeks, and we can talk more about it, okay?"

She shrugged her shoulders and wiped her face with her cashmere scarf.

"I've got to do this in my own time. Give me that. You know how much I hate to be pressured into things, babe. Now, clean yourself up. You look a mess. We're almost there."

Storie opened her purse on the floor in front of her and took out her cosmetic bag. She stared in her compact for several seconds. Her makeup was no longer perfect. She retouched her face quickly before he arrived at the sliding doors.

She put her headphones on, opened the door, stepped out, walked to the back, and removed her suitcase from the trunk. Chance parked the car.

Her squeaky-wheeled suitcase dropped twice, as she dragged it through the airport. Tears wanted to drop, but she fought them off, as she prepared to board her flight.

"Come on, give me a hug. I'll call you tonight."

She draped her headphones around her neck. Chance embraced her loosely. His cold lips pressed up against her forehead. She laid her head on his chest to listen to his slow heartbeats. She moved away from him and walked toward the airplane rep, checking in passengers.

Storie looked back at him one more time, before handing her boarding pass to the rep, and placed her headphones back on.

Chance took his hand out of his faded blue jeans pocket—while shrugging his shoulders—and lifted his hand up with a stone-faced expression.

As soon as she stepped onto the airplane and found her window

Un-Goodbye

seat, huge tears plopped down, saturating her lap as if she had been sprayed with a water hose. She stared at the raindrops dancing in a zigzag pattern against the windowpane, which put her under a deep sleep spell.

When she woke up, the airplane had taxied into its terminal.

She drove towards her dorm with a mission.

After Storie unpacked, she placed the engagement ring in a box with a one-page handwritten letter sealed with forget-me-kisses.

The End

Heavy Eyes

Silencer

My lips are super-glued around you.
I'm not allowed to utter even a whisper.
My doors remain locked when I know you're approaching.
My heart stops when I hear your breathing.
I can no longer daydream…

I just evoke sleep terrors from the very thoughts of you.

I know now I'll never wake up from those because if I did, you would
be standing right in front of me.
I, too, would transform into stone…

Silencer

Beast

It came without any invitation and crawled into her little bed like a
vicious viper.
It planted its toxic fangs until the poison invaded one organ at a time.
It stripped away everything she once was.
She began to lose her coordination and then fell down.
Her appetite lessened until it vanished.
She only craved water…
Its mouth covered hers and sucked out the little life she had left.
Her body no longer belonged to her.
The appendages of her ribcage could be counted, visually, through her
pink t-shirt.
The visit came…
The vet ran tests and shared the scenarios, but the last one burned in
my mind. His words continue to echo:
*"It's probably cancer, and to reduce her suffering, you may wish to
consider euthanasia."*
So, we took her home, and that night she paced and whined.
She was declining more.
She could hardly stand and her barks were gone.
So, the last visit came with the vet.
She lay down on the table for the first time ever and looked up at me.
This is when I knew.

Heavy Eyes

The vet injected her tiny leg vein with a hypodermic needle as pinkish liquid swam up and down within the syringe.

It took only five seconds, and she was gone.
I held her little limp body in my arms until the time came to give her to the vet.

I terminated her suffering, but mine had just begun…

Beast

Flood

Forced to speak to you, as soon as I recognized your crooked smile in the crowd—I just wanted to flee, but it was too late.

Loose stares you projected upon me, as if I was that same helpless victim from years ago.

Over and over again, I chanted in my mind… *Remain calm and be strong.*

Only a few more minutes of this unexpected torture of you giving a lecture titled *I'm so perfect, and guess how great my life is…*

Do you ever grow tired of placing yourself on a pedestal?

Heavy Eyes

Excluded

An invitation arrived last Tuesday
Saw the name and instantly knew
Did not know what to say
Placed it in the mail stack
It grew...
No need to open something from someone who never took the time to
know
Me...

Excluded

Heart
Stopper

Once upon a time, in 1955, a 16-year-old tomboy caught the almond
eyes of a handsome soldier from across the dance floor.
There he stood, leaning against a wall.
His tall chiseled mocha body swayed rhythmically to the slow songs,
with his hands clasped behind his head, staring at her all night.
A few days later, he met her at the record store.
He walked her home, and they talked on the porch under the cherry
moonlight.

She became his steady.
He gave her a sunflower and a sterling silver bracelet with their
initials engraved on the back to symbolize his commitment.
She longed to give him her greatest gift.
He convinced her to postpone.

The time was approaching for him to return to his Army post, many
miles from Texas.
So, one night, she prepared a very special basket full of mystery.
She wore one of her prettiest dresses.
She walked by his Hudson under the willow tree.

Heavy Eyes

She noticed the foggy windows.
She pressed her petite face up against it and saw…
There he was, with her best friend, practicing with silent echoes.
She ripped her promise bracelet off in horrific awe.

She ran all the way home and cried all night.
He drove to her house the next morning with a sealed box.
Her mom called for her, but she refused to see him before his flight.
Years passed, and the box remained unopened on top of her icebox.

She found out from a friend that he died in the line of duty.
She thought of him more then.
She wondered what her life would have been if she had been first in
his arms of beauty.
Now, she clings to their encounters without sin…

Heart Stopper

Death of the One
Musketeer

Sisters we're now and always will be.
Never to abandon each other.
Not even a Wayne Honey could tear us apart.
Sisters we're now and always will be...

Harper, Crystal, Marjorie, and Far shouted the sacred vow out loud, holding hands in the quad of Volster Lake University, where they all met four years before, during orientation.

That was their last night together before graduation.

Marjorie presented each with a special gift, a sterling silver butterfly locket. A silly group picture of them from their freshman year was tightly secured in each locket.

They laughed until their sides cramped and promised to talk to each other at least once a month and to meet up each year for a girl's weekend.

Far flew into Volster Airport and waited for Harper to pick her up for their first college homecoming celebration. She found a comfy space on a bench and pulled out a bridal magazine from her hobo bag, as a cool breeze automatically turned each page for her.

As she flipped through the magazine, she recalled how they were

Heavy Eyes

inseparable and always rescued each other. Honestly, she performed the majority of the rescues.

Harper's boy-toys always tap danced on her heart for a short time. She really knew how to pick the bad wolves.

Sleepovers were always in high demand in one of their rooms with tons of junk food and music to help Harper forget about her latest bad breakup.

Harper only shared her darkest secrets with Far.

One night, Harper called Far around 2:00 a.m. She could barely make out her words, due to her uncontrollable crying and mumbled speech that dominated the short conversation.

She begged Far to come to her dormitory, so she walked almost a mile in snow up to her knees. She knocked on the door.

Harper stumbled down the stairs, wrapped in a thick blanket. Her wet and swollen scarlet eyes possessed a faded glow, as she opened the door slowly and beckoned Far to follow.

They walked up the stairs to Harper's room in the attic. She shut the door and locked it.

"Harper, what's wrong?" she asked, as she shook the excess snow off her boots and peeled off her winter gear.

No words were exchanged at first.

Harper walked into the bathroom and handed her a white stick. She plopped herself onto the twin bed, rested her head in Far's lap, and sobbed.

"Far, what am I gonna do? I'm pregnant."

"Listen, you know these tests aren't always 100% accurate."

Harper picked up her wastebasket, and it was half full of test sticks.

"Yep, no need to guess. They're all positive. I know… I am. The worst part of it all… I'm not sure who's the dad. Maybe Professor Murphy, the boy I met at the Triple-Dare Theta Annual Island Party, or the video guy in town who gives us free rentals on the weekends."

"Harper, seriously, Professor Murphy? He's, like, old enough to be

Death of the One Musketeer

your granddad."

Harper squinted her eyes and said, "That's not the issue, Far. I just know I can't keep it. My parents will kill me. You have to help me!"

"You know I'll help you. It'll be okay," Far insisted, as they embraced.

"Promise. Promise me you'll never tell anyone, including Marjorie and Crystal," she begged.

"I won't."

Within the next few days, Far sold her great aunt's diamond earrings to a local antique dealer downtown and drove Harper almost a hundred miles from campus the following Saturday morning to the secret place.

The next week, Harper stayed in her dorm room. Crystal and Marjorie were both studying abroad in Spain that semester.

Every night, she begged Far to read her *Cinderella*, her favorite story. She always fell asleep before the ending.

After her recovery, they never talked about it.

Harper honked the horn so loud that the magazine flew above Far's head and landed on the ground.

I've Done Everything for You was blaring from her red Bugatti. Harper jumped out of the car and ran towards Far. They hugged for several minutes as if more time had passed since they'd last seen each other after graduation.

When Far sat in the car and fastened her seatbelt, she slowly held out her hand, as an 8-carat princess-cut diamond glittered across the glass.

"Jackson finally did it!"

She squirmed with excitement in the Italian leather snow seats.

Silence filled the car.

"Harper, aren't you going to say anything? You're happy for me, right?"

"Yeah. I just never thought Jackson would commit. Never mind me, I got a lot of stuff on my mind. We have to celebrate tonight. I'm

Heavy Eyes

happy for ya," Harper snapped.

She gripped the steering wheel tighter and pressed down on the accelerator harder.

"I know you. Tell me. What's wrong?" Far asked.

"It's nothing. You just surprised me. You never mentioned it during our recent phone calls. That's all. Now, let's get to the girls."

"It just happened, Harper. I wanted to tell you in person. You're the first. I've always considered you my best friend."

Harper remained silent during the entire trip, as did Far.

When they met up with Crystal and Marjorie, Far showed them her surprise. Their reactions were almost identical.

"What's wrong with y'all? Talk to me!"

They shrugged their shoulders and shared how happy they were for her, matching stiff smiles adorning their lips.

They decided to go to a frat party that night.

As they were getting dressed in their hotel suite, she overheard Harper telling the girls, "Jackson isn't..."

"Jackson isn't what? Say it!" Far snapped.

"Nothing."

"I can't believe you. Out of everyone, you're the one I thought would be genuinely happy for me. I see now that I've been the fool for so long. You can't be honest with me. I've done so much for you over the years. Why?"

Harper stared down at the floor, turned the hair dryer on full blast, and pushed the door closed with her foot.

Far opened the hotel door and slammed it behind her. She walked toward the campus and sat down on a bench in the quad, reminiscing about the vow they took. She looked on the corner edge of the bench and found their engraved initials.

Upon her return, she slid her key into the slot and opened the door once she heard the click. Something was off—all the luggage had disappeared except hers.

Death of the One Musketeer

Far called Harper several times, only to hear her sassy voicemail message play back. The same happened when she called Crystal and Marjorie.

Sunday morning came quickly, and no one was around to drive her back to the airport that afternoon. She tried calling Harper and the girls one more time, but she got no answer.

She called a cab a few hours before her flight. In the back of the musty cab, she ripped the locket from her neck and threw it out the window, into the air. A swift breeze scooped it up and cradled it in its arms. It carried Far's broken memories out of sight within seconds, as streams of tears followed.

Years flew by, and she never heard from any of them.

Jackie's curly ponytails with yellow loose bows tied at the ends swung back and forth, as she pulled at Far's apron to give her some freshly baked chocolate chip cookies. Far placed six of them on a plate and poured three glasses of milk. Far carried them on a wooden tray towards the living room couch.

Jackie crawled across hers and hubby's laps.

"Mommie, please… read me *Cinderellie*."

As Far read from the book, she thought about Harper and wondered what her life would be like if she and the girls were still a part of it.

She thought about writing and calling them once or twice over the years, especially Harper, but she always retreated from those actions. Harper always knew that Far was the Queen Bee on campus and thought that she could control or get anyone she desired. She definitely controlled Crystal and Marjorie with ease. Deep down, Far always knew how much Harper despised her because Jackson proposed and married her.

Jackson confessed to Far about Harper's cheating proposal to him one night after a junior fraternity formal they attended; Far and Jackson dated sophomore and junior year off and on. She never confronted Harper, but Harper knew that Far was aware of what she'd done,

Heavy Eyes

without speaking a word between each other.

Far never imagined that would be their finale that night many years ago. Though, after all, they were once the four musketeers.

The End

Death of the One Musketeer

Unjustified Heartbreak

Heart nailed on a cracked wall
Arrows shot over and over again, piercing it, until it bled out
Heart dragged over hot coals
She found it.
Held it up, but chunks fell and splattered onto the ground
Decided to FedEx it to a special place, where she heard broken hearts
are fixed
Scooped up all the broken pieces in her hand and placed it in a white
cardboard box
She sealed it with tape.
Drove to the post office to mail it off
Waited in line for a while, until the clerk motioned her to his station
When she placed the package on the counter, the clerk asked, "Is
there anything perishable or fragile inside?"
"Why, yes, there is," she replied.
"What is it, Miss?"
"My broken heart."
"Oh, my. I see you are mailing it to *Mended Heart Express*."
"Yes, I heard that was the best place to mail a broken heart."
"You must not know."
"Know what?"
"*Mended Heart Express* closed yesterday. It was all over the news."

Heavy Eyes

She looked down at the package.
"I'm so sorry, Miss."
"No, it's not your fault. Thank you."
She picked up her box, turned around, and walked out the glass door, carrying her broken heart.
She whispered, "It probably wouldn't have mattered, anyhow. My heart died years ago, when I gave it away."

Unjustified Heartbreak

Temporary
Wish

I would:
Run the Boston Marathon backwards
Walk on 100 feet of hot coals blindfolded
Swim the English Channel in January
Hitch a ride from Italy, Texas, to Pasadena, California
Lose 50 pounds and have $250,000 in plastic surgery from head to toe
Climb Mount Everest
Buy you 1,500 pairs of *Jimmy Choos*
Give you all I had.

I would do anything.

If only you truly noticed me, for one night…

Heavy Eyes

Infinite
Stranger

Not One:
Meaningful phone call
Single invitation
Sincere visit without obligation

Why all of these personal games?
I used to wish for a bond to be cemented between us.
It never transformed.
Today, I possess empty tears for you.

It's your loss.
No longer mine…

Infinite Stranger

Fired

Feelings of inferiority flowing through a tormented soul
Intensely simmering with rage, tears, and muffled echoes
Refusing to give full explanation of the unnecessary torture
Erasing your entire existence here with a permanent marker
Dying a slow social death of betrayal…

Heavy Eyes

Evaporated
Love

His love letters no longer smelled of *Cool Water* cologne.
Calls became shorter, with long pauses in between
Visits transformed into regrets
Manuel ended his love overnight without a receipt.
Years passed by like tornados rolling over a Kansan terrain
If only he could make things right…
Love her again without his selfish detours and escapades
To go back to the place where they first met in order to start over
again
No genie to grant his wish…
He stood there, staring at her from across the busy street.
Time moved on, and so did Ella…

Evaporated Love

Locked
Out

How dare you broadcast false accusations about my world, while
shielding your
monstrous filthy sins?
You don't even know me.
Really, you don't.
Please stop pretending!
I'm so tired of your slithering lies piercing my soul over and over
again,
like the dripping fangs of a 12-foot diamond-back rattlesnake.
Is it because I possess stability, and you ache for that?
I'm tired of guessing and suppressing my true feelings and thoughts,
so this is my personal instant message to you:
Nevermore to be in your presence…

Heavy Eyes

Flypaper

Everywhere he stepped, he always found himself stuck.

He could drive a million miles round-trip and all over again.
No changes.
He remained there with a glass heart full of dark liquid.
He knew it would break at any moment without any assistance.
So, he decided not to play anymore and burrowed himself deep.

Everywhere he stepped, he always found himself stuck.

First his feet, then his hands
He pulled and pulled, but nothing helped.
He couldn't even roll over anymore.
He gave up and stayed in that one position until his glass heart finally
broke and spilled out.
It loosened the sticky grips from all his body parts.

Yet, he remained…

Flypaper

Shattered

A billion whispered lies dragged through our town that you sculpted
all around me.
Dirty tricks played on and off the playground
You painted innocent walls with gooey, sticky untruths…
Bright red lipstick smeared on your distorted lips with a fake smile, as
the large shimmery knife dangles back and forth in your hand behind
your back.

Heavy Eyes

Bloodsuckers

You sit on my shoulder with your piercing claws plunged deep.
Blood dyes my new champagne silk blouse
You guide my fingers on each keystroke.
I'm your marionette on short strings.
You pull them tight, dislocating another bone.
Counting each mistake
Videotaping my every move with your secret cameras…
You shout out:
"Cross those T's."
"Dot those I's."
"Finish that report up yesterday."
"Tidy up that space."
It is perfect already.
You slap my hands with a long whip superglued with upside down
thumbtacks.
You bend down close to my ringing ears and whisper,
"Nope, do it again!"
Tears swim down my face
You reach inside of my shriveled-up heart
to turn off my tear-sprinkler.
I fall over
You call the *Cleaners* to throw me in the dumpster
Tomorrow, you start over with a new toy…

Bloodsuckers

Trust

Turbulent flashbacks
Run across my mind day and night
Until I
Surrender my broken self
T*his too shall pass* echoed in my chaotic dreams…

Heavy Eyes

Miss
Blue

Lately, it's been so hard for Blue to wake up.
She only wants to befriend her bed.
Not just for the seven to eight recommended hours, but for 365 days and nights.
No need for her to dream or wish
Perpetual tangled thoughts of misery and despair plague Blue's world...
She conceals her true self from her friends and family.
They have no idea where Blue lives or what she really feels.
She's an expert in her complicated masquerade.
When she's alone, she stays in her safe haven, counting each crack in the ceiling and pulling the thick covers toward her face, until they reach her puffy pink eyes.
Blue only daydreams of her next secret rendezvous with her best friend.

Miss Blue

Finish
Line

I ran and ran around the track.
I couldn't breathe anymore, so I stopped a few inches from the finish
line to look back at you.
Three runners were behind me.
No use in taking first place because I would never be first in your
world.
Just a second-class playmate, when your Fakers were too busy to play
The Gossip Game…
So, I forfeited the race by tripping over my empty deeply scarred
heart, and before landing facedown, I caught my last glimpse of you
before my heart ceased its tick-tocking…

Heavy Eyes

Love
Punisher

Seven days and 18 hours

Stacked cards into a replica of the Eiffel Tower
You huffed and puffed and blew it into the air.
Built a six-foot sand castle in your image
You sprayed it down.
Waxed and polished the car
You broke a beer bottle and dragged it up and down its body.
Washed all the house windows
You gathered up a wagon of baseball-sized rocks and chucked them
into each one.
Planted a garden of petunias, purple irises, and a rainbow spray of
roses
You poured kerosene and set them on fire.
Downloaded your favorite tunes on a flash drive
You smashed it in half and tossed it into the street.
I decided to write you a letter to ask you why.
I started and then stopped.
I ended up with over a hundred balls of paper encircled around me.
Maybe tomorrow, I'll try again

Love Punisher

No!

Maybe tomorrow, I'll be gone.

Heavy Eyes

Chances

I was touring the local carnival last Friday night.
Guess who I bumped into?
Love…
She invited me to take a ride on her fastest roller-coaster.
I accepted.
Jumped on
'Round and 'round I went
Boy, she was fast!
I counted three loops and two steep hills.
I rode again.
Love took me around faster this time.
I held on tight to her slippery cold bar.
Once the car slowed down, I jumped off as soon as I could.
I had my share of cotton candy, salty pretzels, candied red apples, and
funnel cakes.
They always gave me temporary satisfaction.
Before I knew it, love found me again.
She asked me to join her and promised she would take it a little
slower on her coaster.
I politely passed on her invitation.
I chose the *Ferris Wheel*, instead.

Chances

Fatality

Pulled in
Pushed away
Hand held
Hand dropped
Sweet kisses
Sour kisses
Unexpected surprises
Anticipated disappointments
Long walks
Short walks
First dance
Last dance
Fixed eyes
Wandering eyes
Intoxicating and secure embrace
Loose embrace
Warm hands
Cold hands...
Yesterday, we were the #1 couple in the 10th grade.
Today, your sharks wait to attack me.
Our once upon a time unraveled and relocated both of us to
disenchanted worlds...

Heavy Eyes

Mr.
Heart-Breaker

February 14th came and went
The day of romance, right?
Roses
Chocolate
Love letters
Salsa dancing
Diamonds
Proposals…
That special night you and your sweetheart celebrate, right?
My sweetheart must have experienced temporary amnesia.
Not one:
Rose
Chocolate
Sticky note with "*I love you*" scribbled on it
Diamond, not even cubic zirconia
Definitely no proposals of any kind…
So, I bandaged up my little broken heart the best I could with a silk
scarf and placed her in my top drawer—allowing her to sleep.
Maybe he wouldn't forget next February 14th…

Mr. Heart-Breaker

Without My
Consent

We traveled to the retail stores on Black Friday this year.
As soon as you opened up your pregnant wallet to complete a
purchase, I saw.

I saw

The forgotten photo…
The lost story of him, which I buried in a vaulted coffin years ago that
you reopened.
The story I had forgotten until now.
How could you still carry the one memory I have tried to erase?
It has been a long time since I thought of him and what could've
been.
We were never destined to be.
You still refuse to believe.
Regardless of the truth, you continue to throw everything back into
my face
like a pot of grits boiling on the stovetop.

Scarring me again and again…

Your devious games will never cease.

Heavy Eyes

You'll play them until the end, without my permission.
One player you truly are
Selfish acts of cruelty ooze out of your visible wand of deception
I know you'll not help me with this erasure.

So, I'll continue to endure memories of *him*.

Without My Consent

Unjoy

Love can make one twirl 'round and 'round until that one thing
terminates all twirling.

Heavy Eyes

Stranded

No reasons given or questions answered.
Left floating in the middle of deep space…
Trying to make my way back to you
Without proceeding with caution
You simply vanished, unconsciously, from our world.
I tried to touch you.
You retreated with your senseless secrets.
Complete disappearance of your entire soul
I kept returning to the very thing
That caused my heart
To bleed, tremble, and crumble
I tried to find you.
Missing—just maybe—I grabbed on too tightly.
False hope became my best friend.
You weren't missing.
Stranger became your new identity.
You never introduced me to the *Real You*.
I chose to ignore us drifting to separate planets.
A one-way ticket to Saturn—the last gift you gave me
So, I mailed your false symbol of commitment back to you.
Sealed with a twisted spell of unregrets and forget-me-not kisses.
The worst part of it all… You never said goodbye.

Stranded

Daydreamer

Long walks under the glistening moonlight, as purple snowflakes, in
the shapes of butterflies and dolphins, gently fall
Watching tequila and chocolate sunrises on Milky Way slides…
500,000 candlelights flying all around to illuminate the path to a
secret garden full of fairies and rainbow-colored unicorns
Exotic snow hummingbirds sing and ignite automatic intoxication in
the air
Trips to candy lands and magical doors…
Kissing endlessly upside down in an April rain shower, under a
turquoise mermaid tree
Watching the birth of 100 new rainbows before night falls
Slow dancing under a canopy of sapphire and diamond star babies
All merely daydreams of my made-up fairytale world…
Unlike Cinderella, my prince never placed my glass slipper on
to live the happily ever after.
Only liquid regrets and bitterness swim through my cold veins…

Heavy Eyes

Confessions

Journey pulled the clothes out of the wicker hamper and separated them into three piles. Before placing the last pair of jeans into the washer, she dipped her hand into Roman's back jeans pockets.

One was clean, and the other wasn't.

Journey found a small envelope; she opened it and pulled out a restaurant receipt, dinner for two.

On the end of it, a note was scrawled: *"Britnee, I can't wait... Love, Roman."*

She reached for her cell and dialed True's number.

He was unavailable, so she left him a message: "I need to meet you now!" she screamed on his voicemail.

She threw her phone in her purse, stuffed the envelope inside, and darted out to her car.

It was 5:30 p.m.

True met her at Mocha & Dreams Coffee Shop at 6:30 p.m.

"Journey, what's the urgency?" True asked as he sat down on the cushy barstool next to her while waving the waitress over. "A pumpkin latte with roasted marshmallows and extra cream, please."

"You recall my ordeal with Roman two years ago?"

She slammed her empty coffee cup down on the table.

"Of course, I do, Journey. We've been best friends since second grade. You were at your lowest with Roman's last escapade. Your 20-

day hospitalization stay at the psychiatric center almost drove me over the edge."

"Yeah, I didn't think I would be walking out of there."

"Please don't tell me… Is Roman cheating again?"

Her eyes began to well up with tears.

"True, I found this in his jeans earlier. His frat brothers let me in the dorm early. I thought I would surprise him by doing his laundry." She handed him the crumpled-up receipt with her quivering hand. "Sometimes, I wish… he never existed."

"You mean that?"

He pressed his full cranberry lips against his oversized coffee cup, staring hypnotically into Journey's swollen grey eyes. He glanced down and read the receipt, wadded it up in his hand, and chunked it to the floor.

"Maybe. Of course, not. You know I never told Roman about you-know-what during my stay at the center," she said, as teardrops rolled down her face. "He visited me once and sent a taxi to get me because he was tied up with one of his frat functions."

True placed his arms around her, held her tightly, and whispered, "Journey, you know I'll do anything for you, right?"

"Yeah, I know. This isn't your problem. It's all mine. Always has been. All I can do now is leave him for good. This is it. I have no more forgiveness left inside of me."

"What if he could never hurt you again?"

"My life would probably then be perfect, without restless nights, and I could mail a goodbye card to my weekly therapist. Look, I'd better get back to my dorm. It's late, and I need to finish two more chapters for my Children's Literature II class."

She wiped her face with her hands.

"You never gave me a straight answer."

"True, I would just like for Roman to suffer a little, you know."

She hugged and kissed him on the cheek with her warm wet ruby

Heavy Eyes

lips; she slid her hand down his neck.

True's heart began to beat faster than a gazelle's heart while being chased by a cheetah. He waved until she was out of his sight. He could smell her light gardenia essence all over his chest.

Journey tossed and turned all night in bed.

The next morning, she walked down to Roman's frat house and noticed his car parked in the front. She knocked on the door, and a new frat pledge told her that he was not there. She called Roman's cell several times with no answer.

That's weird. He usually gets back to me pretty fast.

Journey phoned and texted Roman several times—no response. She then called True and got no answer. She walked back to her dorm and threw on a scarlet velour sweatsuit, before driving to True's apartment. She knocked on his door with trembling fists.

No one answered.

She jumped back into her car and tried to reach Roman again. As she dialed the last digit, she saw True drive up behind her in her rearview mirror. She almost fell facedown onto the gravel driveway, as she stepped out of her car, gasping for air.

"I've been trying to get in touch with Roman all morning with no luck. Roman's car is at the frat house, but no Roman. Please tell me you didn't do anything. I was just so mad at him last night."

True remained in his car. He rolled his tongue around in his mouth, paused, and stared up at her for several seconds, without any words.

He said, "I took care of everything. You'll never have to worry about Roman's extracurricular activities. I did what you wanted to be done, but you could never say it until last night."

Journey bent down, reached her hands inside his car, and grabbed his shirt with both hands.

"Where's Roman, True?"

"Let go and follow me."

Journey withdrew her hands, stood up, and walked back towards

Confessions

her car. She jumped in, turned the key in the ignition, and shifted it into *Drive*.

Her palms were sweaty, as she gripped the steering wheel tighter and tighter.

A storm started out of nowhere. Raindrops slammed against her window. Her windshield wipers swished back and forth at a rapid speed.

After driving out of the city and down a long and twisted muddy road for 45 minutes, they parked in front of an abandoned barn.

True popped open an umbrella, casually stepping out of his car, while Journey flew out of her seat and ran towards him.

"Where is he?"

Her entire body and lips trembled, as the rain saturated her clothes.

"You're soaked. Get under here with me."

"No, True! Show me now!"

"There." True pointed at the shabby barn. "Wait."

"What?"

Journey stopped in her path towards the barn and jerked her entire body around.

"Roman wasn't cheating on you. I planted that receipt. I knew you wouldn't leave him unless you thought he deceived you again. Don't know why you've tolerated him this long, with everything he's put you through."

True shook his head.

"What!"

"Listen, I did it for us. I've always loved you."

"You're insane, True!"

She sprinted towards the barn, dropping her keys. She swung the massive wooden door wide open and found only an industrial-sized freezer, as True walked up behind her.

"What are you waiting for? Go ahead," he whispered close to her ear while rubbing his palms vigorously together.

She opened the heavy lid slowly. A thick plastic sheet covered the

Heavy Eyes

top, and Journey reached down and peeled it off. True stood over her, with a flashlight shining down into it.

Roman was underneath the ice. His pale face absorbed the bright light rays. She looked into his cold brown eyes, which were barely open. He blinked. She looked closer, and he blinked repeatedly. His fingers slowly moved as if he was trying to claw his way out of the ice. He was still breathing.

"True, you placed him in there alive?" she asked, crying. "Hand me that damn thing!" She chipped the ice away with the flashlight. "Are you that heartless? I just wanted him to suffer a little, not die! What are you?"

The light bounced to the ground in her clumsy attempts to free Roman.

"Well, this is how we take care of a constant problem back home! I did leave a tube of oxygen in his nostrils, but the O2 tank is practically empty by now."

He swept the flashlight up with his right hand.

"How could you do such a horrible thing?"

"I did you a favor. He's been emotionally killing you since freshman homecoming night. He snuck out the back with that slutty friend of yours, Marissa Hampton, a few hours before you and he were announced homecoming king and queen of our high school."

"What?"

"Oh, you didn't know? I really am doing you a huge favor, then."

"Please, just stop it, True!"

"No, you, stop it! Journey, you've been so blind about my feelings for you, just as blind as thinking Roman ever loved you. I did all this, so we can now be together," he said, wrapping his large arms around her.

"True, you went too far. I could never be with you! I don't love you like that."

She squeezed out of his bear-hug and pushed him out of the way,

Confessions

snatching the flashlight from his hand.

"Dear God, what have I done?" she cried out.

She jumped inside the freezer like a gymnast, dropped to her knees, and slammed the flashlight feverishly against the ice over and over again with all her 136 pounds poured into the motion, and then it began to fall from her tight grip.

Ice chips flew up like mini razor blades, piercing her face.

"Roman, I didn't mean for this to happen!" she screamed.

The ice coffin finally broke apart enough that she was able to pull him halfway up between her trembling thighs and out of the freezing water.

He coughed up a gush of water and whispered from his shivering blue lips, "Journey, I'm sorry for everything. You were the only one I ever loved."

His eyes froze suddenly, staring up at her blood-splattered face.

The End

Heavy Eyes

Trapped

Torn out dreams
Rolling in iridescent, ebony flames
Again and again
Pieces of her undefined and
Punctured with hypodermic needles filled with the
Evil juices of envy, jealousy, and hate
Damaging her wings and transforming her into a flightless bird…

Un-Kiss

Her lips talked to his lips from 9:00 p.m. to midnight without
touching…
Before the tango engagement, she pulled away.
She left him on the dance floor.
It was best.
She tattooed him inside her heart in the sixth grade, but she wasn't in
his heart—she wasn't the chosen one.
She knew that one night would transform into more consequences
versus
sincere dedication and loyalty to only her.
So, the next morning, she waved him on, as red rose petals were being
thrown over the homecoming queen and him, homecoming king.
Infinite tears splashed onto her sapphire-crystal pumps…

Heavy Eyes

Doubt

Seeds planted
Heavy clouds blew in from the North
Unstoppable weeds sprouted up overnight
Violent thunderstorms and tornadoes tumbled in
Homes, cars, and lampposts plucked up and instantly vanished in one
blink
Those ugly weeds still remained.
They're rooted everywhere.
I tried to yank them up.
Once
Twice
Never mind…
They won.

Doubt

Enemy

Razor sharp smiles cut me from across the crowded room
Plots of evil schemes forecasting in your twisted mind
Venomous lies planted on your merciless forked tongue
You lurk around doors slowly, like an anaconda in the wet marshes.
Perching yourself on the stair banister to eavesdrop on exchanged
secrets
Piercing my existence with your stainless-steel fangs full of *liquid
cyanide*
Trapped in your vicious world of infinite torment...

Heavy Eyes

1958

Love Tales ———————————————————————————

Dedicated to

Lindsey Elaine & Brandon Kitzmiller

Love Stew

2 pounds of forgiveness
1 cup of chopped patience
½ teaspoon of magic
2 cups of sacrifice
1 stalk of laughter, cut into ½ inch pieces
3 cups of romance with passionate raspberry kisses
1 teaspoon of impossibilities
2 cups of tears
⅓ cup of warm and tender hugs

Now, mix until blended well together…

Remember to simmer when needed.

No need to overcook.

Love Stew

Southern Lover's
Tale

I am the:

Fire set ablaze by your voice and touch with passion and intensity
Complete waterfall overflowing into an empty pit, contemplating
thoughts of
love and devotion
Flock of doves, soaring into the twilight skies, anticipating my dream
40,000 ballerinas, dancing eternally by the silent unchanged melodies
that all lovers hear
Moonlight reflecting off the midnight glass
Colors that made up the rainbow that you saw last
Sunlight that rises and falls with sweet memories
Far South awaiting the return of her Far North
North ignited all these visions just by his simple gaze, a touch of
magic, and love flying all around South…

1958

Awoken

I walked a tightrope backwards
with a den of 1,001 rattlesnakes slithering and hissing underneath me.
I slipped and caught the rope with one hand…
Held on as long as I could before I felt puffy burning blisters forming
I looked up into your golden watery eyes from afar, and that's when

I knew…

Awoken

You

Where would I find another you?
Maybe if I traveled around the world twice or to another galaxy?
Two of you could never co-exist.
I know that God only made one you for me.
So, if I ever lost you, then chaos would dominate my world, until my
last breath…

1958

One

Your oversized tender hands swam through my soapy hair as you
washed slowly.
I barely possessed the strength to stand there.
I never worried about falling from that place.
I knew you would be there to always catch me in your *Captain
America* arms,
even at my weakest moment.

One

Second
Chance

Betrayal of the heart for almost five years…
Consistent ripping at his soul with her jagged tongue
Dreams to escape his barbed wire world haunted by her
Emptiness floods his mind full of darkness and entrapment.
Redemption finally threw him a rope down and pulled him up and out
of his deep cold well,
to feel the sun's warm rays
on his face again…

1958

Dancing
Flames

Your blues sway back and forth
Stretching all around
Piping up and down
I enter the room, and you suddenly transform into a sparkling
fireworks trio
Your eternal S.O.S. love signal…

Dancing Flames

Stampede

Shaken by your bursting cranberry
Thunderbolt kisses… you doused
Arrows in dripping honey to
Meet my beating heart once more…
Piercing it intensely and causing
Explosive fireworks to
Dance in front of me
Each time I reminisce about my first Sweet Sixteen kiss with you back
       then and right now…

1958

Dream
Destination

Let's run away together…
Where, you ask?
Hmmm…
What about…
The Caribbean
Vegas
San Diego Zoo
The Great Lakes
Mount Kilimanjaro
Alaska
Greece
Straight to the moon
Wait!
I know… I know just the perfect place.
The most magical place on Earth that I could ever travel to…
Why didn't I think about this before?
Lost in your arms, exactly where I wish to run to…
Now, losing sleep will only be in my distant memory.

Dream Destination

Union

Your touch ignited my silent volcanoes to erupt and melt all the
glaciers surrounding my crumbled-up heart.
Your titanium arms cradled me, oh, so tenderly.
You rocked me into a deep slumber.
Raindrops dancing off the windows woke me.
I found moonlight rays encircling your beating heart.
This is when I knew.
I knew…
I finally found
my home.

1958

Exposed

Follow my purple candle glow around the moon's twisted staircase,
until you find my inner mystery, which can only be solved by the
touch of
your warm sweet nectarine-tasting lips onto mine.

Thousand

There he was, just standing, watching me from across the room
Hypnotizing me again with those baby blues like the very first time…
Orchestra played our song in the background. I thought, *How could he
    love me?*
Useless for me to think such foolish thoughts… He walked up to me
    and
Swept me off my feet with just the touch of his open hand next to
    my face. He whispered, *"Wherever you are, I am, too."* I fell
    backwards.
And he caught me without hesitation…
Never have I felt like this with anyone. Uh-oh! Uh-oh! Uh-oh! I guess
Destiny finally gave me a real chance to experience a true love…

1958

1958

As soon as our
fingertips kissed,
you
were
mine
then
and
in
all
of
time…

1958

Boundless
Questionnaire

Which work was your favorite?

Which work would you like to be considered for longer transformation?

Why did you choose that work?

What did you like most about **Boundless**?

Thank you again. If you enjoyed **Boundless**, I would so appreciate if you would take the time to leave a review on Amazon. It can be short, or more if you so desire. I enjoy hearing from my readers. Feel free to answer the above questions or write anything you wish to share via my email and/or Facebook instant messenger.

Extras

Also by Miracle Austin: *Doll*
Available on Amazon and www.miracleaustin.com

~DOLL REVIEWS~

A Tour De Force in YA!

"I loved this novel from start to finish; the characters were developed thoroughly. I believe that adults can enjoy this book as much as teenagers. I loved how the character Tomie (Toh-me) was such a relatable character to me. I was bullied in high school myself, and I used to *daydream* about being a *witch* and *casting spells* on my tormentors, so this book was right up my alley!!!

The author, Miracle Austin, is in the *realm* of the greatest YA horror writers, such as **Christopher Pike** and **R.L. Stine**. I really cannot wait to read *Doll 2*, as I am interested in where Miracle will take us this time!"

~Chanel Harry, author of the *Skin Witch: Tales of the Soucouyants*
*****

Addicting!

"I was introduced to your book, *Doll,* the Friday before Spring Break by my reading teacher. During the week, I've been reading it, and I couldn't stop. I saw the *Doll* cover, the synopsis, and the word Louisiana, I got excited. I have a weird passion for voodoo based books or shows.

The story is a wild ride from the beginning to the end! I was always on the edge of my seat and the thing that Opal did nearly gave me a heart attack! I also enjoyed the two endings, those features were very unique and I loved them.

Miracle Austin must do a sequel!

P.S. For my Language Arts class, we have to do a diorama—mini essay about a book and a couple of paragraphs on the scene we choose.

Reviews

I chose *Doll*. I'm doing the prom scene. Thank you for the excitement you brought with your book." ~Emily, junior-high teen *****

All around perfection!

"Even the book's dedication really hit home! It definitely does only take one person who believes in you to give you the confidence to accomplish anything!

Miracle really nailed the description of high school life (at least my experience of it)...It really took me back! I can relate each character to a person in my past, the accurate portrayal of schoolyard cliques...We all know the types! The book left me with feelings of nostalgia from my school days.

As for the story itself, I read it one day. From page one, I couldn't put it down. The content flowed so smoothly! Just enough detail to paint a picture, but leaving room for your own imagination. It was so easy to get lost in this magical world. Miracle has written her own magic book with *Doll* because it definitely put a spell on me!

I tried to sleep and finish it the next day, but it just pulled me right back in! So, I made coffee and finished the book...it was more than worth the read!

Her short story, bonus in *Doll*, *The Triple Dare* was unique with an unexpected twist, left me wanting more..." ~Brandon Kitzmiller *****

Must Read!

"...With a flawless plot, descriptions and style, this book is the perfect combination of horror, suspense and a little teenage drama and romance. A definitely must-read for this year!" ~Vanessa *****

Extras

Little
Sneak Peek

I wanted to share a few reviews from my debut YA/Paranormal novel *Doll* and thank you all who've read it. I so appreciate the amazing reviews and comments about my novel, including the choice of the reader's favorite ending.

Therefore, based on the reviews, comments, and instant messages received, I decided to pursue a mash-up of both endings for ***Doll 2: The Revealing***. By the way, if you haven't read *Doll* yet, then skip this sneak peek because it contains a few spoilers. I so hope that you enjoy this short excerpt.

DOLL 2:
The Revealing

COMING SOON: FALL OF 2017

DOLL 2:
The Revealing

I bet your junior year in high school was pretty ordinary and normal—not a lot of supernatural twists and turns, right?

Well, my junior year was extremely supernatural!

Oh, I forgot to tell you my name… Tomie Dupuy, pronounced *Toh-me Du-pay*.

I have three words for you, to describe my junior year at Frost High—***big unexpected outcomes***…

Let me tell you all about it.

Cupid opened my eyes and pierced my heart—with a little resistance on my part—and I fell for my long-time friend since junior high, Sari Green.

Sari and I befriended a fellow outcast Opal Dawn, and let me tell you… She possessed some unbelievable tricks. She murdered the meanest, most popular girl Pepper Fox, during Frost High's junior prom and almost murdered my girl, too.

Mr. Ray, a veteran bus driver at Frost High, turned out to be a shape-shifter and my *MEGA, Messenger/Elite Guardian Owl*. He's meant to guide me along my journey in discovering my powers.

Lisette, my powerful witch cousin from Monroe Creek, Louisiana cast an epic spell on Opal—she transformed her into a tiny doll—in order to terminate her evil magic before placing her in a secure location.

I discovered my late mom was an extremely powerful witch and

DOLL 2

how her marriage to my dad was forbidden. I also discovered that I was a late bloomer, *T.N.W., Teen Newby Warlock*.

My dad informed me that my ancestors, the Dupuy Silver Slayers, were relentless witch hunters. Right up my alley, right?

If you think my junior year was magically complicated, just wait until you experience my senior year…

✳ ✳ ✳

"Mr. Ray, I have so many questions to ask you. Why didn't you tell me who you were before now?"

"Tomie, it wasn't time for me to tell you. You wouldn't have believed me, anyhow, because you weren't ready to accept who you really were."

"Yeah, you're right. I wasn't, not until prom night. After I witnessed Pepper's awful demise on the dance floor and then the way you showed me how to use my powers to save Sari."

"Tomie, there's something I need to show you now."

"But there's so much I want to ask you, Mr. Ray."

"No time for that right now, Tomie!"

He sat down in a chair, took his glasses off, closed his eyes, and then opened them. They changed to a reflective golden color, and as he tilted his head up, a bright light shined onto the ceiling, emanating from them.

"Watch and listen carefully, Tomie!"

I looked up, and it was as if a movie projector was playing from Mr. Ray's eyes. I noticed a parking lot and knew where it was immediately—Pizza Beat, where I used to work before Pepper fired me. I saw Mr. Fox in his office, glancing down at his watch a few times as if he was waiting for someone.

Doll 2

After a few minutes and a zoom-out through the walls of Pizza Beat, an older woman approached the glass door entrance and knocked. I couldn't make out who she was at first because her face looked fuzzy.

As the scene panned back to Mr. Fox, I saw him rise from his chair, then walk around his desk and through the restaurant, towards the entrance. He welcomed the woman in, locked the door, looked both ways, closed the blinds, escorted her back to his office, and closed that door, as well.

When she sat down and began to speak, I knew exactly who she was—Opal's grandmom. Her voice was raspy and loud. A cigarette levitated from inside her purse and landed in between her open crinkled lips, painted with nectarine lipstick. She then snapped her fingers, and the cigarette lit up.

Mr. Fox's eyes widened, and he knocked a coffee cup over onto the floor.

"You shouldn't be surprised, Cage. Remember that night when Resella experienced that unexplainable accident at the Frost Country Club when she was pregnant with Pepper?"

He nodded his head, without saying a word.

"I know what you desire, and I need something from you."

He leaned in closer and asked, in a low growl, "What, Verlinda?"

"I know who murdered your only child."

She dragged her chipped black nails across his desk—a piercing sound echoed for a few moments. He stood up and placed both hands on his desk, leaning over, so his face almost touched hers. She blew a thick swirly grey cloud into his face, flicked her finger, and pushed him back down into his chair.

"I like my space. Listen up. You know that young boy, Tomie Dupuy, who used to work here and told you that night at the hospital how he didn't know anything about Pepper's terrible accident?" she said with a smirk.

"Yes, I know him."

DOLL 2

"No, you don't. If you really knew him, you would know that he's a liar and a murderer. He and his meddling cousin, Lisette Laveau, murdered your precious Pepper and did away with my Opal. If you truly seek revenge, then you have to do it my way, with no law enforcement involved. Understand?"

He nodded, as one teardrop coasted down his bright raspberry cheek. He pounded his fists down on his desk.

Verlinda whispered, "Bad magic always wins, and I possess the perfect plan."

Their images soon faded from the ceiling.

Mr. Ray opened his eyes, placed his glasses back on, and looked at me.

He said, "We must leave right now and begin your *training* with Lisette!"

(To Be Continued...)

Doll 2

LONESTAR
Unordinary Girl

COMING SOON: SPRING OF 2018

Lonestar Unordinary Girl

CHAPTER 1:
The Delivery

A little ol' country gal was about to meet Loola-Mae Jo Ray—*a mighty mouthful,* I bet you're saying to yourself—her mama, for the first time.

Loola-Mae's water broke, so, her brother Jethro scooped her up in his wobbly arms and laid her down on top of some blankets in the backseat of his 1955 Chevy truck.

Peering into the rearview mirror at his sister, as snuff filled his hairy jaws and splattered onto the mirror with every word, Jethro yelled, "Loola-Mae, I gotta make a quick stop at Dusty Shadows Inn."

Sweat beads flowed in a zigzag dance from his crinkled-up forehead, towards his bushy sideburns.

"Are ya kiddin' me, Jet?"

"Aw, come on, sis. Dusty's expectin' me, and I gotta pick up a package."

"I promise, if ya make me have this baby in the backseat, I'm gonna…"

Shaking her tiny fist in the dry warm Texas night air, she let the threat drift off into silence.

Jethro swerved into the gravel parking lot, stopping perfectly between two cars.

He jumped out and screamed, "I'll be back in a jiffy, sis. I promise. I'll leave the radio on for ya."

Lonestar Unordinary Girl

"Make it snappy, or else!"

He pulled up his faded Levi's—they slid down his slender waist again almost immediately—and shuffled into the inn, almost tripping over his spurred armadillo boots.

Before Loola-Mae could respond again, she felt a kick. She pushed once and then twice.

"Touchdown!" she screamed.

She looked between her legs and saw the greatest gift God ever gave her.

"Well, knock me down and steal muh teeth," she whispered to herself while wrapping her baby up in a receiving blanket she pulled from her overnight bag.

Loola-Mae held her gift close to her chest.

"What should I name ya, my sweet baby girl?" she asked softly, wiping away some of the blood and waxy film that was clinging to the baby's face with a clean towel.

As she was pondering, she overheard two women fussing in the parking lot. Loola-Mae stared at them while rolling down her window. They began to pull on each other's tight clothes and stiff hair.

One of the women shouted, "I can't stand you, Bullah. Your daddy was right all along, ya Jezebel!"

Something clicked in Loola-Mae's head.

"That's it. Jez-abell... Jez-abell Billie Jo will be your name, baby girl. You're Mama's special little booger," she murmured, as she planted a kiss on the baby's forehead and began to sing along to the radio, playing in the background.

"Trixiebelle, oh, Trixiebelle... Yep, she's madder than hell. Crazy Billy Ray been a two-steppin' again with that trashy Georgia Rale."

Staring up into her mama's bright eyes, Jez-abell cooed and whispered, *"Run, duck, everyone. Told ya, boys, she's fixin' to shoot that..."*

She snapped her tiny fingers together and bobbed her head up and

Lonestar Unordinary Girl

down with a huge grin, accompanied by loud cooing.

Loola-Mae's jaw dropped, and her eyes bucked.

"Yee-haw, my baby girl's a genius!"

"Hey, Bullah, help me up," the hollering woman from before pleaded. She dusted her skintight jeans off and pulled her glasses out of her denim pocket to place them on her slender face. "Did ya hear that?"

"Nope," Bullah said while pulling her cheap wig down over her ear and popping bubble gum into mega-sized bubbles.

"It's comin' from over yonder in that car. I know a youngin's lungs anywhere," Heneritta squealed.

They both tiptoed in their cheap pumps to the back of the car and found Loola-Mae and Jez-abell.

"Hey there, honey! What a cute booger ya have there! What's her name?" Bullah asked, leaning over the window with Henrietta.

"Jez-abell Billie Jo." Loola-Mae's grin was so proud and wide that her front gold tooth popped out, striking the left corner of Henrietta's glasses. "Oops, I'm sorry."

"Nonsense, honey. Don't worry about it. They're just cheapies. I got a dozen at home, different colors to match my outfits, of course. Anyhow, ya sure ya wanna name her that?" Bullah asked.

"Yeppers! I heard ya call your friend that. I think it's a real fancy name for my sweet possum here," Loola-Mae said, as she made cooing sounds to her new little booger.

"Sure, real fancy," Henrietta said, raising her eyebrows and elbowing Bullah slightly. "Well, congratulations, darlin'. Need us to drive ya to the hospital, or somethin'?"

"Ah, how sweet of the two of y'all. I feel just fine, hardly any pain. She's my first, too. My brother Jet should be comin' out any second now to take us to the hospital. He just drives me nuts, a lot! No, all the time."

"Ya wouldn't be referrin' to Crazy Jethro Ray?" Henrietta asked with a smirk slapped on her face.

Lonestar Unordinary Girl

"Why, yeah. Ya know my baby brother?"

"Do I ever?" Henrietta hollered out.

The girl gossip bonding time terminated, as a loud *pop-pop-pop* sounded, and flying bullets soared like mini torpedoes out of Dusty Shadows Inn's front door.

Jethro sprinted towards the car, ducking right and left. Loola-Mae never saw him in that big a hurry for anything in his life.

He slid nearly under the truck as if he was making a homerun on a baseball field while grabbing and hanging on to the driver's side mirror. Thank goodness, he wore those spurred armadillos that night. They served as his safety brakes.

"Sis, we gotta get outta here," he squealed, out of breath. "Whew-wee, you had her! She's sure pretty, but we really gotta go right now! Hey, there, Henrietta and Bullah," he said, as he swatted Henrietta on the rear and winked twice at her. "Call me."

Henrietta's smirk transformed into an unforgettable smile, as though she was a young teenage girl, finally being kissed for the first time by the heartthrob she'd been fantasizing about since freshman year.

Jethro swung the driver door wide open, jumped in, and slammed it shut. He threw an object loosely wrapped in newspaper under his seat, revved her up, placed her in *Reverse*, and sped out of the gravel parking lot, leaving multiple grey clouds of smoke behind.

"Whatcha gone and done now, Jet?" Loola-Mae asked with a huge frown.

"Loola, I promise. Nothin'! Some strange fellas were askin' weird questions about you and the new baby girl. Boy, they smelled funny. Phew! When I didn't budge with the answers, they threatened me and pulled out their guns. I started runnin', and they started shootin'. Dusty promised to slow them down for us."

"Jet, we can't leave Honey Springs. Plus, I need to go to the hospital and get checked out."

"Don't worry. I got us a plan. We'll head to a hospital outside the city limits."

"Nothin's makin' sense to me, Jet. Why am I runnin' with you? This just ain't the time. Ya always find ways to get me involved in your problems every darn time."

"Loola, listen. We gotta. This ain't just my problem. There's somethin' I need to tell ya, but not now."

"Yeah, I got somethin' to share with you, too. Tell me somethin', Jet, or I'm gonna make you stop this car right here, right now!"

"All right… all right. You, babygirl, and me ain't safe here anymore, and it's time for us to meet Sylver Foxx…

(To be continued…)

Acknowledgements

I want to thank my precious mom for sharing her youthful and current stories/experiences—both continue to inspire me all the time. I also want to thank each of you so much for your beautiful support:

Troy Gee   Chanel Harry
Lorelei Buckley   Claudette Peercy & James Peercy
Dan Foytik & the Wicked Library
Gloria Bobrowicz & Sirens Call Publications
Julianne Snow   Ian Michael Fuggle
Barry Skelhorn & Sanitarium Author Family
Irenka Vlajnic   Chris Jones
Beth Teliho   Erica Smith
Tracy Guillory   Kiarrah Guillory
Heather Violet VanZandt   Julee Murphy
Emily Hernandez   Rose Caramaya
Vanessa Kings   Katara Johnson
Maureen Billings   Laurie Murray
Kathleen Rodgers   Deb Storey Pyles
Annabelle Pyles   Tich Brewster
Tracy Stone Lawson   Kristen O. Iten

Acknowledgements
(Cont'd)

Paula Baker
www.thevoicesproject.org
Break Fate Publishing
Waco Wordfest
Janis James
Kelly Parker
Tres Kennedy
Nina D'Arcangela
Deborah Oren
Letha Hanover
Lee A. Forman
Chrissy Moon
Debbie VanZandt
Ethan Cooper
Roxanna Kirkpatrick Batson

Martha Boss Coth
www.13Horror.com
The Stray Branch
Yellow Chair
Katherine Boyer
Elaine Barris
Lauren Murray
Dark Oak Press
Blackberry Magazine
The Dark Eclipse
www.HelloHorror.com
Poems-for-all
Moonja Book Promotions
G. W. Carver Middle School
Amy Hubbard

All Social Media Buddies and readers of my works...

~Mari Rohweder, Kitten Jackson, Molly Phillips, and Mia Hoddell, my magnificent creative team, I couldn't do any of my creative magic without any of you. Thank you all!~

Acknowledgements

About the *Author*

Miracle Austin works in the social work arena by day and in the writer's world at night and on weekends. She's a YA/NA cross-genre hybrid author, but adults can also enjoy her works. She's been writing since junior high, and *Drive* by The Cars is one of her biggest inspirations to write. She enjoys writing free-verse poems/mini-stories and short stories. Horror and suspense are her favorite genres, but she's not limited to them.

Doll is her debut YA Paranormal novel; it won 2nd place in the Young Adult category in the 2016 **Purple Dragonfly Awards**.

Doll 2: The Revealing is anticipated to release in the Fall of 2017.

She enjoys attending diverse book festivals and comic conventions, where she has been honored to be one of the panelists on some. She hopes to present at many more teen book events and conduct school visits in the future.

Miracle resides in Texas with her family and looks forward to hearing from her readers.

Website: **www.miracleaustin.com**
Email: **shadesoffiction@miracleaustin.com**
Twitter: @MiracleAustin7
InstaGram: MiracleAustin7
Facebook: Miracle Austin Author

~Works Previously Published~

Pens first appeared in www.leaves-of-ink, © 2013
Unfallen first appeared in Blackberry Magazine, © 2013
Last Pass first appeared in Sanitarium Magazine #007 (Antho), © 2013
Infinity first appeared in Sirenscallpublications.com #10, © 2013
Monster first appeared in Sirenscallpublications.com #10, © 2013
Confessions first appeared in Sirenscallpublications.com #11, © 2013
Dishonorable Path first appeared in The Dark Eclipse #26, © 2013
Enemy first appeared in The Dark Eclipse #27, © 2013
Wingless first appeared in www.thevoicesproject.org, © 2013
Dark Place first appeared in The Dark Eclipse #28, © 2013
Meat Lover's Special first appeared in www.13Horror.com Vol#3, © 2013
Solo first appeared in The Dark Eclipse #29, © 2013
Stalker first appeared in The Dark Eclipse #30, © 2014
Study Break first appeared in Dark Oak Press, © 2014
Lights Out first appeared in HelloHorror.com, © 2014
Meat Lover's Special appeared in The Dead Walk (Zombie Antho), © 2014
Alone first appeared in www.thevoicesproject.org, © 2014
Meat Lover's Special appeared in The Wicked Library Podcast#415, © 2014
Krisper first appeared in Sirenscallpublications.com (Womeninhorrormonth), © 2015
Invisible Ones first appeared in The Stray Branch, © 2015
Awoken (former title *The Revealing*) first appeared in Poems-

Works Previously Published

for-All#1327, © 2015
Side Effects first appeared in Waco Wordfest, © 2015
Meat Lover's Special appeared in The Wicked Library Podcast (Encore), © 2015
Slippers first appeared in Yellow Chair Review, © 2015
Crave first appeared in SirenscallPublications.com, © 2016
Lock first appeared in SirenscallPublication.com (Womeninhorrormonth), © 2016
Last Pass appeared in The Wicked Library Podcast# 624(**DoubleFeature**), © 2016
Lights Out appeared in The Wicked Library Podcast#624(**DoubleFeature**), © 2016
Damaged first appeared in SirenscallPublications.com #28, © 2016
Creep first appeared in Moonja Book Promotions, © 2016
Ex-Change first appeared in Moonja Book Promotions, © 2016
One-way first appeared in Moonja Book Promotions, © 2016

Works Previously Published

~Helpful Resources~

(If you and/or a friend ever need someone to talk to…)

AIDS and HIV
National AIDS Hotline
1-800-232-4636

Alcohol and Drugs
Al-Anon/Alateen
1-888-425-2666

Bullying and Cyberbulling
1-800-273-8255

Depression
National Hopeline Network
1-800-784-2433

Eating Disorders
National Association of Anorexia Nervosa and Eating Disorders
630-577-1330
National Eating Disorders Association
1-800-931-2237

Grief and Loss
Crisis Call Center
1-800-273-8255
Tragedy Assistance Program for Survivors
1-800-959-8277

Homelessness and Runaways
Boys Town National Hotline
1-800-448-3000
National Runaway Switchboard
1-800-786-2929

Mental Health
National Institute of Mental Health Information
1-866-615-6464

ChildHelp USA National Child Abuse Hotline
1-800-422-4453

National Domestic Violence Hotline
1-800-799-SAFE (7233)

Rape, Abuse, and Incest National Network (RAINN)
1-800-656-HOPE (4673)

School Violence
SPEAK UP
1-866-773-2587 (SPEAK-UP)

Suicide
National Suicide Prevention Lifeline
1-800-273-8255

Teen Parenting
Postpartum Support International
1-800-944-4773

Helpful Resources

<u>Teen Pregnancy</u>
<u>American Pregnancy Helpline</u>
1-866-942-6466

<u>Baby Safe Haven</u>
1-888-510-2229

<u>Birthright International</u>
1-800-550-4900

<u>Thursday's Child National Youth Advocacy Hotline</u>
1-800-872-543

READER'S NOTES

www.ingramcontent.com/pod-product-compliance
Lightning Source LLC
Chambersburg PA
CBHW030400180626
46812CB00005B/1862